"Whose baby is it? And why did they dump it here?"

Dylan's voice was laced with disgust. The teenager glared at Joanna as the infant—dressed in a fluffy pink jacket and quilted overalls—began to wail.

Taking a deep breath, Joanna slid her hands beneath the little girl and lifted her from the car seat.

Rigid with fury, the infant shoved away with both hands and kicked her little feet. "Shh, it's okay," Joanna murmured. She turned to Dylan. "See if there's a note or something in her bag."

He unzipped the bag, held it upside down and shook it, but the crammed contents didn't budge. With a deep sigh he reached in and began to withdraw the contents. Diapers, disposable wipes, three sleepers, T-shirts, socks, a can of powdered formula, two bottles and two sipper cups. Then he pushed his hand into the main compartment and pulled out a tightly folded piece of paper.

Relief washed through Joanna as Dylan spread the paper out on the table. Here would be the explanation.

"I'm sorry I didn't call first. I just couldn't. I figured you wouldn't be interested," the note began.

The last paragraph told Joanna what she needed to know.

Ben Carson was going to have quite a surprise waiting for him when he got home.

Dear Reader,

The loss of a child is the ultimate personal tragedy. The grief is so overwhelming, it seems as if there will never be a brighter day. Yet, in time, the unbearable pain eases and one can finally move on—never forgetting, forever changed, but able to pursue new dreams and find happiness again.

It's been several years since the loss of her baby and the end of her marriage, and Dr. Joanna Weston is now ready to start a new life. Great opportunities await her in California, but first she plans to cover a pediatric clinic in the rugged mountains of New Mexico for three months while the physician is away. An escape artist of a horse and a Great Pyrenees pup the size of Texas are all the family she needs now—or so she thinks, until she meets a footloose cowboy who couldn't be more wrong for her.

I enjoy exploring the issues of family and the special bonds between generations. I'm also intrigued by how many obstacles a person will overcome to forge a strong, romantic bond with someone else. I hope you'll enjoy the story of Ben, a cowboy who finds himself with an unexpected family, and Joanna, who needs to leave the past behind in order to find a love she never dreamed possible. I also hope you'll read the other stories in the six-book BIRTH PLACE series. Darlene Graham, Brenda Novak, C.J. Carmichael, Kathleen O'Brien and Marisa Carroll have all written fabulous books that you won't want to miss!

I love hearing from readers, and if you send a business-size SASE, I'll send you my latest promotional items.

Wishing you all the best,

Roxanne Rustand

www.roxannerustand.com
www.booksbyrustand.com
www.ditzychix.com
Box 2550, Cedar Rapids, Iowa 52406-2550

Christmas At Shadow Creek

Roxanne Rustand

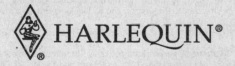

HARLEQUIN®

TORONTO • NEW YORK • LONDON
AMSTERDAM • PARIS • SYDNEY • HAMBURG
STOCKHOLM • ATHENS • TOKYO • MILAN • MADRID
PRAGUE • WARSAW • BUDAPEST • AUCKLAND

ISBN 0-373-71165-4

CHRISTMAS AT SHADOW CREEK

Copyright © 2003 by Roxanne Rustand.

Visit us at www.eHarlequin.com

Printed in U.S.A.

Acknowledgments

Research could never be complete enough without
the insights and help of so many friends, old and new.
Many thanks to the wonderful Cataromance e-mail loop
members who shared their experiences and challenges in
dealing with asthma in young children: Pam B, Judith,
Debbie, Sylvie, Sandra, Cindy and Sara.

Special thanks to New Mexico rancher Genora Moore;
New Mexico rancher and author Kelley Pounds; and
Dr. Joan Harding, Emergency Room Physician, who all
answered my endless questions with admirable
patience and concern for detail. And finally, thanks to
Diane, Anna, C.J. and Brenda—for your advice,
assistance and support when I needed it most.
I feel so blessed for knowing you all.

Dedication

To the five other authors in this series—
Darlene Graham, Brenda Novak, C.J. Carmichael,
Kathleen O'Brien and Marisa Carroll—who made working on
THE BIRTH PLACE an absolute pleasure from first day to last.
As always, to Larry, Brian and Emily,
and to Andy and his family, who live too far away.

And finally, in memory of Christiana Leigh...
because this one's for you.

Books by Roxanne Rustand

HARLEQUIN SUPERROMANCE

Coming soon: OPERATION: SECOND CHANCE—Harlequin Superromace
#1185 (Available February 2004)

CHAPTER ONE

DR. JOANNA WESTON WAS finally ready for new beginnings and the chance to take firm control of her life. *Absolute control.*

The words conjured up a sense of power. Peace. Healing. All of which she hoped to find here in Enchantment, an isolated town in the mountains of New Mexico.

She'd long since dealt with the end of her marriage. This temporary job in a pediatric clinic would help her ease back into her beloved medical specialty. But there would never be a day when she didn't remember saying goodbye to her newborn son, Hunter.

Two years ago, now—and it still seemed like yesterday.

"Come on, buddy," she murmured as she slid the halter from the horse's head and patted him on the neck. "You've had one heck of a long trip."

So had she.

After a thousand miles of driving, a flat tire and a two-day layover to replace her SUV's carburetor, she'd begun to wonder if they would ever arrive. And once they'd hit the mountains…she shook her head in disbelief.

Towing a heavy horse trailer for the first time in her life, she'd taken the steep, hairpin turns at a crawl and had coasted gently into each stop. Every five hours she'd pulled over so her latest acquisition—an old paint gelding—could clamber out of his horse trailer to stretch his tired muscles.

He should have been grateful to find himself in New Mexico and not in a glue factory.

Instead, he took one look at the split-rail fence surrounding his new pasture, broke into a lope and cleared it with ease. His tail raised like a banner of victory, he gave a few hard bucks before disappearing into the aspen-and-pine-studded foothills surrounding Joanna's cabin. Hills that steadily climbed higher into the Sangre de Cristo Mountains. Uninhabited, unfenced and endless, from what she could see.

Stunned, she leaned against the tailgate of the horse trailer. Would Galahad come home? With what little she knew about horses, she doubted it. He clearly thought he was headed for horse paradise and wasn't looking back. At the rate he was going, there'd be no hope of catching up to him.

Apparently wanting to join Galahad on his adventure, her massive Great Pyrenees pup, Moose—another recent addition—strained at the cable she'd fastened to a corner post of the cabin porch. His deep barks echoed through the empty landscape, and with each powerful lunge, dried pine needles showered from the roof of the porch. If she'd turned him loose in the fenced yard around the cabin, he'd probably be gone as well.

Oats. Would the old gelding come to her if he smelled oats?

She spun around and jerked open the door of the trailer's tack compartment, stepped inside, grabbed a sack of mixed feed and lugged it over to the small, pine-log barn. The sweet scent of molasses filled the air as she ripped open the top seam of the paper sack and emptied it into a new garbage can.

Snagging the halter and rope she'd hung on a nail by the door, she scooped up a small bucket of the mix and hurried through the pasture gate by the barn.

Behind her, Moose's frantic barking rose to a deafening level. The pup had instantly bonded with the old horse, and he desperately wanted to follow his new friend. *Not a chance, buddy.* What if there were coyotes out here? Mountain lions?

With Moose's puppy mentality, cloud of white fur and seventy pounds of awkward exuberance, he'd be very easy prey.

She crossed the parched grass of the pasture at a jog, muttering under her breath. The same impulsive behavior that had led her to attend that San Diego horse sale in late August had also made her step on the brakes while passing an animal shelter a few days afterward. "Buying a family?" Allen had chided coolly at the last county medical meeting she'd attended. "You really ought to consider therapy, Jo."

Something she'd seriously considered after he left their marriage last year for a twenty-two-year-old arm charm with a Victoria's Secret body and the giddy smile of a teenager. But moving here was probably the best therapy she could have found. And an old horse and faithful dog had to be better company and far more dependable than Allen.

As she climbed through the gnarled fence rails at the far side of the pasture and entered government land, she bent to break off a wiry stem of sagebrush. The peppery, pungent aroma of the tiny silver-green leaves tickled her nose. Ahead, dark pines rose like sentinels and stands of aspen gilded the hillsides with splashes of brilliant October yellow.

The thinner air at this altitude smelled so pure and crisp, scented with juniper and pine and sun-warmed earth, she felt a sudden pang at the fact that she'd have to leave all of this at the end of December—just a few short months away.

Taking a deep breath, she started up into the hills...but no hoofprints marked the hard, rocky soil. She called Galahad's name and shook the feed bucket every few minutes, but heard only the soft rush of wind through the branches above and the whistling call of canyon wrens coming from the rocky cliffs ahead.

Wild beauty surrounded her—rugged and vast and unspoiled—but danger lurked out here as well. Now, after an hour of searching, lengthening shadows hid precipitous cliffs and perhaps even a mountain lion or pack of coyotes that could bring down an old horse with ease. And Galahad's splashy black-and-white coat and long white tail would make him stand out in this environment. He had raced for freedom, but where was he going to find food? Water? She'd had him for only six weeks, and he'd started to put on some weight, but his gaunt body didn't have much reserve.

After another fifteen minutes, she stopped in the shade of a massive boulder and decided she hadn't been particularly wise, either. A water bottle would have been a good idea, given the arid climate and heavy dust that rose with every step.

Unaccustomed to Enchantment's altitude—over eight thousand feet in town and even higher here—she felt breathless and a little nauseous. A headache started throbbing behind her eyes. The sun was already settling low on the horizon.

Calling Galahad's name one last time, she listened for distant hoofbeats, but heard nothing. With a heavy heart, she turned to go home. When she reached the cabin, she would call the police department in Enchantment to report her lost horse. Maybe someone would see him, and at least report his general location.

An unexpected splash of red caught her eye as she started down a different path.

Through the shadows, she could make out the form of someone slumped against a boulder a few dozen yards away. She stilled as dozens of old news reports rushed through her thoughts. Serial killers. Escaped convicts. Crazed survivalists. Any of whom might decide to hide out in remote areas.

The city girl in her sent urgent warnings. *Time to get home. Now.*

But the splash of red wasn't moving.

What if this was an innocent hiker bleeding to death after a fall? Or an older person who was confused and lost?

Wishing she had her cell phone—though the reception had been poor even back at the cabin—she edged a few feet closer.

She could see the guy better now, but he was facing in the opposite direction and didn't seem to be aware of her. Western hat, dark hair, a flannel shirt of red plaid. Spurs glinted at the heels of his western boots. Obviously he hadn't been hiking.

He slowly rose to his feet, using the rocks at his side for support, and settled his hat lower on his head. He began hobbling in the opposite direction.

Joanna had done volunteer work at an inner city clinic before starting med school, and wasn't fool enough to walk into a trap, but her hesitation faded when she saw a gash on the side of his jaw and the ragged tear along the thigh of his jeans. "Hey!" she called out. "Are you okay?"

His head jerked around and he stared at her in obvious surprise. Beneath the shadow of his hat brim she saw a strong, square jaw, narrow nose and warm brown eyes. He was in his mid-thirties, maybe. An easy grin lifted a corner of his mouth.

"Lose your horse?" She approached slowly, still keeping her distance.

When his gaze fell to the halter slung over her shoulder and the bucket of grain in her hand, his mouth twitched.

"Apparently you lost yours. Let me guess—a big, skinny, black-and-white paint gelding."

"You saw him?" Relief flooded through her. "Really? Was he okay?"

"Oh, yeah. Well enough to be heading this way at roughly the speed of light."

Relief turned to horror as she contemplated the laceration on the man's face and the bloodstains on his shirt. "Oh my God—he made you fall off your horse? I'm so sorry!"

"I didn't fall off her," he said carefully. "She hit the ground first. Your paint barreled around those boulders and knocked my filly right off her feet. I don't know which horse was more surprised."

Remorse slid through her as she imagined how badly this man could have been hurt. *Killed,* maybe. "Gosh—he's really so gentle. I'm sure he didn't mean any harm."

She thought she saw the guy roll his eyes at that one. "No harm done. Except that now both horses are probably hightailing it up into the hills, or heading toward my ranch. Together."

"You think Galahad followed? Really?"

"Galahad?"

She felt a touch of warmth slide up her cheeks. "I…um…visited my first horse auction six weeks ago. I told the guy next to me that I thought Galahad was pretty, and he said that only the kill buyers would bid on him because he was lame."

"You bought a *lame gelding?*" His voice filled with disbelief. "At a *sale?*"

"If I hadn't, the kill buyers would have gotten him. I knew he couldn't be ridden, but there was just something about him that I couldn't ignore. I figured I could give him a good home for the rest of his life." She lifted her shoulders. "Anyway, he's a sweet old guy."

"Well, ma'am, I'm sure he is." Given his smile and the

patient expression in his dark brown eyes, he probably considered her a foolish city slicker.

Not that it mattered. After Allen, she had absolutely no use for any man with a superiority complex—and that pretty much took care of every man she met. If this guy thought she was too sentimental, so be it.

"It's gonna be dark in less than an hour, ma'am. You'd better get home." He reached for his back pocket, wincing as he retrieved a worn leather wallet. From inside he withdrew a business card. "I'd sure be glad to help you get home, but my transportation left without me."

"I'm so—"

He waved away her second apology. "Don't worry about it. Call tomorrow and I'll let you know if your horse turns up at my place. Or," he added as an afterthought, "you can let me know if my filly shows up at yours."

"You should let me take a look at your injuries," she murmured as she accepted the card. *Ben Carson, Shadow Creek Ranch. Quarter horses and Charolais cattle.* "Do you feel dizzy? Did you hit your head?"

He raised an eyebrow

The laceration on his cheek was still bleeding a little, and when he didn't answer, her concern deepened. "I'm a doctor, for heaven's sake. Consider this free roadside service. Your lucky day."

"Lucky," he echoed dryly. "But no thanks."

"I don't live all that far from here. At least let me give you a lift home."

"No, ma'am." He started limping away, but the slick leather sole of one of his boots slipped on the rocks, sending a volley of pebbles ricocheting down the rocky slope. Swearing under his breath he leaned over, his hands braced on his thighs.

Men. If there was a gene for bullheadedness, it surely

had to be linked to the Y chromosome. She walked over to him and waited patiently.

"My place is quite a few miles away," he said on a long, drawn-out sigh. "How far away is your car?"

"Maybe a couple of miles at the most."

"You're at the Wilsons' rental cabin?"

Surprised, she nodded. "I've leased it until the end of December. Can you manage on that ankle? I could go for help—"

"*No.*"

She weighed the options. Could she find him in the dark if she left him behind and went for help? What if he passed out and couldn't answer someone calling his name? "All right," she said finally. "We'll take it easy. Do you need to lean on me?"

"Nope."

His response was no surprise, but it certainly made for slow progress over the rugged terrain. By the time they made it over the last hill above her place, darkness had fallen, relieved only by a sliver of moon and a heavy blanket of stars. Moose broke into a new frenzy of ferocious barking as they came into view.

"He's just a pup," she apologized. "He misses Galahad."

"My God. What is it? A polar bear?"

"Great Pyrenees. He'll be double that size in no time. Isn't he cute?"

"Yeah. Real cute." He nodded toward the SUV parked by the cabin. "Is that your Tahoe?"

"Yes, but can't I just check you to make sure—"

"My hired hand will be home from town soon, and I need to get there first." He gave her a tired smile. "If he sees that filly come home without me, he'll start a search party."

With a sigh of resignation, she helped him into the SUV

and rounded the front of the truck. Moose's barks changed to frantic yelps as he watched her prepare to leave.

"Poor guy. He's afraid of the dark," she called out. "I'll get him."

In a moment, she'd loaded the pup into the rear of the vehicle and had climbed behind the wheel. Moose whined and tried to turn in circles in order to lie down, but gave up and sat with his massive head resting on the top of the bench seat in front of him. Drooling.

"I would guess," Ben said, eyeing the panting dog, "that most anything out in the dark would be afraid of him."

"He's just a big baby. So tell me, Mr. Carson. How far is your ranch?"

"Nine miles south of town, then two more backtracking to the northwest. The ranch buildings aren't that far from here, but there aren't any direct roads."

His voice was deep and mellow, with a dark, intimate tone that sent a little shiver across her skin. "There don't seem to be *any* direct routes around here," she said with a smile. "I've seen more hairpin turns and steep grades in this area than I saw all the way between here to California. This is beautiful country."

"And treacherous." Ben leaned against the headrest, his skin pale in the dim light of the dashboard. "We've already had some good snows at the upper elevations."

At the end of her long, twisting lane, she glanced at the man next to her.

With his Stetson held in his hands, she could see the strong line of his jaw, the dark crescent of lashes that had drifted downward minutes after she'd started the vehicle. A lock of nearly black hair had tipped over his forehead, and she almost reached over to brush it away before catching herself.

Handsome? Oh, yes. And until he'd become a tad impatient with her offers of help, she'd seen hints that he was probably quite a charmer. Not that she was easily charmed.

In the darkness, the curves and steep grades were hard to see, so she white-knuckled the steering wheel and leaned forward to peer out at the swath of light in front of her headlights. After nine long miles she slowed to a crawl. A few moments later, two tall, heavy posts appeared at either side of a gravel road. The name, Shadow Creek Ranch, was carved in the log suspended high over the road.

"This is it," Ben murmured. "Just a couple miles to the northwest, and we're there."

Startled, she turned to look at him. "I thought you were asleep."

"No, ma'am. Just thinking about the chores I have to do."

The SUV rattled as she drove it over the bars of a cattle guard. "Don't your hired hands do them?"

"Rafe is my only full-timer. He helps me run the ranch, but most of my time is spent training horses. There's always more than enough to keep us both busy." He gave a short laugh. "I should have been feeding broodmares and moving cattle this evening instead of trying to hobble home on foot."

In the bright illumination of the headlights, the wire fence flanking both sides of the road gleamed like silver. Ahead she could see a number of lights that probably marked the location of a house and surrounding buildings. "I'm so sorry about Galahad causing trouble. I still can't believe a lame horse could run that fast."

"Don't worry about it. If I'd been on anything but a green-broke filly, there wouldn't have been any problem." After a moment, he cleared his throat. "Thanks for the ride home."

She cut a rueful glance in his direction. "This is all my fault, after all."

A few minutes later, she pulled into a broad parking area between a collection of ranch buildings. Straight ahead, the porch light of a small house blazed on, and the silhouette of a wiry man appeared in the doorway.

Joanna opened her door, intending to help Ben out of the SUV, but he shook his head. ''That dog of yours will probably tear up the upholstery if you leave him alone. Just wait here a minute, and I'll find out if our horses showed up yet.''

The SUV rocked as Moose whined and fidgeted. Joanna laughed. ''Good idea,'' she said.

She watched Ben survey the parking area closely, then hobble over to confer with Rafe.

They appeared to be having a rather animated discussion, with the older cowboy shaking his head and throwing out his hands, palm up, pointing toward the road.

Unable to hear the conversation, she studied her surroundings. Beneath the illumination of several security lights overhead, there appeared to be a building large enough for an indoor arena, plus an assortment of barns and corrals. Everything looked neat, well kept. To the right, the lights of a sprawling house twinkled through the wind-tossed branches of the surrounding trees.

In a few minutes, Ben returned to the SUV, radiating tension he hadn't shown before. He braced one arm on the roof of the vehicle and bent to peer inside. ''He hasn't seen either horse. Tomorrow morning we'll go out and find them.''

Worry fluttered through her midsection. ''Maybe they disappeared up into the mountains forever. Maybe they didn't like each other and went off in different directions.''

''Not likely.'' He nodded toward the northwest, where the Sangre de Cristo Mountains lay in darkness. ''After four years of drought, there's damn little grazing up in the foothills, and my filly was born here. I expect she'll head this way toward her dinner and her old buddies.''

"If not?''

"Manny Cordova is an old horseman who lives a few miles from you to the north. I'll let him know, just in case the horses end up in his area. I'll also call the Enchantment police and the county sheriff.''

Even in the dim light, she could see that Ben's eyes were filled with worry. What had he and Rafe discussed? She'd bet her favorite stethoscope it was something other than a few missing horses. "When I get Galahad back, I'll do my best to keep him home.''

Ben's pensive gaze flicked toward the ranch road leading to the highway. "That'll only happen if you rebuild that fence of yours. Ole Galahad obviously doesn't consider it much of an obstacle.''

Fencing? "I'm just *renting* the place.''

Ben lifted a shoulder. "You could run electric wire. That would keep him away from the fences, and you could take the charger with you when you leave.''

"When I go back to California I'll move him to a nice, safe boarding stable.'' She paused, then gave Ben a hopeful look. "Could I just board him with you while I'm in town? He wouldn't be much trouble.''

"Nope.''

She gestured toward the barns and arena. "I thought you were in the horse business.''

"Training and breeding, not public boarding.''

"But—''

"Sorry.'' He stepped away from the Tahoe. "Check the bulletin board at the feed mill in town. I'm sure you'll find some other places close by. If you can't, I'll check with some friends. Manny might know of someone.''

He seemed almost wary now, and she wondered why. "How about for just a day or two? As soon as I figure out how to put up that electric wire, I'll be all set. That is," she added sadly, "assuming that Galahad is found."

Folding his arms, Ben studied the toes of his boots. Finally, he gave a long sigh. "All right. And I'll send Rafe over to help with your fence so it gets done right."

He didn't seem very enthusiastic, but at least he'd agreed to help her out.

Which is all she wanted—or needed—from a New Mexico cowboy whose world revolved around livestock and perhaps a hot time at the local roadhouse on Saturday nights.

Right?

CHAPTER TWO

ENCHANTMENT'S MAIN STREET, Paseo de Sierra, charmed Joanna with its array of coffeehouses, art galleries and gift shops. Old-fashioned boardwalks and pots of flowering plants by many of the doorways invited leisurely browsing.

At eight o'clock in the morning there were few other cars on the road, so she drove slowly, taking in the fascinating storefronts. A few looked like quaint cottages, some were of rustic timber, but most were of the area's ubiquitous earth-tone adobe.

At both ends of Paseo de Sierra, the downtown area gave way to chalets and log cabins displaying outdoor-adventure equipment of every conceivable type. Fishing. Hunting. Backpacking. Mountain biking. Given the crisp bite of early-October air at this high altitude, the bright assortment of skis and snowboards were probably already doing brisk trade.

She continued down the quiet street, studying the street signs, and turned up Desert Valley Road, a heavily shaded lane that wound past several law offices and well-kept homes. At the corner of Copper Avenue, she stopped in front of the Enchantment Pediatric Clinic where she would soon be working. She hesitated in front of the one-story adobe building, then drove on. *Later—I'll be ready just a little bit later.*

The tap dancing in her stomach told her otherwise. Returning to pediatrics meant once again facing her old sorrows.

The lane narrowed, winding through stands of cotton-woods cloaked in bright fall yellows. Soon, hardwoods gave way to pine and juniper scrabbling for a foothold among massive boulders and rocky outcroppings. A deep, sagebrush-strewn ravine fell away to one side.

The lane ended at a tumble of boulders and a rugged ascent that would be possible only on foot. To the right, a graveled circle driveway led to the front steps of a two-story adobe building.

Peaceful and unadorned, save for the turquoise trim around the mullioned windows and the overflowing pots of salmon and hot-pink bougainvillea flanking the front door, it could have been mistaken for a staid insurance company or accounting firm if not for the small white-and-turquoise sign in front that read, The Birth Place.

During her phone conversations with Birth Place founder Lydia Kane, Joanna had thought the woman sounded compassionate and dedicated. But while those qualities were important, so were high-tech birth suites and well-staffed hospitals, where the latest technology might save a mother or baby's life. Why would anyone choose anything less?

The moment Joanna walked into the building, she felt her preconceptions start to shift.

The gleaming Mexican-tile floors of the entry and waiting areas were decorated with colorful Navajo-print rugs, while southwestern prints and cheerful health posters—English and Spanish versions—adorned the walls. Flames danced behind the glass doors of an adobe fireplace in the corner, taking away the early-morning chill. The warm scent of peach tea wafted from the reception area.

Warm, welcoming, homelike, the atmosphere enveloped her in an unexpected sense of comfort.

The young women—midwives?—coming and going down the hall with stethoscopes draped around their necks and clipboards held at the crook of their arms were casually dressed, but even at a distance they appeared to be professional and confident.

A dozen Hispanic, Native American and Anglo women, most in varying stages of pregnancy, filled the leather-upholstered furniture in the waiting room. In the corner, a group of young children played with a bright assortment of toys.

Joanna caught a glimpse of a hugely pregnant woman in the hallway at the left, who surely had to be in labor. Waddling slowly, she braced one hand at the small of her back and the other on her belly. A young woman in clogs and a long denim dress walked with her, talking to her in low tones.

Another employee, a short, plump Hispanic woman, wearing a jack-o'-lantern print lab coat over jeans and a T-shirt, sauntered into the waiting room and smiled at a woman who appeared to be in her early forties. *"Buenos días, Señora Martinez. ¿Se acuerda de mí?"*

The older woman smiled and tilted her head in thought. *"Sí. ¿Lenora?"*

Nodding, Lenora exchanged a few more pleasantries with her. The two of them soon disappeared into an exam room down the hall.

Behind the high reception counter, a middle-aged brunette finished speaking into a phone and cradled the receiver. She glanced up at Joanna with a welcoming smile. "I'm Trish. Can I help you?"

"Is Lydia Kane here?"

The receptionist's smile faltered, and a haunted expression flitted across her broad face. "If you're…um…with the media, I'm afraid she's…not available right now. You could leave your name…"

Media? "I'm Joanna Weston." Clearly flustered, Trish appeared almost ready to bolt. Joanna resisted the urge to reach out and comfort her. What on earth was going on here? "I'll be filling in for Dr. Davis for a few months."

A blush darkened Trish's cheeks. "Oh, gosh. I'm sorry. I should have known. Please wait here. I'll find out if Lydia can see you now."

She leaned forward and spoke into an intercom on her desk. Moments later, a tall, imposing woman appeared at the end of the hallway and strode toward Joanna.

"Welcome to Enchantment, Dr. Weston. I'm Lydia Kane." She extended a strong, tanned hand, her piercing gray eyes fixed on Joanna's. "We've been looking forward to meeting you."

From her steel-colored hair, caught in a loose bun, to her primitive sandals and the hand-woven, natural fabric of her casual slacks and pullover top, she radiated serenity and strength. Joanna could easily imagine her as a flower child of the sixties, one who'd milled her own flour, baked her own bread and demonstrated for world peace.

Her handcrafted jewelry—hammered-silver bangles at her wrists, large silver hoops in her ears and a charming rose-colored pendant on a long silver chain—reinforced the image.

"I'm delighted to meet you. If it hadn't been for your phone calls and encouragement, I might not have come here." The compassion in Lydia's eyes touched Joanna's heart. "This was...a difficult decision for me."

"I think you'll find it was the right one."

Was it? Her closest friends had thought so. When they heard about the opportunity in Enchantment, they'd urged her to accept, and had practically packed her bags. They'd seen Allen's condescension, his disregard for her feelings, and had figured a thousand miles would make all the difference.

But she knew the truth.

She'd developed immunity to Allen long ago. What

wouldn't change, no matter how far she traveled, was that her old grief would follow, as inescapable, as absolute, as the rise and fall of the sun each day.

After Hunter's death, she'd channeled her grief into providing the best possible care for her young patients—more than professional dedication, it had become an obsession. Then losing the Goldsteins' baby so soon after Hunter had torn her heart in two. Wracked with sorrow and self-doubt, she'd left pediatrics to work at a walk-in clinic in a retirement community where she saw mostly the elderly.

But maybe, after covering Dr. Davis's Enchantment Pediatric Clinic for a few months, she'd finally be ready to restart her career back in California with a job she'd dreamed of since her earliest days in medical school.

Dr. Hazelwood of famed Anderson Pediatric Clinic in San Diego, had offered her a position on his staff, and the clinic's close association with the university meant there would be fascinating opportunities for field research in addition to her pediatric practice. *Important* research that might help countless children in the future. A dream come true; an opportunity she couldn't pass up.

Lydia's voice pulled her back to the present. "We certainly need your help while Dr. Davis is gone," she continued. "By the way, I'm sorry our clinic administrator—Parker Reynolds—isn't here to greet you." She smiled fondly. "He got married just before you arrived, and he's taken his new wife and his little boy to Florida."

"I'll enjoy meeting him, but since you're the clinic's founder, I imagine you can give me all the information I need."

A shadow crossed Lydia's face. "I don't deal with administrative matters anymore."

"But you're on the board, if I remember correctly."

"I stepped down several months ago. For…personal reasons."

Perhaps the same reasons the receptionist had been so guarded? Carefully sidestepping the issue until they could speak privately, Joanna said, "One of your staff members found the ideal place for me to stay. It's a charming little cabin with a lovely view of the mountains—and it couldn't be more perfect."

Lydia's smile didn't quite reach her eyes. "That would be Kim Sherman, our accountant. She's absolutely the most efficient person we have on staff."

"I believe it. She had the place cleaned and my electricity and phone service started before I arrived." Joanna shook her head. "I owe your accountant a dinner."

"Well…" Lydia pursed her lips. "It's a nice thought, but don't be surprised if she refuses. She doesn't socialize much—all she seems to think about is work."

"Is she shy? Maybe I could just send her flowers."

Lydia laughed at that. "Believe me, she isn't shy. She's been here just a few months, and she's really making us watch the bottom line. She's also quite a barracuda when it comes to collections—something I've never done well."

"I'm afraid I don't know much about your operation, here. Dr. Davis and I mostly discussed the pediatric clinic. So…you assist with home births?"

Lydia regarded her thoughtfully. "You sound a bit hesitant."

That was an understatement, because any added risk to mother or child seemed too high a price to pay in the name of alternative, holistic medicine. "I do feel more comfortable with a pregnancy and delivery being supervised by an obstetrician."

"We're trained and licensed to operate independently, but we're associated with Dr. Ochoa, an O.B. at Arroyo County Hospital, as well as Dr. Davis. We immediately refer when there's increased risk for mother or child, but midwives consider birth a natural event that can usually take its own course, even in a home setting. It's wonderful when the husband and the rest of the family are closely involved.''

An all-too-familiar weight settled in Joanna's chest at the memory of Allen's reaction when their newborn's severe heart defect was diagnosed. Allen had been distant, retreating behind his professional persona, and she'd never forgiven him for that total lack of empathy and support.

''Joanna?'' Lydia's forehead creased with concern. ''Is there something wrong?''

''No—not at all.'' She tried to remember where the conversation had been leading. ''I'd…love to see the rest of the place. Is it busy?''

''We average an eighty-client caseload per month.''

Joanna gave a low whistle as she and Lydia started down the hall. ''A lot for such a small town.''

''But they're not just from here. We take patients who live within an hour radius of the clinic. Sometimes,'' she added, ''we have patients who come from farther away to stay in Enchantment so they can use our services.''

''And your staff?''

''The office staff, plus four midwives.'' Lydia stopped by an unoccupied exam room and ushered Joanna inside. ''Not quite the standard clinic, is it?''

The room held the expected sink and supply cabinets and exam table. Not so expected were the soft coral walls, the mural of a playground, the comfortable couch and upholstered chair in the opposite corner. ''This is lovely.''

''We have the usual equipment for exams, of course, but much of our time is spent talking to our clients. We want everyone to be as comfortable as possible.''

Despite her initial reservations, Joanna's curiosity was piqued. ''Do you do many home visits?''

''We accommodate our patients' wishes as much as possible.'' Lydia smiled. ''We do home births, we have birthing rooms here, or we attend our patients' deliveries at the hospital, if need be. The woman's primary midwife follows her through the entire labor and delivery."

"Long hours, then."

"Yes, but this work is a calling, not just a career. The joy of bringing babies into the world is beyond anything else." Lydia's voice conveyed a sense of deep satisfaction. "Midwives are also allowed to offer birth-control counseling and do annual gynecological exams."

Which would account for the older women out in the waiting room, Joanna realized. Farther down the hallway, she stopped in front of a crazy quilt of hundreds of photographs on a large bulletin board. Babies of all ages. Older children posing with newborns. Parents cuddling infants.

Everything she had hoped for and lost on that gray day in December two years ago. "Your success stories?" she managed to say.

"We have an excellent track record." Lydia led the way toward the other end of the building. "Of course, we immediately transfer any high-risk cases to the obstetrician. We're an alternative, but we aren't in competition with the medical community. We want only the best outcome for mother and child." She waved toward several open doors. "These are our birthing rooms."

Joanna stopped to peer inside them both. The decor was bright and cheerful, with ferns hanging at the windows and colorful Navajo-print blankets folded at the foot of each bed. Each room had a counter and cupboard along one wall, and a waiting bassinet in the corner. "Very nice," she murmured.

"We want these rooms to seem like home for those who choose to deliver here." Lydia paused at an open doorway marked Business Office in the central administrative area. Inside, a petite blond woman in her mid-twenties sat facing a computer screen, her forehead creased in concentration. "Kim Sherman, I'd like you to meet Dr. Joanna Weston."

The young woman pushed her wire rims up with an index finger and gave an almost imperceptible nod to Joanna. "Lydia, I need to talk to you about your accounts receivable stats, when you've got a minute."

Joanna stepped into the room and approached the desk with her hand outstretched. "Thanks so much for all your help with my cabin, Kim. Your choice was perfect."

Kim gave a slight shrug, but didn't accept Joanna's hand. "No problem."

"And thanks for arranging the cleaning lady, too," Joanna persisted. "The place was spotless when I moved in."

"Kim has been a godsend to the clinic," Lydia interjected smoothly into the awkward silence that followed. She gave the accountant a warm smile. "I'll be in my office after lunch, Kim."

At the sound of a man's voice at the reception desk, Joanna turned to see a short, burly man with thinning red hair combed carefully over his shiny scalp. He nodded to several of the pregnant women in the waiting area, his smile widening when he noticed an elderly woman sitting with a girl who might have been her granddaughter. "*¡Buenos días,* Señora Marquez!"

He moved closer to her, his voice lowering to a confidential tone, but when his gaze flicked around the room and landed on Lydia, he stilled and raised an eyebrow.

Lydia gave him a curt nod, then shepherded Joanna toward her office a few doors down, shutting the door behind them.

"Is he an employee?"

"No, that's Stuart Pennington. He sits on the board of The Birth Place."

And he probably had some strong opinions on how to

run it, given Lydia's brisk tone. "You certainly have a lovely office."

The southwestern theme continued here as well. Collector-quality pottery graced the small tables at either end of a cushioned leather sofa. Between the sofa and chairs sat a low coffee table covered with stacks of magazines on parenting and several issues of the *Journal of Midwifery and Women's Health.* Books on obstetrics, holistic-health issues and pediatrics overflowed the bookshelves lining one wall.

A painting of a Native American mother and child hung above the sofa, and on the massive oak desk were dozens of framed photographs. Family? Clients? The overall effect was as soothing and peaceful as the woman herself.

"Would you like some herbal tea? Coffee?"

Joanna glanced at her watch and shook her head, wishing she could prolong her visit. "I should probably get over to my office. Can I just ask what you expect from me during the next few months? I know I'll mostly be seeing patients at the children's clinic, but I'd like the transition from Dr. Davis to be as seamless as possible."

"If we have any problems during a birth, you'll be contacted immediately, of course. Otherwise, you'll be seeing newborns at your clinic for their first checkups. Dr. Davis does house calls for the new mothers who can't make the trip to town. He wasn't too keen on the idea at first," she added wryly. "But over time he has become a good advocate for us."

House calls. A step into the past, and one she would enjoy while here. "I look forward to working with you, Lydia."

Lydia settled into her chair and studied Joanna with a thoughtful expression. "If you're interested, maybe you could give some classes for new moms while you're here. Doctors Davis and Ochoa have been talking about starting a program for some time."

"And…you're losing patience with them."

Lydia gave a low, throaty laugh. "I want everything done yesterday for my moms and babies. It would be such a benefit—especially for our young teen moms who've grown up on frozen pizza and carbonated soda. Some of these kids come from difficult home situations themselves, so we try to work with them from every angle. We have classes with Celia Brice, our local psychologist, and Alice Richards, our social worker, but you could provide a whole new medical perspective."

"And when I leave, Dr. Davis will be obligated to continue?"

"Exactly." Lydia chuckled. "I think it's the women in this world who get things done, don't you?"

Joanna nodded in agreement. "I do have one question. When I first walked in here, the receptionist seemed alarmed and asked if I was with the media. Why was that?"

Lydia's expression cooled. "We've…had a few changes here."

When the older woman didn't elaborate, Joanna sat up straighter in her chair. "I'll be associated with your clinic. I need to know what's going on."

"The Birth Place serves a great many low-income families, and a lot of them fall through the cracks between welfare and the ability to pay on their own. We depend on substantial donations every year. We recently lost some of our financial backers."

"Why?"

Lydia seemed to choose her words with care. "Tough economic times, I suppose, with the years of severe drought we've had around here." She gave a negligent wave of her hand. "That loss of funding may have affected the confidence of some people in the community. Rumors fly in a small town, and now our patient count is down by ten or fifteen percent. A temporary situation…but the board is concerned.''

"Stuart?" Joanna guessed.

Lydia's mouth thinned. "He's one of our more…conservative members, but his family is also one of the biggest contributors, thanks to his wife. He married into local money—one of the big ranching families in the area."

"So he wields a bit of power."

"A bit. So, Joanna, tell me about your trip out here. Any problems?"

Warning bells sounded in Joanna's head when she walked out of the building a few minutes later and tried to sort out the enigmatic woman she'd just met. There'd been veiled sadness in Lydia's eyes, and perhaps a touch of anger as well. Despite direct questions, her answers had been too vague.

What could have motivated her to step down from a position at the clinic that meant so much to her?

CHAPTER THREE

AFTER LEAVING The Birth Place, Joanna drove down Desert Valley Road to the Enchantment Pediatric Clinic. Peaceful, tall pines shaded this building as well, and the bright yellow front door set against the rust-red adobe gave the clinic a cheerful air.

Inside, the reception area was cool and dark, set with plastic chairs, speckled brown linoleum and a scattering of children's books and toys strewn on a square of orange carpet in one corner. The gift for creating a welcoming atmosphere obviously hadn't extended to Dr. Davis.

A young woman sitting at the front desk looked up and smiled. In her late teens, probably of mixed Anglo and Hispanic heritage, her lustrous black hair swung from a high ponytail and she wore a crisp white uniform. "Are you Dr. Weston?"

The note of awe in her voice made Joanna smile. "I am—and you must be Nicki?"

"Yes, ma'am…I mean, Doctor. Gosh, I never thought— I mean, I knew you were a lady, but—" She ducked her head with obvious embarrassment. "I mean, you're a lot younger and prettier than I thought."

A feeling of uncertainty had settled in the pit of Joanna's stomach as she stepped in the front door, but the awkward shyness of the young girl at the desk disarmed her completely. *I can do this, it will be all right.* "Thanks. Although I have to admit that after the long drive here and some…um…problems with my horse yesterday, I feel as though I've aged a few decades overnight."

"The horse that got away?" Nicki grinned. "Gina told me all about Galahad last night."

"Gina?"

"You didn't meet her?" Nicki frowned. "Maybe she was out on a home visit or at the hospital this morning. She doesn't look at all like her brother Ben, 'cause she's this bitty little gal with *red* hair, but you'll like her a lot."

Ben Carson? Small world. Feeling as though her head was starting to spin, Joanna gave it a slight shake. "That's…good."

Nicki laughed. "Sorry. My sisters always tell me I should let my brain catch up with my mouth. Trish over at The Birth Place called to tell me you were on your way here. Gina's the newest midwife they have, and she's really cool. I baby-sit her two girls sometimes, when she has to be out on evening or night calls."

"I see."

"Oh, hold on." Nicki shuffled through a stack of haphazard notes on her desk, then held out two pink telephone-message forms. "Dr. Davis called, and gave me the number where he can be reached in New York. You can call him if you have any questions about the clinic, and he's real sorry he couldn't be here to show you around. A Dr. Allen Holcomb called from California…" She searched her desk again, with increasing agitation, before holding up a third note with a gusty sigh of relief. "And here's a note from Ben—" she breathed his name as if he was a major movie star "—who says he found your horse, and that you should call his cell phone as soon as you get in. I wrote down his number for you."

Alarm snaked through Joanna. Had he found Galahad dead? Killed by some mountain lion or bear? Had the poor old gelding broken a leg? "I need a phone."

Nicki jumped to her feet. "Sure—in Dr. Davis's—er, in *your* office."

Four exam rooms, a laboratory, consultation room and a small employee lounge flanked the wide hallway leading to the rear of the building. Nicki ushered Joanna through the last door, into a spacious office dominated by a massive carved mahogany desk, leather upholstered chairs and two stained-glass floor lamps in dark jewel tones. An immense, original painting of the Sangre de Cristo Mountains on one wall completed a setting of luxury and comfort completely missing from the waiting room out in front.

Joanna moved behind the desk and settled into the executive-style chair. "Thanks, Nicki."

"Eve is our nurse and she'll be in at noon. I'll bring you tomorrow's charts, if you want to see what your first day will be like."

"Thank you."

The girl waggled her fingers and quietly closed the door behind her.

Tomorrow's charts.

Joanna's heartbeat thrummed in her ears as she remembered that last hospital call two years ago in San Diego, when she'd desperately tried to save a newborn's parents the kind of grief she was dealing with herself. Despite her best efforts, the baby had died, and losing him just months after her own son's death had devastated her.

The next morning, she'd turned in her notice at Ocean View Pediatric Clinic.

"You can't take this job personally," Allen always said. *"Some patients you just can't save. Keep your distance."*

It was what anyone in medicine had to do to stay sane, she supposed, because getting too close, caring too much, was a dangerous thing. But she'd never been able to manage that kind of emotional detachment—except by leaving the medical specialty she loved most.

Shaking off the past, she read the scrawled number on the slip of paper and dialed. After the fourth ring, Ben's familiar deep voice answered.

"We found your horse," he said. "He's okay…so far."

Relief washed through her. Last night she'd had a hard time falling asleep, and this morning she'd awakened imagining what might have happened to the gelding. "Thank you so much," she said. "But what do you mean so far?"

"He's…uh…temporarily in one of our corrals."

"And you want me to bring him home as soon as possible." Joanna chewed her lower lip, trying to remember where she'd seen the ranch-supply store in town. "I'll go buy the electric fence charger tonight."

"Plus the wire, and the insulators—the kind you can nail to wood posts. Tell the clerk that you need enough supplies for however many acres you have there, so you get enough."

Joanna found a notepad on the desk and jotted down the items. "Got it. Anything else?"

"Make sure it's a weed-burner unit. One with a good strong jolt."

The thought of hurting Galahad made her wince. "Is that necessary?"

"Only if you want to keep him home and out of trouble. He's gone over my five-foot fence twice this morning. The first time, he wandered over to the house, stood on the patio and stared in the kitchen windows. Nearly scared my poor aunt Sadie to death. The second time, he figured out the latch on the feed room and ripped up two fifty-pound sacks of supplement. He's kept Rafe and my nephew, Dylan, busy most of the day. We finally put our stallion in his box stall so we could use his exercise run for Galahad because the fence is higher."

"Oh," she said faintly. Galahad had been so thin, so old when she won the high bid on him. He'd definitely been limping at the time. Who would have guessed that he'd turn into an equine Houdini? "Weed burner it is."

He must have heard the hint of reluctance in her voice, because he gave a heavy sigh. "Look, it won't hurt him. One zap of a hot wire and he'll stay clear. As long as you keep it plugged in," he warned. "I swear, some horses can sense the current without touching the fence. If it's off, they grab the wire with their teeth and start pulling it from the insulators."

"Sort of like payback time?" Joanna laughed. "Sounds like revenge to me."

"They aren't that smart. Once the wire's down, they usually get tangled in the coils. This evening I'll send Rafe over to help you put up the fence. Five o'clock okay?"

"Perfect. I can't tell you how much I appreciate the help."

"I'll just appreciate seeing that horse leave," he muttered.

The connection ended.

Nicki knocked softly and eased into the office to place a stack of charts on the desk. "Sorry to interrupt, ma'am."

Joanna dropped the receiver into its cradle. "You didn't interrupt anything at all. Tell me, do you know Ben?"

"Of course. Everyone around here knows everyone else." Nicki gave a dreamy sigh. "He's hot."

"Really?" He'd been a little distracted by the loss of his horse, but she'd seen hints of an easy, confident sort of bad-boy attitude—the kind of guy who knew what women wanted, and expected them to fall at his feet. Exactly the kind of man she was smart enough to distrust.

"You didn't notice?" Nicki stared at her in disbelief. "He's the biggest catch in Arroyo County!"

"I guess I didn't see him at his best. My horse has tried his patience."

"People bring him training horses clear from California

and Texas, so one old horse shouldn't be much of a challenge.'' She winked. ''He does have quite a reputation around here, but it sure isn't for being cranky. He has women…'' Nicki's voice lilted upward suggestively, then trailed off. Her mouth curved into a grin. ''He's too old for me, but his nephew, Dylan, is pretty cute. If I was four years younger, I'd go after him like a rocket.''

''I haven't met him,'' Joanna said dryly.

Nicki hovered at the door for a moment, apparently savoring the mental image of young Dylan. She gave an embarrassed shrug. ''I'd…um…better get out to the front desk.''

Joanna had just started to review the second chart on her desk when she heard the front-door chimes.

Seconds later footsteps rushed down the hall and Nicki appeared at the door with another chart in her hand. ''Dr. Weston? I know you weren't planning to start working until tomorrow, but we have a two-year-old patient in the waiting room…do you mind? I could send her over to the hospital, but…'' She chewed at her lower lip. ''I don't know if Val would take her daughter there.''

Joanna held out her hand for the chart. ''Why not?''

''Um…'' Nicki's gaze slid away. ''Val's had some problems, and…''

''What kind?''

''Some trouble with the law. With the county social workers. They even took Shanna away from her for about six months, but she's doing better now.''

''Drugs?''

''Just weed. And alcohol, I think.''

Just? Joanna shook her head slowly. ''Is she a friend of yours?''

''Yeah—but I don't mess with that stuff, believe me,'' Nicki said fervently. ''So will you see them? She thinks it's Shanna's ears again.''

"Of course. Bring her into an exam room."

With a short nod, Nicki headed back down the hall. A few minutes later, Joanna finished reviewing the child's medical history and closed the chart.

Low birth weight. Had Val been smoking during pregnancy? Using?

Below normal on the growth curve. Did this mother bother to provide adequate meals? *Numerous upper-respiratory infections.*

Even in the most caring families these conditions could occur, but Val's history was likely a major factor in this child's status.

When Joanna stepped inside the exam room, her heart skipped a beat. The tiny child perched on the table shot a frightened glance at her, then dropped her head and cowered over a threadbare stuffed bunny. Her curly brown hair was wild, her ragged tennis shoes were untied. Even from a few feet away, Joanna could smell tobacco in the child's clothes.

So her mother had money for cigarettes, but not to buy the child decent shoes.

Reining in her frustration, Joanna gave the little girl a cheerful, reassuring smile, then turned toward the thin teenager sitting on a chair in the corner with her chin lifted in defiance. From her skintight, spaghetti-strap crop top, to her gleaming belly ring and low-slung jeans that might have been shrink-wrapped to her long legs, she couldn't have appeared less maternal.

The fact that she'd plopped into a distant chair without staying close to her daughter was confirmation of that fact. The child needed comfort, reassurance. At the very least, she needed to be watched so she wouldn't fall to the hard vinyl floor.

"You're the *doc?*"

"Doctor Jo." Joanna moved forward and did a quick

assessment as she offered her hand to the girl. "And you're Val?"

"Yeah." Val straightened up in her chair and awkwardly returned the handshake.

She smelled of cigarette smoke, too, but her pupils appeared normal, her hand was cool and dry. Her speech was clear...her breath free of alcohol. A quick glance at the girl's forearms revealed no evidence of needle tracks. *Thank God.*

"Shanna's ears hurt," the girl muttered. "She kept me and my grandma up all night."

"Why don't you come over here, so she'll know you're close by," she said. "It's important to be close to your mom when you hurt, right?"

Val shrugged, but slowly rose to her feet. "She needs that medicine again. Do you have samples?"

Joanna glanced at Nicki, who still stood at the door. Nicki nodded toward a high cupboard over the sink. "We might, but let me check."

The little girl ducked her head lower, and silent, fresh tears spilled onto her faded red shorts. Her shoulders trembled.

Nicki had set out an otoscope and stethoscope on the table, but Shanna appeared almost petrified, so Joanna lowered her voice to a singsong, playful level. "That is one of the *prettiest* bunnies I've ever seen. Hmm...does he have ears?"

Shanna gripped her bunny tighter.

"Did you know that sometimes, if we're really lucky, we can peek inside a bunny's ear and find *elephants?*"

The child wiggled her dangling feet.

"Have you ever seen my magic spyglass?"

Raising her chin a few inches, she shot a furtive glance toward Joanna's hands.

"Would you like to see inside your bunny's ears?"

Val gave an exaggerated sigh. "She usually screams, but you can just *make* her sit still."

"I'd rather have fun, wouldn't you?" Joanna kept her voice level. "So coming here can be easier." She flicked on the otoscope light and danced the tiny beam across the exam table.

After a long hesitation, the little girl loosened her grip on her bunny and searched Joanna's face, then her shoulders relaxed. She edged the stuffed animal a few inches away from her chest.

With an exaggerated show of effort, Joanna examined the rabbit's ears. "Whoa! I thought I saw some giraffes, but they ran away. Would you like to try?"

When the child gave a jerky nod, Joanna positioned the otoscope and bunny for her. "See anything?"

The child squinted the wrong eye. Repositioned herself and tried again.

"Any luck?"

She straightened, and gave Joanna a solemn look. "Bears."

"Cool! You have one amazing bunny, there. Can he and I peek in *your* ears?"

Though she stiffened, Shanna sat quietly while Joanna checked her left ear. On the right, she cried out and flinched. No wonder—the tympanic membrane was inflamed and bulging.

After checking the child's temperature and lungs, Joanna gave her thin shoulders a quick hug. "What a good girl you are! I'll bet we have stickers here someplace. Would you like one?"

Lifting her down to the floor, Joanna reached for a box of stickers on the counter and handed it to her. "Find the best one, okay? And get one for your bunny, too, because he was really a good helper." To Val, she said, "Her lungs sound clear, but she has an infection in the right ear and she's running a 101.1 fever. She needs to be on antibiotics."

"How long?"

Joanna turned to the supply cupboard and scanned the contents, thankful when she found an adequate number of samples and a new dosage syringe. "One teaspoon of this—see the mark on the syringe? Twice a day. For ten days."

She wrote the directions on a sheet of paper and dropped it into a small bag with the bottles and syringe. "Be sure to come back in two weeks for a recheck. Any questions?"

"No." Val grabbed Shanna's hand and started for the door.

"I'm glad I got to meet you, Val. If you ever have any questions please stop by, okay? About anything. Raising young children can be a challenge, and I'd love to help."

"Uh…thanks."

"Remember—two weeks. Bye, Shanna."

The child glanced over her shoulder and smiled, but her mother gave her hand a firm tug and they disappeared down the hall.

Out in the waiting room, Joanna heard Nicki talk to her friend for a while. A moment later, the front door of the clinic opened and closed.

No wonder Lydia wanted to offer more classes for new and expectant moms. Joanna leaned against the exam table and closed her eyes. A cold tide of emotion washed through her, leaving emptiness in its wake. Would Val bother to return? If Shanna wasn't crying about ear pain, probably not.

What future did that adorable little girl have? Or her mother, for that matter?

Unwanted children were born every day. Children were abused, or neglected, or simply ignored. *I would have been such a loving mother—devoted and determined to give my child the best I could afford.* Why was life so unfair?

With a sigh, Joanna turned on the tape recorder lying on the counter and dictated a progress note on Shanna, then she went down to her office and gathered her things. Tomorrow, she would be ready to work.

Right now, she needed to go home.

THE MOMENT BEN CARSON laid eyes on Joanna Weston yesterday, he'd been intrigued…despite his better judgment.

He liked women. He liked the scent of them, the softness of their skin, their gentle laughter. He loved the way they could talk, and tease, and make a guy feel like he wanted to conquer the world for them. He'd always figured on settling down someday and having a family.

But those dreams had gone south three years ago, with the abrupt and breezy departure of the woman he'd loved, heart and soul. The woman he'd planned to love for the rest of his days.

He'd been thinking *forever.* Apparently Rachel had been thinking *just for now—until someone richer, more successful came along.* When her dream guy showed up at Ben's ranch with two outstanding Doc Bar-bred colts and an unlimited bank account, she'd taken one good look and packed her bags.

She might as well have crammed Ben's heart in one of those suitcases along with her shoes, because since then he hadn't found the energy, interest or ability to go beyond a casual flirtation. Anything more just reminded him how painful the whole process could be.

A system that had worked just fine until Doc Weston came down that trail searching for her blasted horse.

Something had turned over in his chest at the first glimpse of her. Like a rusted engine, his dormant heart had managed a faltering little kick start, and maybe even started to beat. But a survivor didn't take chances, and Ben had reacted instinctively.

He'd turned down Joanna's offers of help.

He'd refused to board her horse.

To avoid running into her again, he'd even offered to help fix her fence so her hayburner would stay put, and she would stay out of his life.

But…that was where he'd slipped off course. He'd planned to send Dylan and Rafe over to help with her fence. It was an easy job, and the kid had helped him run hot wire in the broodmare's pasture just last week.

Better yet, he could have sent Rafe's dad, Felipe, who sometimes came to stay with his son for months at a time and enjoyed making a little money now and then. Felipe had seen seventy summers and wouldn't find himself thinking the doctor was too damn fine to be all alone at her isolated cabin.

But the afternoon had come and gone, and Ben hadn't gotten around to telling anyone about the fencing job. They'd been busy, he'd been busy. Then everyone had headed to Slim Jim's for supper, and he'd stayed behind. Hell, it was just easier to do it himself and get it done right.

That she had all that curly blond hair escaping her ponytail and those pretty blue eyes had no bearing on the job at hand. Especially not when she was such a city slicker. What kind of fool went to a horse sale and bought a lame horse? Buying a sound one in that setting was risky enough.

The fact that her gelding seemed to think it was a steeplechaser and refused to stay corralled—despite its diagnosis—meant he might turn up at the ranch again and again, in search of equine company.

Which meant Joanna would be turning up at the ranch, too.

As Ben pulled to a stop in front of her cabin, he made

a firm vow to himself. He would install the electric fence, haul her horse back up here and go home. Period. No idle conversation over a cup of coffee, no casual flirtations with the new neighbor.

But the moment Joanna stepped out of her cabin onto the wide, covered porch, with that huge white furball, his intentions were shot straight to hell.

Coffee sounded nice.

Flirting sounded better.

"Hi, there," she called out. "Sorry I'm running late. I had to take care of some errands, and I got sidetracked by the most beautiful scenic drive I've ever seen. Want to come in for a moment?"

Rolling down his truck window, he wavered for only a heartbeat as his common sense warred with rising curiosity about her. "No, ma'am. I can wait here."

Her laughter floated toward him, soft and sweet. "I'll be just a minute."

Translated, that likely meant a good half hour. If he moved fast, he could get most of the insulators done before she came outside, avoid a lot of chitchat, and be on his way much sooner.

Her dog launched himself off the porch steps when she disappeared into the cabin. He barreled up to the woven wire fencing surrounding the yard and threw himself at it, his front paws hanging over the top as he barked furiously and wagged his tail.

Ben opened the door of his truck and reached for the fencing pliers and leather gloves on the seat, settled his hat low on his head and stepped onto the graveled parking area. The dog's barks escalated when Ben slammed the truck door and headed for the plastic sacks from Elkhorn's Hardware Store that had been left by the pasture gate.

He'd hammered plastic insulators onto just six of the fence posts, when he heard footsteps come up behind him.

Joanna watched him hammer another insulator into place. "If that's all there is to it, I can do this myself and save you the time. Just show me how to hook up to the charger and I'll be all set."

He'd planned to get this job done fast and head for home. Neighborly assistance, and nothing more. But finding Joanna was just as eager to cut this short made him realize that maybe he didn't want to leave right away, after all.

"Two can get it done faster." He reached in the sack, withdrew another insulator and held it against a fence post as he drove a nail home through the center. "Once we finish the corral, you can keep your horse in it until the rest is done."

"Thanks." She studied the cut on his face, then glanced at his leg. "That laceration looks good. How's your ankle?"

"No problem." Her dubious expression made him chuckle. "Out here, a little sprain or strain is nothing. Some ranch hands suture their own wounds, dose themselves with antibiotics from the feed store and think doctors are for pansies."

She lifted a hand to her chest in mock horror, her eyes twinkling. "I'd forgotten just how tough you cowboys are."

He made damn sure he didn't limp on his way to the next fence post. "There's an extra hammer by the gate, if you want to get started."

"Yes, sir."

She retrieved the hammer and started working around the corral in the opposite direction.

Fascinated, he lost his concentration and whacked his own thumb twice, because she was just so darn interesting to watch. With each precise swing of her hammer she bit her lower lip and frowned, giving the task her full concentration, but it was those snug Levi's and those long, slender legs that kept capturing his attention.

When the wiring was done and hooked up to the charger, she grinned at him and offered her hand for a quick handshake. "It was sure nice of you to help me. I really appreciate it."

"No problem." And it sure wasn't, if it meant that her horse stayed where he belonged from now on. Ben needed to be left alone. No interruptions, no casual visits that might distract him from what really mattered.

This year he'd had to face reality. After years of drought followed by a plummeting cattle market and with heavy taxes coming due in two months, he needed to concentrate on the ranch and his training horses, and on those who depended on him.

There just wasn't time for anything else.

CHAPTER FOUR

"I DIDN'T ASK TO COME HERE." Dylan's jaw lifted to a stubborn angle, but he didn't quite make eye contact. "And you aren't my dad. You can't tell me what to do."

"But I have to keep you in one piece until he gets home from the Middle East." Mindful of his taped ankle, Ben stepped lightly up into the saddle and settled the nervous buckskin filly with a hand on her neck. "He said," Ben added with a smile, "that this would be a great opportunity to bond with your favorite uncle."

"As if I had any others," Dylan muttered under his breath.

"Make the best of it, kid." Ben nodded toward the mountain range looming to the north and west. The late-afternoon sun lit the distant stands of aspen to molten gold. "How different could anyplace be from New York? Next weekend, we can ride up into the backcountry and camp if you'd like. Have you ever gone fly fishing?"

The mutinous line of the fifteen year-old boy's mouth didn't waver, though he gave a noncommittal shrug.

Ben could hardly blame him for being angry. His mother had died when he was five, and with a divorced father who worked as a foreign-news correspondent, Dylan had probably spent more time being shuffled off to nannies and housekeepers than he'd ever spent with his dad.

"If you don't want to, that's fine. But no matter what, you've got to follow the rules. You can't take a car or pickup again. Anywhere."

"So I'm stuck here."

"You're welcome to ride Patches or use a four-wheeler, but you don't leave here without letting someone know exactly where you're going and when you're coming back."

"I'm not a five-year-old." Dylan shoved a hand through his hair. "I can take care of myself."

"But this is rough country. This ranch is almost a thousand acres. What happens if you drive over the edge of a ravine? Get thrown from your horse?"

"I can walk."

"Right. Unless you're hurt."

As convinced of his immortality as most other teenage boys, Dylan lifted an insolent shoulder.

"We could search for days and not find you. The temperature's dropping into the forties at night. People *die* of hypothermia."

"Don't forget the poisonous snakes," Dylan sneered. "I bet there's one under every rock."

"Not quite. We do have prairie rattlers here in the foothills. Timber rattlers as you get up into the mountains. A bit farther south, diamondbacks in the rocky canyons. But the days are getting too cool to see much of them." Ben tugged his hat lower over his forehead and counted to ten before he spoke again. Hadn't his brother, Phil, ever reprimanded this kid? Ever taught him basic manners? "I just want you to understand and use common sense."

The boy gave a defiant jerk of his head.

"And I'd appreciate basic courtesy toward your great-aunt Sadie."

The boy was already a good five foot ten, though still as angular and awkward as a yearling colt, but at the mention of his indiscretion yesterday the boy's teenage bravado slipped away and a dark blush crept up his cheeks. Now Ben could picture him as a much younger child—before he'd developed a chip on his shoulder and the attitude of a renegade biker.

"I didn't, like, mean it or anything."

"That doesn't make it okay. She can't help it if she gets a little confused." Ben gave the kid a dismissive head to toe glance. "Are you man enough to apologize to her?"

The arrogant expression returned in a flash, and the boy turned on his heel and stalked toward the main barn.

Apparently not.

Teenagers. Full of pride and independence, but no common sense. While Ben was helping with the fence at Joanna's last night, Dylan had taken one of the pickups and driven into town. Without a driver's license. Without a word to anyone. *"I needed to go the library,"* he'd said when he finally showed up a half-hour after dark. *"There wasn't anyone around to take me."* Then he'd pointed an accusing finger at Sadie and announced that he'd told her, but she obviously couldn't remember anything important.

Whether he'd told her or not, he'd still driven illegally. He'd also thoughtlessly hurt a sweet old lady who'd never said a cruel word against anyone in her life.

With a deep sigh, Ben pivoted the buckskin to the left and eased into a slow jog around the arena, driving her into the snaffle bit with leg pressure until her head dropped nice and low. When she relaxed and got down to business, he shook out some slack in the reins.

Horses were so much easier than people. Some bloodlines tended to be cranky, some flighty. But whatever the genetic predisposition, gentle, firm and consistent handling from the moment of birth made all the difference in the type of horse they became.

People were far less predictable. The best families could have children who slid into the morass of drugs and wild behavior. Seeing it happen with his friend's kids had tempered Ben's thoughts about parenthood long ago. Meeting his nephew had now confirmed his opinion.

Ben hadn't seen his brother for years. After their parents' divorce, the old man had taken Phil and headed for the West Coast, and had shown little interest in his two younger kids.

Phil, Ben and Gina had only recently started keeping in touch by phone and e-mail, and Phil had sure seemed proud of his son. So what had happened?

The buckskin moved smoothly under him as Ben took her through several big figure eights to work on her flying-lead changes. At the far end of the arena he cued her into a neat rollback, then poured on the speed down the center of the arena and dropped her into a sliding stop that left a pair of twenty-foot tracks. She bobbled out of it at the finish, taking a few steps to balance herself, but already she'd shown a lot of improvement this week.

After a few 360s, where she spun in a tight circle around the axis of her crouched hindquarters, he settled her with a stroke on her neck and headed for the gate. A few miles up in the foothills would do wonders to keep her fresh and open to her next session.

From the stallion run off the main barn, Joanna's paint gelding whinnied loudly. As Ben rode into view, Galahad bobbed his head up and down until he found a space to peer between the two-by-six oak planks.

This enclosure had a seven-foot fence, and was too small for him to take a run at it. So now he was contained, and he sure wasn't happy about it. His whinnies had echoed over the vast hills all night, shrill enough to awaken the dead in the neighboring town of Red River.

This evening Ben would take him to Joanna's place—thank God—so he'd be back where he belonged.

Last night Ben had helped her with the fence until after dark. The chore wasn't fun in anyone's book, but there'd been a certain amount of satisfaction in watching the doc wield a hammer with determination that more than made up for her lack of skill. Talking to her had been even better. She'd been surprisingly well informed about local environmental issues, current events and everything else they'd covered in those few short hours.

Ben smiled to himself at the memory. Maybe he owed her old fence-jumper a vote of thanks. Working with Joanna had been more entertaining than anything Ben had done for a good long while.

He'd ridden past the barns and had started to dismount at the gate for the north pasture, when he heard Dylan yell his name. Twisting in the saddle, Ben glanced over his shoulder and saw the boy outside the barn, leaning against the hitching post with his left foot cradled in his hands. Was he *hurt?*

Ben reined the filly into a pivot and loped back to the barn. "What's up?"

"I stepped on a nail." Dylan's face was a mask of worry. "Isn't that like, real bad, around a barn?"

"In the *barn?*" Every stall was bedded with deep pine shavings, every aisle swept. The exercise runs were inspected and cleaned daily. A stray wire, nail or broken board could mean sutures at the very least, disability or death at the worst for an unsuspecting horse, and Ben left nothing to chance.

"I…um…followed one of the kittens, and she disappeared into that pile of boards."

Those were old boards, from the corral Ben had torn down and rebuilt over the past two weeks. He hadn't yet finished pulling the nails out of them. "Do you know when you last had a tetanus shot?"

The boy turned a lighter shade of pale. "No."

"Your dad gave me the name and number of your doctor. We'll need to check that out." Ben dismounted. "Take off your boot."

"Jeez. It *hurts*. And…" He seemed to take on a greenish tinge. "It's sort of sticky in there. Like my foot is bleeding."

"Good."

Dylan shot him an accusing look. "You're glad?"

"Not that you're hurt," Ben said patiently. "It's good when a puncture wound bleeds a little to clear out some of the dirt."

Dylan gingerly pried off his boot, then peeled off his bloodstained white sock. Blood still seeped from the small, neat hole at the bottom of his heel.

Ben bent to inspect the wound. "I think I'd better call your aunt Gina to see what she says, and also check your vaccination records."

"You mean, like, I won't have to see a real doctor?" Dylan's voice filled with hope, then his expression fell. "But Gina just delivers babies. What does *she* know about anything?"

Ben bit back a sharp response. "She was a nurse for five years before she became a midwife. She knows a hell of a lot. And she's your aunt, so she cares about what happens to you. Can you make it up to the house?"

Dylan winced as he tugged the sock back on. "Yeah."

"After I put this filly away, I'll come in and make some calls. Go wash that foot really well, with lots of soap. Put on a clean pair of socks." Ben flicked a glance at the boy's ragged grunge-rock T-shirt advertising a band that must have been exhumed after a long stay six feet under. "And find a different shirt."

The rebellious sneer returned, but Dylan turned away and started for the house without a word.

By the time Ben got up to the house his nephew was sitting on a chair in the kitchen with new socks and a pair of old running shoes on. He hadn't changed his shirt, and from the defiant tilt of his chin he didn't plan to, either.

Aunt Sadie fluttered anxiously by his chair. "I had him use gauze squares and some adhesive tape. And some antibiotic cream." She wrung her hands. "But I don't know how deep the wound is. I remember the time when poor Hank got cut on the baler. That abscess—"

"Dylan will be fine," Ben interrupted gently, remembering all too well the graphic, oft-retold stories of Hank's various calamities. The boy hardly needed anything more to worry about right now. "I need to go to my office and make a couple calls. Could you make some lemonade?"

"Of course, of course." She scurried across the room, wiping her hands on the apron she always wore over her brightly flowered housedresses. Barely five feet tall, she was plump and motherly as a banty hen, with short white hair soft and wispy as goose down. "I even have a can thawed in the fridge."

Ben beckoned to Dylan as he started for his office. Once there, he settled down behind his desk and motioned the boy toward a chair. "Did your dad ever tell you much about Sadie?"

Dylan shrugged a shoulder.

"Years ago, Sadie and Uncle Hank lost a daughter in a car accident. A few years later, Hank died when his tractor rolled on him. Since then, Sadie's always expected the worst when anyone gets hurt. I hope you were patient with her."

"What, you think I can't be nice?" Dylan slumped in the chair. He scanned the room, his gaze settling on the framed certificates on the wall above him. "You went to *college?*"

Ben pulled open a drawer and thumbed through files until he found the new one labeled Dylan. "Yeah. Agricultural economics, New Mexico State." He spoke without glancing up as he paged through the contents. "I've got your insurance card here, and the name of a clinic on Williams Avenue in New York. Do you still go there?"

Dylan visibly cringed.

"You don't like the doctor?"

The sullen scowl on the boy's face spoke volumes. "He's a real jerk."

Ben almost smiled at that, guessing the feeling was probably mutual. After four weeks with the boy living at the ranch, he could imagine just how much the poor doctor enjoyed dealing with Dylan.

A long-distance call to a nurse at the clinic revealed Dylan was due for a tetanus booster.

He caught Gina on her cell phone just as she was flying out the door of The Birth Place to visit a homebound client.

"Take him to the pediatric clinic," she advised breathlessly. "I hear Dr. Jo is really nice. The E.R. at the hospital will mean a lot more waiting, because Dr. Selby is the one on call today. He won't hurry over for something like this."

Selby. Gray-haired, gruff and impatient, he seemed to think his word was the voice of God. Ben had a good idea of how Dylan would react to the imperious old coot. "Good idea."

"If my client is in false labor, I'll be back in town soon and will stop to see if you're still there. Bye."

As he hung up the phone, he gave a rueful shake of his head. He'd met Joanna the day she arrived. Last night he'd helped her with that fence. Today would make three days in a row that he'd run into her for one reason or another.

Good thing he had his priorities straight, or he might have been interested in getting to know her better.

The chirpy teenager who answered the phone at the pediatric clinic—Gina's young friend Nicki, he realized after a moment of disorientation—breezily announced that she could fit Dylan in if they arrived before five-fifteen.

Ben hung up the phone and found Dylan gazing at him with a curious expression.

"So why are you out here in the middle of nowhere?" the boy asked.

"Why?"

"I mean, like, there's hardly anyone out here and nothin' to do. You went to college. You couldn't find something better than this?"

Better? What could be better than this ranch, in the shadows of the mountains, with a view of Wheeler Peak rising above all the others on the horizon? Or this crisp, early-October weather? Or training top contenders for the reining-horse show circuit? The kid just didn't understand.

"You know, Dylan. While you're here, we could work on your people skills and really surprise the folks back home. What do you say?" Ben softened his words with a grin as he rose from his desk. When Dylan glowered at him, he added, "I'm going to change my shirt and grab a clean one of mine for you. Unless you want to choose one of yours?"

The boy stayed in his chair just long enough to telegraph his mulishness before launching to his feet and stalking to his room, the intended impact of his departure dampened by his limping stride.

Ben sighed heavily as he stared at the year-at-glance calendar on the wall. *October 7.* Two months to go—maybe longer, if Phil's overseas assignment was extended.

"He's had a hard time of things," Phil had said before leaving. *"I'm gone a lot. He's too old for a nanny, and he's been running with a bad crowd. I swear this will be my last foreign assignment until he's in college."*

Only after Ben had pressured him for more information had Phil vaguely alluded to the boy's three juvenile-court appearances for vandalism and shoplifting, and warnings from the judge that the next appearance would lead to significant time in a detention center.

He'd asked for a safe haven for his son, away from the dangers of running loose in a big city. A place to store him, until Phil decided to stay home and be a father.

Like parent, like child, Ben thought grimly. Heaven knew, Ben, Phil and Gina had grown up with about the same lack of parental involvement. What kind of life was that?

Now Ben had two more months to make a difference in the kid's life. To try to get past that all-too-familiar wall of anger and hurt, and reach the boy inside. And when Phil came for his son, Ben would try to get through to him as well.

With Dylan's juvie record and a group of troublemakers waiting to welcome him back, this kid needed all the help he could get.

"HOWDY, STRANGER," Joanna drawled when she walked into the exam room, ignoring the shimmer of pleasure that slid through her. "Didn't expect to see you again quite so soon."

Ben stood near the window, leaning against the wall with his Stetson hanging at his side in one hand. "My nephew had a run-in with some old boards out behind the barn at my place."

In the small room he seemed larger, broader than he had before. His black Polo shirt hugged the curves and planes of his well-muscled chest and flat belly, while the short sleeves molded the muscular bulk of his upper arms. A silver trophy buckle—big as a dessert plate—gleamed at his narrow waist.

"I'm glad you brought him in." She shifted her attention to the teenager standing by the exam table. "You must be Dylan."

The boy gave her an insolent glance.

He was clearly a Carson, from the thick, wavy black hair to those dark-chocolate eyes, and he had that same sensual curve to his mouth. Both he and his uncle had strong, stubborn jawlines that promised determination, but where Ben's nose was straight and narrow, Dylan's had a bump in the center. Probably the result of a fight, she surmised.

He'd removed one boot and sock, but apparently had refused to climb onto the table. "It's nothin' much," he muttered. "I'm okay."

"I imagine you are," she said mildly. "But since you came all this way and even took your boot off, let's take a look." She moved closer and patted the paper sheet on the table. "Can you hop up here?"

His mouth curved into a scowl, but she caught a flash of worry in his eyes. Why did he think he needed to act so tough? Where were his mom and dad? Bracing one hand on the pad, he vaulted easily onto the table.

"Scoot back, Dylan, so your leg is resting on the table. Are you allergic to latex?"

When he shook his head, she pulled on a pair of latex gloves and peeled away the adhesive tape and gauze on his heel. Beneath, she found a puncture wound of about three millimeters in diameter, with inflammation reddening the area. "Did you see the nail after you stepped on it? Was it complete—pointed tip and all?"

He nodded, wincing as she examined the wound for signs of deep injury. "How far did it go in?"

He held up a hand, with perhaps a half-inch space between the pads of his thumb and forefinger.

"I hear the wound bled pretty well, so that's a good thing. I'm going to use a syringe to irrigate this with saline solution," she said, giving the boy an encouraging smile.

His eyes widened. "With a *needle?*"

Ben pushed away from the wall and came over to stand

beside his nephew, resting a large, tanned hand on the boy's shoulder. "Without. Right, Doc? That's how we'd clean a deep wound on a horse."

"Right." Joanna gave Dylan a pat on the leg as she reached for the tray of supplies Eve had set up for her. She lifted a 50 cc syringe of saline and started flushing out the wound. "See? This works like a nice little water jet."

He cringed at first, but relaxed a moment later and gave her an embarrassed half smile. "That wasn't so bad."

"You're a good patient." After covering the wound with gauze, she secured the area with paper tape. As she continued talking, she jotted notes on a slip of paper. "Keep it clean. Soak your foot for fifteen or twenty minutes in warm, soapy water tonight and tomorrow, and check every day for signs of infection—redness, heat, discharge, increased pain. Understand?"

Dylan nodded.

"Given the source of the wound and the date of your last tetanus shot, you need a tetanus booster and some oral antibiotics."

Swallowing hard, Dylan gripped the edge of the table with both hands. Ben stepped in front of him and grinned. "Ever see your dad in a doctor's office?"

The boy shot a glance at him.

"Nope?"

Dylan shook his head.

"I probably shouldn't tell you…" Ben gave him a wink. "But when your dad was a kid, he *really* hated this stuff. He's six years older than me, and I remember once when he was…ten, maybe, he was supposed to have a shot of some kind. One thing about Phil, you always knew when he was upset."

A hint of a wry smile tipped up a corner of Dylan's mouth. "Tell me about it."

"He wrestled himself away from the nurse, the doctor

and Mom, and took off. Only he took a wrong turn and ended up at a dead end instead of out the front door. Mom caught up and threatened him with laundry and kitchen duties for the next month if he didn't behave.''

Dylan's shoulders relaxed and he gave a short laugh. "Did it work?"

"Must have. We got to stop at the Dairy Queen on the way home."

Maybe it was a masculine-pride thing—wanting to best his dad—but the boy didn't so much as flinch when she injected the booster. She'd just reached over to dispose of the syringe and needle in the container on the wall, when a petite redhead appeared at the door.

"Hey, Ben, Dylan. How's it going?" Her short, curly hair bounced as she entered the room and gave Dylan a quick hug. "I hear you're out at the ranch helping Ben find stray nails. Good job!"

A dull red flush rose on his neck. Mumbling something unintelligible, he slithered off the table.

"Have you two met?" Ben asked Joanna, tipping his head toward his sister.

Gina's warm smile revealed perfect white teeth and a set of deep dimples. "Not yet."

"I've heard about you, believe me." Gina thrust out a hand. "Gina Vaughn. You'll probably be seeing my two girls as patients, and we'll likely run into each other over at The Birth Place. Have you met Lydia? Any of the others?"

A bit taken aback at her exuberance, Joanna nodded. "Lydia and Kim, so far."

"Lydia's a gem, isn't she? Without her, there wouldn't be a clinic, believe me. We're all glad you're here, by the way. I don't know what we could have done without a replacement for Dr. Davis." Gina blew at her bangs. "So are you staying just for the three months...or longer?"

"Just while Dr. Davis is gone."

Nicki appeared at the door and waved a chart. "The Hallowells are here," she mouthed. "Room two."

Handing Ben a prescription for antibiotics, the note she'd written about wound care, and the billing form, Joanna shifted her attention to Dylan. "You're all set. The tetanus booster might make your arm a bit sore for a day or two, but that's not unusual. If you have any problems, be sure to have your uncle bring you in, okay?"

"Um…I'll wait for you guys outside," Gina said, giving Ben a friendly nudge with her elbow and a quick, speculative glance. In a wink she was gone.

Dylan fled a second later, leaving Ben and Joanna staring after him.

"Not that he's eager to leave, or anything," Ben said dryly. "I know he enjoyed every moment."

The first time they'd met, she'd thought Ben was a good-looking cowboy, one who probably charmed the boots and bandannas off the cowgirls wherever he went. Nicki's obvious hero worship and her reference to his reputation had confirmed Joanna's assessment.

But now she'd seen him comfort his anxious nephew without stepping on the boy's ego, and she'd seen a glimpse of the warm relationship he had with his sister. Maybe there was more to the man than she'd first thought.

"Be sure to bring him in if he has any problems," she murmured as she headed for the door. "There's always a chance of infection, or even delayed osteomyelitis."

"Wait." Ben's low voice stopped her in her tracks. "I want to thank you for fitting him into your schedule."

"No problem."

"I'll bring your horse back this evening, if that's okay."

For a moment she imagined Ben coming to see *her,* and the thought sent a warm glow through her. But, she reminded herself, he was just bringing Galahad home. And that—given her priorities—was all she should wish for. "Thanks. Just leave the bill in my mailbox if I'm not home by then."

His eyebrows rose. "The bill?"

"You boarded Galahad for two days. You helped with the fence."

"Out here that's just being neighborly." He shot her a grin of pure devilry as he sauntered out of the room. "I'm sure you'll return the favor someday."

CHAPTER FIVE

GINA WAS STILL GRINNING when she walked into her small home on the south edge of town an hour later and shouted a greeting to her girls.

She'd seen Ben eyeing the new doc with interest, and had noticed Dr. Jo slide a few glances in his direction as well. Maybe this time—with a little help—Ben would make a wise decision. He sure hadn't done too well on his own.

When Zach came home from work she'd ask him about having company Saturday, and maybe she'd invite them both for dinner. Dylan, too, because heaven knew that kid needed more contact with family. She'd seen him a number of times during the month he'd been here, and he *still* had his James Dean rebel attitude firmly in place.

The kids' after-school baby-sitter, Sue Ellen Zeman, waddled into the living room wearing one of her usual, flowing muumuus in a wild Hawaiian print.

"There's a note on the kitchen table for you," she said, her eyes filled with worry. "Your husband was here over an hour ago and packed his bags. Is everything okay?"

Finding an older baby-sitter for the three-thirty to six o'clock time slot after school wasn't easy. Sue Ellen was dependable and didn't charge much, but she watched a lot of soap operas and tended to hunt for local drama where there was none. She was also one of the biggest gossips in town.

"Fine. We're absolutely fine," Gina hedged. "Zach drives semi, so of course he's on the road a lot. He's just taking more long-distance runs.'' A lot more, over the past three or four months. And when he was home... Gina shelved her worries and gave Sue Ellen a bright smile. ''Did he have a chance to say goodbye to the girls?''

''He left just as I came, but the school bus hadn't stopped yet.'' Sue Ellen clucked her tongue. ''Another five minutes, and they could have kissed him goodbye.''

So he'd timed it pretty close. Tearful farewells with the girls clinging to him were the worst part of his job, he'd always said. Now he was taking the coward's way out by avoiding his wife *and* children, and hadn't even bothered to dial Gina's cell phone. ''He must have been in a hurry,'' she said breezily. ''Where are the girls?''

''In the backyard, playing on the swings. Regan is worried about a school project due tomorrow. Allie can't wait to ask you about her costume for the Halloween party at school.'' The older woman rolled her eyes. ''I hope you're handy with a needle and thread.''

''My skills amount to hems, buttons and episiotomies, so thanks for the warning.''

Sue Ellen chuckled as she headed for the front door. ''I think she wants to be a pumpkin. Just think about suturing if you decide to make the costume for her. Lots and lots of sutures.''

Gina waved goodbye and waited for the front door to close before going into the kitchen. The note, simply folded over and without an envelope, was propped between the salt and pepper shakers.

Her hand hovering above it, she took a deep breath. With shaking fingers she lifted it and smoothed the paper against the palm of her hand. *I got a run to Flagstaff, and one to Colorado Springs. You've got my cell number.* Zach.

No ''Dear Gina.''

No ''Love you, Zach.''

Not even an estimated day of return. He might as well

have been leaving a note for a plumber or the news-paper boy.

He was letting her know exactly where he stood.

Would she one day find a note between the salt and pepper shakers saying he wanted a divorce?

Outside, the girls' laughter filled the air as they played in the fenced backyard. Through the open windows she could hear Maria Corvallis scolding her own daughter about some boyfriend, and the sounds of the Peterson boy's old truck rattling down the street, gears grinding as he tried to shift it out of first.

Everyday sounds. Life rolling on as it always did. Except that Zach was subtly pulling away, his mind made up, and his focus on a future that didn't include her. All because she'd chosen to follow her childhood dream.

"Mom!" Seven-year-old Regan burst into the tiny kitchen, her strawberry-blond ponytail flying behind her. "You're home!" Her freckled face lit with excitement, she threw herself into Gina's arms. Allie—two years younger—followed on her heels and they all rocked into one big embrace.

"Was it a fun day, Mommy?" Allie planted a big kiss on Gina's cheek. "Did you catch lots of babies?"

She couldn't help but laugh. "No, none today. Not yet, anyway." There might be, though, if Bonita Schweitzer went into labor. She'd reached forty weeks and the baby had dropped considerably over the last few days. "Remember, if I have to leave, Nicki or Sue Ellen have promised to come over. Okay?"

"Even in the night, right?"

Gina dropped a kiss on each daughter's forehead. "Even in the night. I'll always come back."

But your daddy might not—and what will we do then?

AT TWO-THIRTY on Friday afternoon, Joanna leaned against the counter in the pediatric clinic lab and took a sip of soda, savoring the icy, refreshing slide of liquid down her dry throat. After five days here, she hadn't yet adjusted to the high altitude and arid climate, still felt a little breathless and headachy when she hurried. And that's what she'd been doing most of the day.

Thankfully her work at the pediatric clinic had gone well so far, all things considered. Dr. Davis had left several weeks before Joanna's arrival, so there'd been a backlog of sports physicals to contend with, routine vaccinations and a number of well-baby exams interspersed with the usual coughs, colds, strep throats and ear infections.

She'd done okay. On Monday, she'd felt that familiar ache when she walked into the exam room and found a five-day-old snuggled at its mother's shoulder. By Thursday, working with the little ones hadn't hurt quite as much.

Maybe her devastating grief was quietly giving way, letting her function without the intrusion of painful memories.

Or maybe she hadn't reached that stage at all, she realized with a weary yawn. Today she hadn't stopped moving since eight o'clock, and hadn't even found time for the sandwich and apple tucked in her bottom desk drawer. *Maybe the trick is to stay so busy you don't have time to think.*

If so, she was sure in the right place.

Eve bustled into the lab, grabbed her thermal cup of coffee and took a hearty swallow. "Mrs. Fiona Pennington is here with Jason," she announced. "Another physical." She shook her head. "Every year it's the same. These people know their kids'll need physicals before they can play sports. They could make appointments in July or August, but what do they do? They wait till September to call for an appointment, and then complain when we can't see them till mid-October."

Joanna put her can of soda in the small refrigerator and

moved to the sink to wash her hands. "Maybe some of the kids aren't sure about sports until after they start school."

"Most of 'em are in these activities from elementary school on. Anyway," she added in a quiet tone, "that's what Jason needs. But don't be surprised if his mother isn't very friendly. She comes from big money around these parts, and lets you know it, too. Her husband is some sort of fancy financial adviser."

"And a member of The Birth Place board, right?"

Eve rolled her eyes. "A vocal one, from what I hear."

In the exam room, Joanna found a scrawny twelve-year-old with neatly cut brown hair, already on the table, in a paper gown and swinging his feet. His thirty-something mother sat in one of the plastic chairs with her long, elegant legs crossed.

A cool blonde, dressed in a classic winter-white skirt suit, her gaze flicked to the wall clock, then settled on Joanna with a hint of impatience. "You must be having a busy day."

"Swamped. I apologize for keeping you two waiting." Joanna studied the chart she'd picked up from the Plexiglas holder just outside the door. *An only child, no significant health problems, other than a propensity for injuries. Fracture of the wrist, 1997. Collarbone, 2002. Severe sprain, 2002.* Warning bells sounded in Joanna's mind as she moved to the table and offered her hand to the boy. "I'm Dr. Jo. How've you been, Jason? Any problems? Anything you want to ask me?"

He awkwardly returned her handshake, his palm cool and clammy, and shook his head.

"How about you, Mrs. Pennington?"

A delicate frown line formed on the woman's forehead as she thought for a moment. "Is he due for any vaccinations?"

Joanna ran a finger down the list of dates and vaccinations on the inside cover of his chart. "He's up to date." She flipped to Eve's notes. "His blood pressure, heart rate and temp are normal…as are his hemoglobin and urine."

After checking his lymph nodes, she positioned her stethoscope and evaluated his lung and heart sounds—all normal—then she had him lie back so she could palpate his liver and abdomen. When she finished, she had him sit up so she could test his reflexes.

"You've had a few injuries in the past. What sport are you playing this year?"

"Seventh-grade football. Track, in the spring."

"Great exercise. How did you break your collarbone last spring?"

He frowned. "Fell off my horse."

"His father bought him a young horse that seemed to shy at its own shadow. We sold it right after Jason got hurt." His mother rose from her chair and came to the table. "He had a severe sprain last year, too, from when we were skiing down at Angelfire."

"Shoulda stayed on the intermediates," the boy said ruefully. "But Dad—"

"He wanted to join his dad on the advanced runs," Fiona interjected smoothly. "But the slopes were icy that day. He's just lucky he didn't break his leg."

Joanna gestured for the boy to hop down from the table. He hadn't appeared nervous, as if he was trying to hide the cause of his injuries, but she never ignored possible indications of abuse. "After I check your spine for any curvature, you'll be through. Can you bend over? Good boy. Now slowly straighten up…"

From the corner of her eye Joanna caught his mother's profile, and realized with surprise that her well-cut suit had masked the fact that she was very definitely pregnant. Her gaze slid to the glittering jewelry Fiona wore.

The slim hand at her side bore long, professionally done

nails, a ring encrusted with diamonds to the point of being ostentatious…and a faint purple stain surrounding her wrist.

Joanna's gaze flew up to meet Fiona's, but the other woman abruptly clasped her hands behind her back and turned away.

"We just need you to sign the health form and we'll leave." Fiona gathered her purse and gave an impatient toss of her head. "I've got another appointment in fifteen minutes."

With Jason in the room, Joanna couldn't ask any questions, but she'd seen that type of bruising before on wrists that had been held in a crushing grip. No one exerted that kind of force with loving intent. Her husband?

If the woman was wise, her next appointment was with a family counselor or a lawyer.

Nicki's voice came over the intercom as the Penningtons walked out the door. "Phone call, line two. It's…um…the elementary school, and they have a bit of a problem. Can you take it?"

The *elementary* school? "Of course. I'll pick it up in the lab."

The school secretary answered, and quickly transferred Joanna's call to the principal. Mystified, Joanna wound the telephone cord around her finger while waiting for him to come on the line.

When he did, his voice was stern. "You need to come after your horse, Dr. Weston. There's a huge white dog with him as well."

"My *horse?*"

"I tried calling your clinic earlier, but was put on hold and couldn't wait."

"My horse is at your *school?*"

"We called the police department, but they've got everyone out at a three-car pileup on the highway. We checked with some local ranchers, and Ben Carson said our description matched your horse.''

''I'll bet he was amused.''

The principal snorted. ''Maybe he was, but we aren't. That horse has been creating pandemonium for the last hour. Ben offered to come after the horse, but when I talked to him he was over an hour away with a semi load of cattle.''

Visions of property damage and personal-injury suits rushed through her thoughts. Million-dollar suits. Multi-million-dollar suits. In this litigious age, who could imagine what might happen? But far worse would be knowing that Galahad might have harmed someone—especially a child. She took a steadying breath. ''Can you tell me what my horse has done?''

''He's been staring in the windows.''

''That's *it?*'' Relieved laughter bubbled up from her chest, but she caught it just in time.

''Imagine the distraction of seeing some big blaze-faced, wild-colored horse peering at them through the windows,'' the man snapped. ''He stands there, and twenty or thirty kids go nuts. He moves along down the building to watch another class, and the first one erupts in disappointment. We don't have *shades* on these windows, Doctor.''

''And…um…the dog?'' Joanna asked weakly. ''A fluffy white one?''

''Right there with him, but with his paws on the windowsill.''

''Oh, dear…''

''See that you get here in a half hour—or *less.*'' He slammed down the receiver.

Stunned, Joanna stared at the receiver before cradling it. ''Eve—I've got to leave for a little while.''

''I heard,'' Eve retorted dryly. ''One of the kids who just came in is chattering a mile a minute about some horse that wants to go to school. He says the principal is really upset.''

"No kidding. Can you try to move our appointments back by an hour? I'll stay as late as it takes to catch up.''

With an efficient nod, Eve bustled toward the front desk.

Joanna had been held up at the clinic on Wednesday, so she'd missed seeing Ben when he'd brought Galahad home. She'd found the gelding peacefully munching hay in his corral, with Moose sleeping as close by as he could, but within the fenced yard surrounding the house.

Though Ben hadn't said a word to her, she discovered that the electric wire had been installed around the entire perimeter of the pasture while she was gone.

Life had been tranquil for all of two days, but now the horse was on the lam again, and this time he'd taken his devoted buddy along. Had he simply jumped over the fence, confident he could clear that uncomfortable buzz of electricity?

She found out when she got home fifteen minutes later and discovered the heavy steel "horseproof" hook-and-eye closure on the pasture gate hanging loose, leaving the gate wide open.

"Good move, Weston," she muttered as she grabbed a halter and hurried to her truck, mentally adding heavy chains and padlocks to her shopping list. "You *really* needed this horse, right?"

Just like she'd needed a dog the size of Rhode Island, the new furniture that she'd bought for her condo in California, the tai chi lessons, and everything else she'd done to fill her thoughts and time over the past two years. Compulsive behavior had brought her modern furniture she didn't like. Memberships she didn't have time for. And now, inappropriate thoughts about her closest neighbor to the south.

It was a good thing that "neighbor" was a relative term

out here. If he'd truly been right next door instead of so many miles away, she might have casually wandered over there during the last couple days, just to chat and see where things might go between them.

Which—if she kept her eye firmly fixed on the wonderful career waiting for her in San Diego—should be exactly nowhere.

After hooking up the horse trailer, she drove back to town. Lost in thought, she pulled up in front of the school on the north end of town…and blinked in surprise.

Classes had let out for the day. Children were everywhere, laughing and running, their bright jackets flying. Some were lined up to get on the row of yellow buses parked out front.

But most of them were gathered in a semicircle at the end of the building. There were teachers down there, too, trying to shoo them away, along with a red-faced, middle-aged man who surely had to be the principal. Towering above them was a lanky, sandy-haired young man with a heavy camera bag slung across his chest and an impressively complex Nikon held in front of his face.

Galahad stood by one of the school windows, his ears pricked and eyes bright, apparently enjoying the attention. Moose sat proudly at his feet.

Grabbing the halter and lead rope, Joanna hurried across the school lawn fielding questions from excited children every step of the way.

"I am so sorry," she murmured as she cut through the crowd. "Really, it won't happen again. I promise."

The photographer lowered his camera and met her partway. "Nolan McKinnon," he said, offering his hand and a broad smile. "The *Arroyo County Bulletin*'s editor. Do you own this horse?"

"Well, I—"

The other man, dressed in a dark navy suit that didn't

quite button over his belly, shouldered his way through the crowd and interrupted her before she could explain. "The school day is now *over,* Doctor," he growled. "We lost almost an entire afternoon here because of that horse."

"Believe me, I'm truly sorry. On the way home I'm buying chains and padlocks for my two gates. This won't happen again."

"You're the new pediatrician, right?" Nolan asked. His smile deepened the dimples in his cheeks and his eyes sparkled with good humor. "What can you tell me about this horse's background? Has he gone visiting like this before?"

"Excuse me—I really need to get him into the trailer before someone gets hurt." She wove through the crowd of children, reached Galahad, and haltered him. His head dropped, as if he knew he'd been playing hooky and now had to face the consequences. "You are one bad boy," she murmured, rubbing him behind his ears.

He leaned into the massage, his eyes half-closed in apparent ecstasy. The editor snapped another three or four pictures.

Joanna felt her cheeks warm. "Isn't there something more newsworthy than this going on in Enchantment?"

He shrugged and flashed another grin. "My reporter is out covering the opening of a new pizza place in town, so I thought I'd check this out. You never know—something amusing might be picked up by the AP wire service."

Joanna glanced down at her smudged silk shirt. "I sincerely hope not."

He laughed. "You look pretty darn good to me."

"Right." Still, she had to laugh with him. "Just promise this won't be front-page news."

He held up two fingers in a Scout salute. "Word of honor."

The crowd of children had thinned out as the buses began

rumbling away. Now the stragglers parted like the Red Sea as Joanna slowly led Moose and Galahad to her trailer.

Nolan continued asking questions until she'd loaded the horse, stuffed the dog into the Tahoe and climbed behind the steering wheel.

She rolled down the window. "I was just curious," she said, giving him a breezy smile. "When I first came to town I heard rumors about something going on at The Birth Place. There was mention of unfavorable media attention."

His affable grin faded.

"Would you know anything about what happened?" she persisted. "People either don't know or won't say, and since I do work with some of The Birth Place clients, I'm a bit concerned."

"I don't deal in rumors. There were a few...and Lydia Kane stepped down from the board afterward. But I never did ferret out any facts." He gave her a broad wink. "With all the good she's done around here, I prefer to give her the benefit of the doubt."

From the corner of her eye, she saw Ben pull his black pickup to a stop across the street and nod to both of them. From under the lowered brim of his hat, she thought she detected a scowl.

Apparently Nolan saw it, too. "Ben's a good friend of yours, I take it."

"We're just neighbors."

"I don't think he looks at all his neighbors like that. Of course, you're a lot prettier than those grizzled ranchers." He winked again and sauntered away, whistling an old Beach Boy's tune.

A glance at her watch startled her into action. She'd been gone an hour, and still had patients to see. If they'd been willing to wait. Shifting her SUV into gear, she pulled out into the street alongside Ben's truck. "Did you come all the way over here because of Galahad?"

"The principal called, but I was over an hour away."

"I'm really sorry. I seem to be causing you trouble one day after another."

"No problem. I had to come into town to meet with Dylan's high-school counselor anyway. If you hadn't arrived, I would have led your gelding down to a barn at the county fairgrounds."

"I still can't believe you came over and finished the electric wire on my pasture. I just wish I could return the favor."

He winked. "I was hoping you'd say that, because I sure could use one. What would you say to spending a night at the ranch?"

CHAPTER SIX

HE WAS BIG, and dark, and way too appealing, and just a sideways glance of those bedroom eyes sent a shiver skittering across her nerve endings. Beyond that, she'd seen the deeper side of him, the man who cared for a teenager who'd try the patience of Job, watched over an elderly aunt and maintained a loving relationship with his sister.

But that didn't mean she would consider a one-night stand.

"I *really* don't think so," she said brusquely, shifting the Tahoe into forward gear. "But I imagine you must have the names and numbers of a lot of gals who would."

"Wait!" He thumbed back his black Stetson. "You have the wrong idea, here."

Men. "Actually, I think *you* do."

"I was wondering if you could hang out at my ranch Saturday evening while I haul some horses down to Carlsbad."

Carlsbad? He hadn't been talking about a wild night after all. She felt the warmth of embarrassment slide up her cheeks.

"I don't mean that you'd have to do any chores," he added. "It's just that I need to deliver a couple of horses to a customer, and Rafe has to take his dad down to Albuquerque this weekend. I'd feel better if someone was with Sadie and Dylan in case I can't get home until Sunday morning."

Of course. How could she have imagined anything else?

She had no interest in him either, yet the realization was vaguely disappointing. "Like a baby-sitter."

"Yes...no—" He broke off with a short laugh. "Don't breathe that word to either one of them, or there'll be hell to pay."

"Aren't they just a bit...*old* for that?"

"Sadie can't provide enough supervision for Dylan, but my main concern is her recent dizziness. Her doctor's trying different drugs for her blood pressure, and so far, the ones that work best have the worst side effects."

"What about Gina?"

"She'd come out, but she's on call this weekend. She swears the full-term moms will all go into labor because of the big cold front coming through." He smiled. "I figure it's possible. We sure see the effect of big barometric pressure drops during calving."

"How can I say no? You've helped me out so much already. Let me know what time, and I'll be there."

His eyes locked on hers and something passed between them that had nothing to do with elderly ladies and teenage boys and the exchange of neighborly favors. "Maybe next week I can take you to dinner? To thank you," he added hesitantly.

She'd first thought he was inviting her to his ranch for an all-too cozy little sleepover, and that would have been way out of line. But dinner implied the start of something, too. Something she wasn't prepared for.

"Not necessary." She gave him a breezy smile and offered her hand. "I owe you, neighbor."

He appeared startled. "Uh...sure."

From the corner of her eye she noticed that Nolan hadn't walked all that far away. He was leaning against a Jeep a half block away, watching them with interest.

Oh, great. Nodding curtly in his direction, she stepped on the accelerator and pulled away. If he was hunting for any juicy gossip to print in his paper, he certainly wouldn't find it here. Not between mere friends.

And how long had it been since she'd had a friend who just happened to be a guy? Allen didn't count. He hadn't been much of a friend or a husband. He'd offered little support after the loss of their baby, and he sure hadn't been friendly since their divorce. There were her colleagues, but they'd been busy with families and fiancés and golf dates, and she'd never seen any of them outside the clinic.

Now she had a horse, a dog and a good neighbor. For the first time—in a long time—she was in complete control, focused on her goals for the future. In three months she would pack her bags, head for home and never look back.

Absolutely nothing else was going to interfere with her plans—not even a cowboy who happened to be handsome as sin.

"YOU CHOOSE. Me, or that goddamn job of yours."

Gina stared at her husband. He'd returned late this afternoon after three nights away without so much as a phone call.

After reading bedtime stories to the girls and listening to their prayers, he'd gone out on the back porch alone and had stood there for over a half hour. Deciding what to say? Trying to postpone a conversation that could only hurt their entire family?

Gina had expected this discussion, but she hadn't expected the bitterness in Zach's voice or his cold, flat expression. There wasn't even a vestige of love or warmth in his eyes. He claimed he was angry over her career—but maybe it was just an excuse. Could there be another *woman?*

"It sounds like you've already decided what you're going to do," she snapped.

"Someone has to make the right choice around here."

The hurt and anger she'd felt over the past months welled up in her throat, making it difficult to speak. *I'm not going to cry. I won't give him the satisfaction.* "And what is that, Zach? What's most convenient and comfortable for you?"

He swore under his breath. "How *convenient* is it for your girls when you have to take off, night and day?"

"They know what I'm doing. They have good sitters—"

"But they never know if they'll wake up and find you gone. And what about me? I come home and instead of supper I find the Marquez girl watching TV on the couch, or old Mrs. Zeman knitting in the living room. No one knows when you'll be back to take over again."

"Most mothers work these days."

"But not your hours. I've had it, Gina." Zach gave an angry slash with his hand. "This isn't a marriage. Not any-more."

"Because of my hours? What about yours? You're gone days at a time. It's never a question of asking me if *that's* convenient. You weren't even here when Regan was born."

"I'm a trucker, dammit. That's what I do."

"And maybe my career is something I have to do, Zach. I've always been here for you and the girls. I always will be. It's just that I've got something else in my life, too…more than a nine-to-five job at some truck stop or the local café. Something I've always wanted."

"Then you've made your choice, and I've made mine."

The enormity of this moment, this shattering of their lives, settled a cold weight in her stomach. She stared at her husband. The father of her children, the man she'd loved since she turned eighteen. She'd tried so hard through the years, wanting him to be happy. Going along with what-ever he wanted. But this time, she deserved more.

"I would have thought," she said slowly, hearing her voice echo from some distant place, "you'd want me to be happy. I guess that's where I made my mistake."

Their eyes met and held for a long moment until Zach finally turned away. "It won't take me long to pack. I'll…keep in touch."

"I hope so, because the girls love you very much."

He paused to look over his shoulder, a muscle ticking along the side of his jaw. Pain and anger simmered in his eyes.

Maybe you'll realize what you're giving up, Zach. Talk to me. His expression softened a few degrees…but the moment was lost when the pager on her belt started vibrating.

She automatically reached for it and read the number on its digital screen, then looked up to find Zach glaring at her.

"A typical Friday night with you," he said coldly.

And then he walked out the door.

"BEN HIRED a *baby-sitter?*" Dylan's disgust was palpable.

"No," Joanna retorted, surprised at the boy's vehemence. "Well—not exactly."

He gave her an outraged look. "So why are you here?"

"Mostly to keep an eye on Sadie, because she hasn't been feeling all that well."

"*Mostly?*" He turned on his heel, stalked down the hallway and disappeared into a room, slamming the door behind him.

Joanna followed and rapped lightly on the door. "I know your uncle meant to mention this to you, but you were out on your horse somewhere, and he heard a weather report about an unexpected cold front with snow. He figured he'd better hit the road."

The stereo in the room came on, cranked up loud enough to preclude conversation.

Sadie appeared at Joanna's side and gave her a comforting pat on the arm. "Boys," she said with a shake of her head. "They take things hard. Don't do so good at talkin' it through, either.'' A soft smile wreathed her face and her eyes took on a faraway look. "Ben is like that. Always carries the world on his shoulders, but never says a word.''

"You must be very close.''

"Lordy, yes. Like my own son, he is. After his daddy took off for California with Ben's older brother, his mother had quite a job raisin' the two youngest. Ben and Gina were with me more often than not, while she worked day and night.''

"Has Shadow Creek been in the family for long?''.

"Belonged to Ben's grandfather, but times got hard, and the place went on the block in '72. When it came up for sale again in '98, Ben was able to buy it back.'' Sadie's voice filled with unmistakable pride. "He did it on his own, with good credit, and hard work.''

Ben's easy smile and casual manner hadn't suggested that kind of backbone. Joanna had imagined that the ranch was an inheritance, or a family partnership of some sort. Now she glanced around with new respect. "He must be doing very well.''

"Yes, indeedy.'' Sadie gestured toward the next several rooms down the hall as she started shuffling toward the kitchen. "He's going to start working on the house, soon as he gets the barns and fencing done. Doesn't have much time, though—he's out working with the horses and cattle from dawn to dusk. Have you seen the rest of the house?''

Shaking her head, Joanna followed her and peered into the rooms they passed. "How many bedrooms does this place have?''

"Dylan and I are over here, plus there's a guest room and Ben's office.'' Sadie rested a hand against a door frame to catch her breath. "The newer wing is on the other side of the living room. Ben's bedroom, a couple of guest rooms and a den are on the other side.''

"It all has such great potential," Joanna murmured. The whitewashed walls were cool and bright, the hardwood floors strewn with Navajo woven rugs. "I'll bet this thick adobe keeps the house cool in summer and warm in winter."

"Sure does. This is Ben's office," Sadie announced, stepping into the open doorway and flipping on the lights. "It used to be his grandpa Lee's."

Curious, Joanna stepped inside.

A huge old desk dominated the left side of the room, while a sofa draped in a horsehide lap robe and two old chairs with antler armrests and leather-upholstered seats were positioned to the right. Bookshelves lined the walls on three sides, interspersed with mounted deer and elk heads. An array of computer equipment worthy of a busy urban business office filled a credenza behind the desk.

"Nice," Joanna said. "I'm not so sure about the animal heads, though. Ben must be quite a hunter."

"Darn things are hard to dust." Sadie chuckled. "I don't think Ben likes 'em all that much, either, but they hung in here when Lee was alive. Ben says he likes things just as they were when he was a boy. Except," she added with a smile, "for all that newfangled computer equipment."

Joanna hadn't intended to pry into the life of Ben Carson when she'd agreed to spend the evening here. Yet, as she surveyed his office, she couldn't help but be more than a little intrigued. Who would have guessed he had such a streak of sentimentality?

Dozens of framed photographs of two young girls filled the end tables at either side of the sofa. Had he been married? "Are these girls…his?"

"No, his sister Gina's," Sadie said fondly. "Regan and Allie. The cutest little girls you'll ever see. When they come out, they follow their uncle like two pups. 'Course, he's like a second dad to them."

Probably why there were Barbie dolls propped on a chair, and bright, childish drawings were taped to the oak-paneled walls.

Sadie pushed up the sleeve of her heavy wool cardigan and checked her watch. "Sit a spell if you want. Find a book to read. I need to get finished in the kitchen."

"Don't you want to sit down yourself?" Sadie appeared tired, her skin grayish. "Are you feeling okay?"

Sadie snorted as she started down the hall. "Fine as frog's hairs. Don't listen to Ben—he worries too much."

And with every passing hour here, Joanna was learning more about him, absorbing more than she wanted to.

"I'll join you in a minute," Joanna called out. "I'm going to check on Dylan."

Hard rock still blasted from the stereo in the boy's room. With a sigh, Joanna knocked loudly on his door. "Dylan?"

She could hear nothing over the pounding, guttural beat of the music that made the door vibrate beneath her hand. At the vision of him slipping out his bedroom window and rebelliously heading off into the night, she knocked louder. Tried the handle. *Locked.* What if he was gone?

"Dylan?"

The center of the knob bore a small, round hole. If need be, she could find a thin nail and unlock the mechanism...

She breathed a sigh of relief as the door cracked open wide enough for Dylan to glare at her. "Yeah?"

"I...just wanted to apologize."

His gaze dropped to the floor. "What for?"

"For upsetting you. Want to come to the kitchen for something to eat before you turn in?"

"No."

"Popcorn?"

The door opened a few inches wider. "Uh-uh."

"Monopoly? Shanghai rummy?"

He shook his head.

"Maybe we could visit a while. You and I are both new here, right?"

He gave a grudging nod.

"How long will you be here?"

He glared at her. "Too long." The door closed.

Wrong question. Joanna leaned close to the door. "I'll be in the kitchen if you decide to join us."

In the kitchen, she found Sadie kneading a fragrant, yeasty ball of dough. "It already smells wonderful," she teased. "What are you making?"

Sadie gave the mass another shove, flipped it over and lifted it into a large crockery bowl. "Caramel rolls for to-morrow morning. Our Sunday-morning tradition."

"I've never been able to make bread," Joanna admitted. "My rolls turn out like hockey pucks and every loaf of bread I make ends up weighing ten pounds. Total disaster—unless someone needs a doorstop."

Sadie smoothed a sheen of vegetable oil over the mound of dough, pulled a clean dish towel from a drawer and laid it over the bowl. "Maybe your water was too hot for the yeast. Or you didn't raise it at the right temperature."

"What's next?"

Sadie pursed her lips. "When this doubles, I'll punch it down and make the rolls. They'll rise overnight." She re-trieved a stick of butter from the refrigerator, peeled off the wrapping, dropped it into a glass measuring cup and put it in the microwave. "You like caramel rolls, don't you?"

"They sound wonderful, but if Ben makes it back late tonight, I'll be heading for home."

"Don't you live alone in some cabin way up in the foot-hills?"

"I have a *big* dog."

"But you could take a wrong turn in the dark and get lost. Some of those mountain roads are hard to follow even in daylight."

Joanna thought about the tight switchbacks in the lane leading up to her cabin, and the two places, hidden in the trees, where she had to make a left turn or face ending up somewhere out in the foothills. "True…"

"What about that dog?"

"I left him in a stall in the barn with food and water. He'll be fine."

"Then it's settled. You'll stay here with us till morning even if Ben does get home." Sadie poured two cups of coffee from the pot on the stove and set them down on the big round kitchen table. "Coffee?"

"Thanks. If you're tired, I can finish up those rolls," Joanna offered as she sat across from Sadie and moved a small vase of fresh flowers to one side, out of their line of vision.

"And miss having another woman to talk to for a spell?" Sadie adjusted the glasses on her nose and peered at the clock over the stove. "It's only nine o'clock." She sipped her coffee. "You know…I remember when Ben was a boy…"

She slid into rambling anecdotes from Ben's childhood, all portraying him in a positive light. If it hadn't been clear before that the sweet old woman was a matchmaker at heart, it was crystal clear now. She kept a keen eye on Joanna's expressions, and each story grew just a bit more outrageous than the last.

"And *you*," Sadie announced suddenly. "Tell me about you. Engaged? Have a special fella back home?"

Caught with her thoughts drifting, Joanna sputtered over a swallow of coffee. "Um…no. Not at all."

"Why not? A pretty gal like you, good job."

"I'm not looking."

Sadie pursed her lips. "The years are awastin', you know. Your time clock's ticking."

Time clock? Joanna hid a smile. There was a gleam in

Sadie's eyes. "I've got lots of time. And really, my career is what matters to me more than anything. I've got a wonderful opportunity waiting in California."

Sadie's forehead lowered in a disapproving frown. "*Family* is what's important, honey. Loving and giving and bein' close."

"That's true." Joanna sipped her coffee, holding the cup in front of her with both hands. "But it doesn't always work out that way for everyone."

Lace curtains hung at the wide windows of the kitchen. Beyond was absolute darkness. At the unmistakable sound of muffled footsteps on the back porch, Joanna froze.

When no one knocked on the door, a tremor of fear went through her. With Ben, Rafe and Felipe gone, there were only two women and a teenage boy in the house. Anyone outside might have been able to peer through the curtains to see them.

"I thought there was a watchdog out there." She stared at Sadie, her city girl's heart in her throat. "How come she didn't bark?"

"Blue?" Sadie shook her head fondly. "She hopped up in the truck when Ben was getting ready to leave. Usually she stays at home, but she seemed to want to tag along and Ben let her go this time."

"A-are you expecting anyone?"

"No," Sadie said placidly, lumbering to her feet. "Why? Did you hear something?"

Joanna lowered her voice. "Footsteps. Outside."

"Really?" An eager smile wreathing her face, Sadie cocked her head and listened. She started for the door.

"*Wait*—" Joanna eyed the cell phone by her purse on the table. How long would it take for a deputy to get out here? "It's awfully late for visitors."

Sadie snorted. "It must be someone we know."

"Not necessarily," Joanna retorted. "Listen first. See if you recognize the voice before you open that door."

"Honey, if it makes you feel better, give Ben a call. He's prob'ly on his way home now, anyway." Sadie reached the entryway and flipped on the porch light, standing on tiptoe to peer through the window on the door. "Funny—there's no one here."

But there *had* been a noise. "Is that door locked?"

"Well, no, of course not." Sadie appeared confused. "We don't lock our doors."

Her pulse pounded in her throat and her knees felt shaky as Joanna grabbed her cell phone and started for the hallway. "*Lock* it, Sadie. Now tell me fast—where are the other entrances? Are they unlocked as well? What about the windows?"

"There's the mudroom…and the sliding glass to the courtyard…" Sadie pondered for a moment. "The screen porch off the family room…"

Joanna spun around and collided with someone's chest.

"Hey!" Dylan stumbled back. "What's going on?"

An image of headline news flashed through her thoughts: Triple Murder at Isolated Ranch. "Someone's outside. We've got to get these doors locked. *Now.* You get the family room and I'll—"

"Goodness," Sadie called out. "There's something out here."

"Don't open the door!"

Joanna was halfway down the hall when she heard its hinges creak.

"Lord Almighty." Sadie's voice trembled. "What on earth…?"

Joanna spun on her heel and hurried toward the kitchen, with Dylan close behind her. From outside came the fading sound of a diesel truck engine. Ben or Rafe—or someone else?

"Wait!" Dylan dived into the utility closet at the entrance of the kitchen and withdrew a baseball bat and a .22 rifle. He thrust the bat into Joanna's hands. "Here. This is all we've got close by."

But Sadie was already backing from the porch through the doorway, lugging something into the kitchen. Once she cleared the entry, the screen door slammed shut.

She straightened and turned around slowly, her face white. "It's—it's a delivery. But—how can this be?"

CHAPTER SEVEN

JOANNA WATCHED Sadie bend over next to a blanket-covered...*car seat?*

The pink blanket shifted as little feet and hands pummeled it from underneath.

With trembling hands Sadie lifted away the blanket. "My dear Lord," she whispered. "It—it's a baby!"

She straightened and wobbled, fighting for her balance until Joanna gently slid the crook of her arm under Sadie's elbow to steady her.

"Geez," Dylan muttered, his voice laced with disappointment. "Whose is it? And why did they dump it off here?"

The little girl—probably around ten months old—was dressed in a fluffy pink jacket and quilted overalls. Her chubby fists flailed at the woolen cap tied beneath her chin until she managed to pull it off, revealing dark, damp curls and rosy cheeks.

She stilled as her gaze traveled up past Sadie's housedress. Her hazel eyes widened as she stared at Sadie's shocked face, then looked at Dylan and Joanna. A terrified wail rent the air. Sudden tears spilled down her cheeks.

"Anyone have an idea who she is?" Joanna cooed to the frightened little girl as she fumbled underneath the shield of the car seat for the release button. "Does she belong to a neighbor—or someone in town?"

Both hands clasping her cheeks, Sadie shook her head. "If she did, why wouldn't they come in?"

Joanna lifted the lap restraint. "Maybe her mom is just outside, parking her car…or getting a suitcase…"

But the sound of that truck or car outside had faded.

The little girl jerked away from Joanna's touch and cried even harder. *Pick her up—she needs you…*

As Joanna stroked the crying child's damp, velvety cheek, memories rushed back as always, stealing her breath and twisting her heart.

Her newborn son's soft weight, so briefly treasured. The soul-wrenching awareness of Hunter's fading warmth as she held him for those few precious moments. The scent and feel of his velvety soft skin. But she needed to put the past aside if she was ever going to get on with her life, and this little one needed comfort. *Pick her up. Pick her up.*

"Aren't you, like, gonna do something?" Dylan stared at her in disgust. "Can't you make her stop?"

Sadie bent forward again, reaching for the baby with arthritic caution. "You poor little lamb. Poor, poor little lamb. Who are you?"

"No—she's too heavy for you to pick up from the floor like this. I—I'll get her."

Taking a deep breath, Joanna slid her hands beneath the little girl and lifted her from the car seat, closing her eyes as she held the baby over her shoulder and patted her with one hand.

Rigid with fury, the infant shoved away with both hands and kicked her tiny feet, fighting to escape, her head flung back in terror. "Poor baby! Dylan, please check the porch. Maybe there's a bag or a note of some kind."

He returned a moment later, with a diaper bag held away from his body as if he was afraid of contamination. "I didn't see anything else out there."

"Can you unzip it and check for identification?" Joanna reached for a tissue from a box on the kitchen counter and wiped the baby's tears and runny nose.

Dylan unzipped the bag, held it upside down and shook it, but the tightly crammed contents didn't budge. With a deep sigh, he reached in and began withdrawing diapers. Disposable wipes. Zinc oxide. Three or four sleepers. T-shirts. Several one-piece outfits, all in pink. Socks. A can of powdered formula, a few bottles and two sipper cups.

"Why on earth would someone bring a baby here?" Sadie muttered over and over. "Of all places!"

"Anything else?" Joanna urged, raising her voice to be heard over the cries of the baby. "Did you find anything else at all, Dylan?"

"Uh-uh." He reached in and swept his hand through the main compartment. Checked the smaller zipper pockets. "Wait—" He lifted the can of powdered formula and squinted through the semiclear plastic lid. "Maybe in here?" Peeling off the lid, he reached in and withdrew a tightly folded piece of paper.

Relief washed through Joanna. Here would be the explanation, the phone numbers. Maybe in a few hours, this little one's mother would return.

The baby gave a huge, wracking sob, her jaw trembling. She yawned deeply, then sniffled, her eyes filling with fresh tears. She gripped a fistful of Joanna's shirt in each tiny hand.

Sadie and Joanna drew near as Dylan spread the paper out on the table.

I'm sorry I didn't call first. I just couldn't—but I figured you wouldn't be interested anyway…

As they all leaned closer trying to make out the cramped writing, the baby struggled in Joanna's arms and suddenly kicked hard. Her little sneaker snagged the flowers in the vase on the table.

Dylan grabbed at the vase but it slipped through his

hands, sending water sloshing across the note. The ink blurred.

"No!" The baby still in her arms, Joanna grabbed the roll of paper towels by the sink. "Get the note—quick. Just blot it—don't rub!"

He quickly tore off a handful of paper toweling and dabbed at the paper, his face stricken. "Geez. I shoulda caught it."

"It was my fault," Joanna said. "You just tried to help. Let's move it to a dry spot on the table." Gently she picked up the note by one corner and transferred it, squinting at the wash of blue ink.

Sadie hovered at Joanna's shoulder, wringing her hands. "Can you read anything more? Anything at all?"

The middle paragraph was smudged beyond recognition, though some of the words might be distinguishable once the paper was dry.

The last paragraph told Joanna what she needed to know.

"Well, it looks like you've got a visitor for a while...maybe for a few months," she said. *Or maybe for good.*

Ben Carson was going to have quite a surprise waiting for him when he got home.

"I'D FORGOTTEN ABOUT how much fun this was with the last baby," Bonita Schweitzer said glumly, staring at the big clock above her dresser.

Her breath caught as another contraction started tightening her distended belly. "Some way to spend a Saturday night, huh?"

"You're doing fine," Gina soothed. "This baby will come in good time, and you'll be strong and ready."

Yesterday, Bonita had experienced erratic contractions for over eight hours that dwindled to nothing by evening. Now she was progressing past the ability to concentrate on anything but the increasing intensity and three-to-five-minute frequency of her labor pains.

"Should we walk?" Gina asked. "Some moms feel better if they move around a bit. You're still at six centimeters, but the contractions are getting much closer."

"I guess." She blew at her bangs. "I want my husband to go through this next time. Fair is fair."

Gina's heart flinched at the word *husband*. Where was hers? It hadn't even been a day, and already she felt more alone than she'd ever felt before.

Pinning a bright smile on her face, she helped Bonita ease out of bed and walked with her through three more contractions.

"I need to lie down," Bonita finally said. "In fact—I want to forget this whole deal. Let's call it off."

"Yeah? You know you'd still be pregnant then. Think about being pregnant forever."

Bonita rolled her eyes and groaned as she awkwardly hoisted herself into bed with Gina's help. From out in the kitchen came the sounds of Bonita's other two children making cookies with their grandmother.

Bonita's face darkened. "I-it's another one. I—" She scrunched her forehead, panting, her hands clenching the sheets. "W-wouldn't you k-know that Bob would be out of town?"

"He'll be home as soon as he can." Gina reached over to the nightstand and turned off her cell phone, then started to massage Bonita's back. "How long did your labor last with Marcus?"

"If I remember right, Joel was eighteen hours and Marcus was around four." Bonita squeezed her eyes shut and panted, sweat beading on her forehead. During the next contraction she cried out and gripped Gina's hand.

Gina wiped her brow with a cool, damp cloth. "You might not have long to go, here."

From the kitchen came the sound of a telephone ringing. A moment later, Bonita's mother peeked into the bedroom. "How's it going?" She took a good look at her daughter's straining face and blew her a kiss. "Good luck, sweetie. I'm praying for you." She glanced at Gina. "When you can, you need to call your brother's ranch."

"What?" Her full attention focused on Bonita, the words barely registered.

"The ranch. You need to call out there when you can. Some sort of problem."

Gina nodded vaguely.

Fifteen minutes later, Bonita's husband, Bob, rushed into the room, his hands reddened from a harsh scrubbing and his eyes suspiciously bright. "I'm here, pumpkin. I'm so sorry I wasn't here sooner." He leaned over to drop a kiss on his wife's forehead, then hovered at her side, murmuring encouragement, talking her through her fierce contractions.

When the baby crowned forty-five minutes later, he whooped with joy. Gina carefully, slowly, lifted the baby's head over the perineum and guided the natural rotation of its body through the birth canal.

"He's beautiful, honey—absolutely beautiful!" Bob's voice trembled with emotion as he laid the baby at her breast and helped Gina cut the cord. His eyes filled with tears, he gave Gina a quick hug. "Thank you—for everything."

"It's a joy to be part of this," she said simply. The baby cried thinly as she applied the required antibiotic eye ointment. "You'll bring him to the pediatrician tomorrow for his exam and tests, right?"

Bonita beamed at her. "Absolutely. Though we already know he is totally perfect."

"Are you ready for the hooligans?" Bob asked twenty minutes later, after Gina had cleaned up Bonita and the baby. "I know they're eager to come in."

Bonita nestled her new son snugly in her arms and nodded. "As long as they don't try to play football with him, I think we're set."

A moment later Bonita's mother ushered in the two awed, wide-eyed boys bearing a platter of misshapen chocolate cookies.

"We made 'em for you, Mommy," Joel whispered. At six, he was tall enough to see over the edge of the bed, but he craned his neck for a better view. "Can we see the baby?"

His four-year-old brother hopped up and down. "Me too! I can't see nothin'!"

With a laugh, their father lifted them both up onto the bed, and Bonita gathered them into a hug with her free arm. "Meet your little brother, boys. Isn't he sweet?"

Gina stayed for another two hours, straightening the room, making sure the newborn suckled well at Bonita's breast. The adrenaline rush—the joy of helping new life begin—would make it impossible for her to sleep until the wee hours of the morning, she knew. Even after six months as a midwife, the experience was as fresh and exhilarating as her first time.

How could she give this up? How fair was it for Zach to demand such a sacrifice? *It's me or that job of yours,* he'd said. *I'm damn sick of you being gone so much when I'm home.*

Not that he was home much. He drove trucks for a living and took off for heaven knew where whenever he could pick up a load. He never thought twice about that.

It was easier when she allowed herself to be angry. But when that faded, her doubts and uneasy sense of guilt grew, and weakened her resolve. It wasn't Zach who'd changed. She had…and now the entire family was hurting. How fair was that?

It wasn't until she was packing up her car after midnight

that she remembered the phone message Bonita's mother had given her.

Her heart tripped.

Had someone gotten hurt out at the ranch? Fear knotted her stomach as she checked the voice-mail messages on her cell phone. One giggly message from the girls at home, wishing her good-night.

One adamant message from Lydia, telling her that there was an important staff meeting Monday afternoon at five o'clock, and everyone had to be there unless they were assisting with labor. Strange. Staff meetings were always held earlier in the day, and usually Trish sent the reminders. Lydia's voice had sounded oddly strained.

No messages from Zach, of course. He'd given her that ultimatum before he left and hadn't called since.

Nothing from the ranch or from Ben's cell phone.

Gina nervously eyed the clock on the dashboard of her car. Hesitating only a heartbeat, she hit the speed-dial button for the ranch.

Please, God, let everyone be all right.

BEN PULLED HIS TRUCK and horse trailer to a stop in front of the main barn and wearily leaned against the headrest.

There'd been some snow on the higher switchbacks, slowing his progress to a crawl both coming and going. Once out of the mountains, he'd been able to travel faster, but he was still arriving far later than he'd hoped.

"One hell of a long day," he muttered to Blue, who'd curled up on the seat beside him.

The dog wagged its tail and studied him with adoration.

"Glad to be home, right?" He reached over to scratch Blue behind the ears, then stepped out of the truck and called the dog to his side. Blue followed him toward the house.

At this hour, Sadie and Dylan would be fast asleep, and the house would be dark and peaceful. And Joanna—

He smiled to himself, remembering that Joanna would be here—probably asleep as well. In the morning, he would see her over Sadie's usual Sunday breakfast of warm caramel rolls and fresh orange juice. Maybe after church Joanna would still be here, and would like to go for a ride up into the foothills. Maybe she'd even decide to go to church with the rest of them, which would give him even more time…

How long had it been since he'd had a woman here at the ranch? He couldn't even remember.

She'd been wearing a billed cap, with an oversize man's sweatshirt and jeans when they first met. The last time he'd seen her, her gleaming blond hair hung loose in deep waves that shimmered past her shoulders, in bright contrast to the crimson sheen of her silky blouse. Gray slacks emphasized the gentle curve of her hips and her long, slender legs.

Upscale.

Not in his league.

Not a remote possibility.

But she was also one of the more intriguing women he'd come across in a good long while. Smart, caring, and one hell of an attractive woman. Strange that she was here alone.

Fortunately he hadn't seen a glimmer of interest in those dark blue eyes. Not a single hint of the usual banter, the familiar signals that women tended to send his way. Her behavior was exactly what he wanted. So why did he feel the sudden urge to see just what it would take to change her mind?

Lost in thought, he was halfway up the walk leading to the porch before it dawned on him that the lights in the house were all blazing. Could someone be sick? Had there been bad news?

Startled, he spun around and surveyed the gravel for strange cars. One of the ranch trucks was parked over by the garage. Joanna's SUV was parked next to it. There weren't any emergency vehicles in sight. Rafe's truck was still gone.

Mystified, he quickened his pace to a fast jog and took the porch steps two at a time. An unfamiliar noise filtered through the door when he reached for the knob. It sounded like…a baby. On TV.

Pulling open the door, he stepped inside and blinked at the bright lights. Sadie, bless her soul, was wrapped up in her favorite flannel robe and sheepskin slippers, sitting at the kitchen table. She appeared exhausted.

"Hey, Sadie, how come you're up so late?" He glanced at the clock on the stove. "It's almost two o'clock!"

Apparently roused by the noise, Dylan wandered in from the living room. His mouth twisted into a sly grin. "This is gonna be good," he said cryptically.

"So why is everyone awake? Is something wrong?"

Dylan laughed. "Ask your friend Joanna."

Impatience and mounting worry flooded through him. "Dammit, tell me what's going on."

"Joanna will be in here anytime. We've been taking turns. Gina's on her way."

"Gina?" Exhausted by his day behind the wheel and the late hour, Ben stared at Dylan. "Maybe you can explain *why?"*

An odd cry rose from somewhere beyond the living room. It sounded once again, then sirened into a wail. Seconds later, Joanna trudged into the kitchen, with dark circles under her eyes and a blanket-wrapped bundle in her arms.

"So," she said coolly the moment she laid eyes on Ben. "The busy traveler has returned."

"What?"

She kept on coming until they were nearly toe to toe. "Here you go, cowboy. You've got an early Christmas present."

His gaze involuntarily dropped to her burden, and he found himself looking down into the tear-streaked face of...

"A *baby?*"

"Gina tells me you're really good with them, so here you go. She's all yours."

Joanna shifted the little girl against his chest. He automatically cradled her, but she whimpered as she stared up at him, her eyes huge and filled with renewed tears. "Where did she come from? Whose—"

"Even I know where babies come from," Dylan snickered. "And about being careful, too."

He was too tired for this. All he could think about was a fast, hot shower and the blessed comfort of his own bed. "Very funny. Now, where's the mom? I need to hit the sack."

Joanna glowered at him as she turned away. "Sadie? You can finally go to bed, dear. Ben can take over." Joanna gently helped the older woman from the chair and walked her to her bedroom door. As soon as she got back to the kitchen, she frowned at Dylan. "You, too, kid. Your uncle and I need to talk. Now scoot."

"Awwww—"

"Now, Dylan, I mean it. I'm beat and I want to go home."

With a last, disgruntled scowl, Dylan left the room. "I can't wait to hear about this tomorrow," he called over his shoulder.

Tired as he was, Ben couldn't help but be impressed. "What did you do to him?"

She folded her arms. "The baby wore him out. All of us. She's been crying for nearly four hours, and nothing has worked except walking with her.'' She glared at Ben. ''And to think I thought…'' With a shake of her head, she stepped around him and reached for the car keys and jacket she'd left on a kitchen chair. ''There's a note on the table from your…your girlfriend. It got a little wet, but you'll catch the drift. Your daughter—''

''Daughter!'' he exploded. ''I don't have—''

The baby had quieted in his arms. Now her face turned to a mask of terror, and she gave an earsplitting scream.

''*My God*, Carson. I thought you were supposed to be good with children!'' He could see the weariness in her eyes and something else—something dark and sad and painful—and he knew that it went far deeper than just the events of this night.

He lifted the child up and searched her sobbing face. Drew a blank. She couldn't possibly be his. *Could she?* Murmuring soft words of comfort, he held her at his shoulder and swayed back and forth until she calmed. ''I think,'' he said quietly, ''that you can at least *imagine* that this situation could be a bit of a shock. Can you grant me that much?''

Chewing her lower lip, she glanced at her watch, clearly debating about staying until someone she deemed competent could take charge. Apparently she figured it would have to be Gina, because she sighed and sank into one of the chairs at the kitchen table.

''When I came to town, I heard about you. How you have girlfriends from one end of the country to the other, and were quite the good-time guy.'' The curl of her lip made her opinion clear. ''I see a lot of cases where irresponsible guys father kids they don't want and refuse to take care of the ones they have. It's a bit of a hot button with me.''

''For what it's worth, I don't know anything about this.'' A sob shuddered through the small, warm child in his arms.

In a moment, though, she relaxed and grew limp and heavy as she gave in to sleep. He lowered his voice. "Hell, I haven't had a serious relationship in three years."

Joanna raised an eyebrow. "How about the casual ones? You know—new town, new bar—'Hey, good-lookin', how about a drink?'"

"Whatever rumors you've heard are just that—rumors. I've let 'em ride, figuring there wasn't much use in trying to stop them—and maybe they'd keep some of the more determined mamas from dragging their daughters out here."

"That must be *sooo* difficult." Joanna took another look at her watch and tapped its crystal. "Fighting off all those women."

"Hey," he said, "someone must have just decided to drop this baby off here, needing to find her a new home. Have you called the sheriff or the Enchantment police?"

"To put your daughter in foster care, when her mother has trusted you to take her in? The woman obviously doesn't know you very well." Joanna reached for a scrap of paper on the table and pushed it toward him.

He stared at her, and for the first time felt a stab of pure fear. Could this be true? How would he ever handle it if it was? Child care. Feedings. Around-the-clock responsibility. He couldn't imagine finding the time and money and commitment—not when he had to work nonstop to keep the ranch going.

Joanna seemed to read his thoughts. "Think about what your old girlfriend felt. How this changed *her* life. She must have been frightened and lonely and overwhelmed. Sounds like she didn't have much money, either."

The baby stirred against him, warm and trusting, and for a moment he wished that she were his. But...

"Read the note," he said hoarsely. "Please."

Joanna snagged the note. "'I'm sorry I didn't call a long

time ago. I just couldn't—but I figured you wouldn't be interested anyway. Remember meeting me in Houston? It was a February—we were both there for that Houlton dispersal sale. Remember how I teased you about that cute tattoo you have…'" Joanna studied him over the top of the note. *"Tattoo?"*

He waved off her faintly amused expression. "Teenage mistake. Stupid thing to do."

That night in Houston came back to him in a rush of images; the remembered scents of smoke and whiskey, the pounding beat of some second-rate, honky-tonk roadhouse at the edge of town.

A woman named Holly had come on to him, all glittery and wild in some sort of shiny red dress and high heels, her smile full of fun and promise. *I heard you tell your friend that your fiancée split,* she'd murmured in his ear as they danced slow and close, her body molded to his. *How about a little company?*

Lord knew they must have hit every dance hall and roadhouse bar from one end of town to the other, and she'd been so hot and insistent that she'd practically crawled in his bed. Given his battered emotions and the whiskey they'd consumed, he hadn't turned her away.

The next day, she was dressed and halfway out the door when he awakened too bleary eyed to think straight.

"Flight to catch, Sugar. Thanks for a great night."

"Wait—your phone number—"

"I got yours. Remember?" Holly had waved a small card in the air, blown him a kiss, and was gone.

Now, Joanna's voice hinted at impatience. "So you remember this weekend, or not?"

"Yes—and it was a mistake." Though feeling the trusting weight of the baby against his chest and breathing in the sweet scent of her made his words seem shallow. "I…spent most of it in the bars."

He'd just bumped into his ex-fiancée Rachel and her husband, who'd both gushed over the news that she was pregnant. Again. She'd been engaged to Ben when the jerk had gotten her pregnant for the first time—while Ben was on a three-week road trip to some big reining competitions in California—and the pain of her betrayal had still cut deep.

Joanna was studying him now, probably wondering if this was more than an occasional occurrence, but since that miserable weekend he hadn't had more than a beer or two on a hot day, or a single bourbon on the rocks when out for dinner...and he'd never been much of a drinker before.

"One weekend doesn't prove I'm this baby's father," he continued. "What else does the note say?"

"Part of it got wet and the ink ran, but it appears the baby was born last December—I think it says the twenty-third. Her name is Molly Michelle. The note is pretty vague, but her mom says something about going to California to start over, and coming back for the baby in a few months."

"Months!"

"She...um...says it's only fair, since you never paid any child support."

Anger flamed through him, and he had to take a deep breath before he could speak. "How could I do that? I never knew the child existed. Never saw or talked to the woman again. What name did she give?"

"Holly Nelson."

"Honestly, I don't even think that was the last name she used."

A soft rap sounded at the door. Gina walked in carrying a sleeping child—her youngest girl, Allie. Regan stumbled in behind her, rubbing her eyes. "Sorry it took me a while," Gina whispered. "I had to pick up the girls so Sue Ellen could go home. Oh, my—let me see her, Ben!"

Ben moved closer and turned so she could see the sleeping baby.

"Wow," she breathed. "She even has the same cowlick my girls do!"

Until this moment, the entire situation had seemed surreal. Like a dream that comes at dawn, where everything seems so vivid and real. *None of this could be happening.*

But at Gina's words he looked down at the baby in his arms. *Really* looked this time.

He saw the family cowlick that had plagued the Carsons for generations. The dark curls in evidence on all his childhood photos and the high forehead…maybe his mother's pert nose.

My God…maybe it's true.

A rush of emotion too powerful to name swept through him, but one coherent thought surfaced above all the rest. *What am I going to do now?*

CHAPTER EIGHT

"Hey, Slick!"

Ignoring the sarcasm from some kid behind him, Dylan jerked a shoulder and kept walking into the high school. *Damn.* Monday morning. Five full days of school till next weekend. Eleven weeks to go.

Since day one in this school, he'd been taunted. About his running shoes. His accent. His clothes. He heard whispers behind his back, and the kids stared at him as if he was a freak, or something. Not that it was anything new. It happened every time he changed schools. After so many moves, he no longer cared. At least not much.

"You look tired. Are you feeling all right?" Mrs. Babcock, his biology teacher, was standing just outside her door. She had to be someone's great-grandmother by now, with those deep wrinkles and gray hair.

"Yeah." *As all right as anyone could be after listening to Ben walking with a crying baby most of the night.*

He started into the room, but Mrs. Babcock touched his arm. "Could you stay after class for a few minutes? I'll give you a pass for your next period."

Great. Twisting a little to break away from her hand, he jerked his head in a brief nod and headed for the corner in the back of the room where he always sat. In every class. As far from everyone as he could get. All of them—whether Anglo, Navajo or Hispanic—had their own circles of friends. This was just one more place where Dylan didn't fit in. Not that it mattered because this place sucked.

He was lucky. By New Year's Eve he'd be leaving this town and all these losers behind.

Nate Welsh—the boy who'd called him Slick—now sidestepped down the aisle between the desks, dropped his heavy backpack to the floor and sank into the desk next to Dylan's with a gusty sigh. "I'd rather be fishing," he muttered under his breath.

His brown, windblown hair stuck up in clumps, and from what Dylan could see, he was in serious need of braces.

"So, you wanna hang out after school?" Nate lounged in his chair and hooked an elbow over the back of his seat.

"Doing what?"

Nate slid him a lazy smile. "Pool?"

"Yeah, right. I'm sure we look like we're legal." Well…maybe Nate could pass. He had a tough-guy attitude that just dared someone to mess with him and the muscular build of a guy several years older.

"No sweat. My uncle owns Ricardo's out by the trailer court. We go in the side door and stay outta the bar, and it's cool. They got three pool tables in back."

Excitement flared up in Dylan's chest. Faded. "I'd miss the bus home."

At the front of the room, Mrs. Babcock started talking about an upcoming test. Nate lowered his voice. "I got a car I can borrow, so I can take you home after."

Home. That was a joke. Where was his home exactly? Which state? Which house and which housekeeper? And now, with that baby out at the ranch, Ben would be even busier. There sure wasn't much point in going home. "Sure," Dylan whispered. "Cool!"

He looked up to see Mrs. Babcock's stern expression fixed on him. "You two don't need this review?" she asked, glancing over at Nate. "You're completely ready for the test?"

Nate grunted something under his breath. Dylan gave a single shake of his head.

After a moment of silent eye contact with them both, she turned to the board and picked up a piece of chalk. "Well, now…who can tell me the difference between meiosis and mitosis?"

It took forever for the bell to ring.

Dylan shouldered his backpack and joined the stampede heading out the door with his head down, but Babcock hadn't forgotten, because she was right at the door, her lips pursed and arms folded.

When the rest of the kids were gone, she shut the door behind them and walked over to her desk, waving Dylan to a desk at the front.

He warily slid into the seat.

"I'm curious," she said, picking up a manila folder and tapping it against her open palm. "How do you feel about school so far?"

"Here?"

"Here…and in general."

This sounds like trouble. Rapidly scanning through the last four weeks, he tried to remember what he might have done wrong. Nothing bad he could think of. Unless she'd gotten word about some of his…troubles…at the last school, this had to be another Great Potential speech. "Okay, I guess."

"Just okay?"

"Yeah."

She nodded as if he'd just confirmed her opinion. "You know, I suppose, that you've been scoring 99's on your annual ITBS tests in math and science since early elementary school."

Yep—just as I thought. He traced a set of initials carved into the desktop with his fingernail.

"You're easily capable of being an A student. And

yet…'' Frowning, she opened the folder and flipped through the pages inside. ''You've gotten Cs on your homework—when you turn the assignments in—and you got a B− on our first unit test. Tell me what I can do to help.''

Send me home to New York.

The passing bell jangled. Through the glass panel in the door, he could see students crowding outside, waiting to come in. Now he was going to have to walk into his math class late, and walk alone through the gauntlet of stares and whispers as he found his seat.

''Dylan?''

He fidgeted in his chair. ''I'll try harder.''

''I hope so. You're exceptionally bright, Dylan. You could win scholarships. Go to just about any college you want. But if you don't work on your GPA…'' She snapped the file shut and dropped it on her desk. ''I'd like you to stay after school this afternoon. I can help you get up to speed with the class. Transferring here two weeks after school started makes things rough.''

Nate and the pool hall…or staying after school. No contest. ''I can't stay after. Not today.''

''Tomorrow?''

Dylan grabbed his backpack as he slid out of the seat and started for the door. ''Yeah…I guess.''

''Three o'clock. This room. And Dylan—'' She hesitated. ''Choose your friends with care.''

''That's a laugh,'' he muttered under his breath as he shouldered his way through the students waiting to come inside. *Choosing* was never an issue.

After eight schools in the past ten years, he knew there wasn't any point. He was always an outsider, always the one who didn't fit in.

Trying to make friends was a big waste of time.

JOANNA HAD EXPECTED Monday morning would be a busy time at the pediatric clinic. She hadn't expected it to start with Ben Carson and his daughter.

"So," she said as she scanned the medical chart Eve had started. "Have you heard from the baby's mother?"

"Not a word, and it's already been two days." Ben lifted the baby higher on his shoulder and rocked from side to side. Even at ten months, she appeared small and fragile in his arms. "I'm hoping," he added in a hushed voice, "that Max stays asleep through this checkup."

"Max?" Joanna eyed the pink cartoon figures at the waistband of the baby's disposable diaper. "You're calling her *Max?*"

"It fits." He brushed a gentle hand over the child's silky hair. "She's a tough little thing. Gina's girls weren't half as loud—and not near as stubborn."

There were lines of exhaustion bracketing his mouth. *Serves you right,* she thought grimly. "Get any sleep last night?"

"Nope, though she dozed off before we got a mile away from home this morning. I almost pulled off the road so I could try to catch a few minutes of sleep myself. But," he added with a weary smile, "I thought I'd better get her in here and make sure everything's all right."

Joanna had to give him points for that. "Eve says her temperature is normal. We'll do a complete well-child exam, and get a CBC to check her hemoglobin…" She flipped the page. "This is all the health history you have?"

"I haven't seen my dad in years. As far as I know, everyone else is fine."

"Max's mom?"

He had the good grace to look uncomfortable. "I…don't know."

He probably didn't even know Holly's middle name.

"I'm sure you'll be hearing from her soon. When you

do, make sure you find out about vaccinations and any health problems the baby has had. Ideally, I'd like copies of her old medical records.'' Joanna set the file on the counter and motioned to the table. ''I need her over there to finish her exam.''

Ben eased the baby down and rested a steadying hand at her shoulder. A strong, protective hand; large and tanned and capable, in sharp contrast to Max's soft skin. ''She didn't wake up when Eve and I got her sleeper off,'' he whispered. ''Maybe—''

But Max's face scrunched into a yawn, then her eyes flew open and rounded with fear as she got a good look at her surroundings. The next second, she burst into tears and twisted into Ben's hands, desperately reaching for him.

''She'll be fine for just a—'' Before Joanna could finish, Ben lifted the baby from the table and snuggled her close, murmuring words of comfort as he stroked her back. ''Guess she likes you best,'' Joanna finished dryly.

''She's not all that pleased with me, either, but Sadie was exhausted yesterday after being up so late Saturday night, and Dylan has avoided Max like the plague. I haven't gotten a thing done since this baby arrived.''

Joanna laughed. ''That's what the new moms all say.''

''But this just isn't going to work. I've got a barn full of training horses to ride. Chores. Heifers to haul down to a rancher in Las Cruces next week. Chores. My days are full from dawn till nine or ten at night.''

''Not anymore, unless you can find a good sitter. Hold still.'' Joanna picked up the otoscope on the counter, and steadied the crying baby's head with one hand as she examined her ears. ''Of course, you could turn Max over to the authorities…''

Ben gave her a dismissive glance. ''And have her end up in foster care?''

''Well, you don't know for *sure* this baby is yours.

Right?'' Joanna reached for the stethoscope draped around her neck. "Eve tells me there are some excellent foster parents in the area. Move your hand just a little…''

He waited until she finished and had slung the stethoscope around her neck again. "She doesn't need foster care. She's got the Carson cowlick, and both Gina and I have the same brown eyes.''

So he's bonded to the little girl already. Hiding a smile, Joanna gestured toward the exam table. "Okay, let's try again. I need Max lying down so I can examine her.''

Max's face crumpled as Joanna lightly palpated her abdomen and the lymph nodes beneath her jawline. This time she just whimpered.

"Good baby,'' Joanna soothed. The baby quieted, but turned her head to keep Joanna firmly in view. "Such a big girl you are!''

When she completed the exam, she pressed the intercom button on the wall. "Eve? We need a CBC in room 1.''

Ben reached into the diaper bag at his· feet and pulled out pink coveralls and a pair of lace-trimmed socks and flashed a boyish, self-conscious grin. "We were running late this morning, so I just changed her diaper and didn't try tackling anything more difficult than her pajamas.''

"She was probably just as happy in them.''

He studied the one-piece outfit in his hands, then turned it upside down and studied it some more. "What do you think—is Max okay?''

Joanna eyed his progress with the coveralls and hid a smile. "She's at the fortieth percentile for height and the fiftieth for weight. She seems fine.''

Ben started awkwardly fishing one of Max's little arms through a sleeve, but she struggled to her hands and knees and plopped backward into a sitting position, the outfit tangled under her bottom. "It's been years since Allie was a baby. I guess I've forgotten how to do this.''

"Here—pick her up. Lay the outfit out on the table. If you put her on top of it and move fast, you can start with the feet and it might work better. Or you can hold her in your lap and try. Feet first."

"I did better with her stretchy pajamas," he muttered under his breath. After several attempts at corralling her waving arms and legs, he managed to get the outfit on and zipped up. "It's a whole lot easier saddling a green colt for the first time, believe me."

Eve appeared at the door. "The Gordons are in two," she said, giving the baby a bright smile.

Max looked up at Ben's face, then gave Eve a wary frown.

"Eve will take care of the CBC, and after that you can go," Joanna said briskly as she started for the door. "Don't hesitate to call the office if you have any problems."

"Joanna?"

She stopped, one hand on the door frame, and looked over her shoulder.

"I appreciate your help Saturday night."

"No problem." With a wave of her hand, she slipped out the door and headed straight for the Gordon family awaiting her in the next room.

For those few hours on Saturday night, she'd held and comforted a distraught little girl whose mother had abandoned her to strangers…whose father didn't even know she existed.

For those hours, because Joanna had lost so much and had grieved for so long, she'd allowed herself to imagine that Max was her beloved child…and that this was a final chance to say goodbye.

And now she knew.

She'd realized it during the wee hours of Sunday morning, when she'd started to drive away from the ranch. It would be all too easy to become involved with Ben's family—especially his newfound baby daughter.

Whatever she'd thought of Ben's reputation before, she couldn't deny that he seemed to accept whatever life brought him. He had a strong and protective soul, something far more compelling than just a handsome face.

And if she didn't stay clear of him, leaving in three months would break her heart.

GINA WAVED to the other Birth Place employees who'd gathered in the lounge. She settled into the soft, welcoming arms of the overstuffed chair and resisted the temptation to tip her head against its marshmallow back.

"Long day?" Katherine Collins, one of the other midwives, dropped into the sofa next to her and gave her a sympathetic smile.

"Long *several* days." Gina rolled her head against the cushion to give Katherine a tired smile. Katherine lowered her voice. "Have you heard from Zach?"

"No."

"He hasn't called the girls?"

Gina shook her head. "They're used to him being gone, and know he doesn't call every day. It's going to be so hard…"

"If you need any help, call me anytime. Day or night." Katherine's voice hardened. "If he doesn't bother to keep in touch with his daughters, maybe you're doing the right thing."

"Am I?" Gina worried at her lower lip with her teeth, willing away the tears that burned beneath her lids. "He's a good man. A good father. He'd never lay a hand on any of us. Do I have a right to throw that away? Am I just being selfish?"

"Maybe you should talk to our psychologist."

Gina gave a strained laugh. "I love Celia. She's a sweetheart to work with—but we're talking marriage problems, here. With her track record…would she know what to say?"

"Her heart is just too soft." Katherine smiled fondly. "She keeps attracting needy guys who want her caring and support more than they want her."

"Celia's scratch-and-dent club?"

"Maybe her personal life is a little rocky at times, but she's a wonderful psychologist. She helped my sister get through her divorce."

Divorce. The word slithered down Gina's spine like an icy hand. "I'm hoping I don't need one of those," she said with a shaky laugh. "But maybe I'd better give her a call."

Lydia strode into the room. "Sorry…long-distance phone call. I didn't mean to keep you all waiting." She scanned the room, nodding to everyone. "Some of you already know this…but we've run into some problems. Financial problems. Kim?"

Somber as ever, the accountant stood and tucked a strand of blond hair behind her ear. She held a sheaf of papers in her hand. "We've had a sixteen percent decrease in new cases over the past month, and a six percent dropout rate. We've also received word from the First Methodist Auxiliary that they'll be diverting their annual fund-raiser proceeds to a children's summer-feeding program. The Enchantment Women's League is also on the verge of pulling out. The impact of these factors will have us at a negative balance by the end of this month. Given our recent property-improvement expenditures, within sixty days, we could be—" she flipped to the second page "—at a deficit of eighteen thousand dollars."

Trish tentatively waved a hand. "But how can that be? Surely the building is paid for…people have insurance, or government assistance…"

"The building is free and clear, but there are utility and

maintenance costs," Kim said, "and the taxes will go up again this year. We provide a number of free services, and some of our patients fall between the cracks—too much money for welfare, not enough to pay their bills. Those people are not turned away."

Lenora fretted with the name badge on her lab coat as she cast a worried glance at the other employees. A widow, she was raising two grandchildren on her nurse's salary. Gina knew that every penny counted in that household. "Surely we won't have to close."

"No, but our revenues, whether from private pay, insurance or public assistance, don't cover our operating costs." Kim glanced dispassionately at every employee. "Given the reduced client load and our high staff-to-patient ratio, we'll obviously have to make significant staffing reductions."

Gina felt that same icy hand grasp her heart. *"Staffing?"*

"That, and other measures."

"Isn't there anything we can do? Surely we can talk to these people. Explain how important their support is...or find new organizations?"

Lydia nodded at Kim and stepped forward. "Kim and I have been working on this for several weeks. We haven't found new support in the community, but Kim is researching grant opportunities and I'm continuing my efforts to reach organizations and business leaders throughout our area."

"What about the reduced patient load? Why is that happening?" Katherine asked, throwing her hands forward, palm up. "We've had wonderful response from the community for years. Even people from a great distance have come here! Remember Ashleigh?"

Everyone nodded, remembering the famed television star Ashleigh Logan who had come here last fall to have her baby, in an effort to elude a stalker. She'd returned to visit The Birth Place several times.

Lydia's face tightened. "There are apparently rumors about unprofessional care. Nothing we can substantiate or stop. I stepped down from the board when this all started in an effort to calm the situation."

"Can't we have informational meetings? Another open house? Ask for a positive article in the newspaper?"

"We've done some of that already. We'll continue with what has appeared most effective." Lydia's hand closed around her rose-onyx pendant, a sure sign that she was deeply troubled. "In the meantime, we've got a choice. Layoffs, or reduced hours. I thought you should all be prepared."

Lenora moaned. Several of the others turned pale. In a town this size, there were few job opportunities.

Gina closed her eyes against the image of Zach's angry expression when they'd last fought face-to-face. She'd thought she owed it to herself and the girls to take a stand— to show she had value beyond being a dutiful wife and mother. With a career she loved, she could try to instill in her daughters a desire to become strong and independent women. Why couldn't he see her side?

Guilt gnawed at her stomach, even as she held on to her determination not to lose sight of her goal.

Whether he admitted it or not, her income had helped them hold on to their small home and provide for their daughters, but it wasn't nearly enough—even with child support—to make ends meet on her own. And since she was the last one hired at the clinic, she'd surely be the first let go. The irony of it all was overwhelming.

Now she might lose her job as well as her marriage.

CHAPTER NINE

ON SATURDAY MORNING Joanna zipped up her cardinal-red down jacket and leaned over her porch railing, breathing in the sharp tang of snow-frosted pine.

A good four inches had fallen since last night, and lazy flakes were still swirling through the trees like a holiday scene in a child's snow globe, while a pristine blanket of sparkling white covered the ground.

Pristine except for where Moose had been romping.

The pup buried his nose in the snow and tossed clouds of it into the air, snapping at the flakes as they drifted down. Out in the pasture, old Galahad dropped to the ground and rolled vigorously. He staggered awkwardly to his feet and bucked, cantering through the snow as if he, too, found it a novelty.

Come to think of it, this was probably the first time the old gelding from southern California had ever seen snow.

A deep sense of contentment swept through her as she watched the horse and dog play. It had been a week now since she'd spent the night at Shadow Creek Ranch. Every day at the clinic had been a little easier...her self-doubts fading, her enthusiasm returning. And now she would have a weekend to relax.

The ring of the cell phone at her hip broke the silence. Ben's anxious voice shattered her sense of peace.

"There's something wrong with Max," he said, skipping the usual greetings. "She's had a cold since Thursday.

Nothing much, just sniffles and some coughing. Now she sounds more congested. She doesn't want to eat.''

"Fever?"

"Not more than a hundred since she started coughing."

"How is she sleeping?"

"By Wednesday she actually slept through the night. Once she got sick, we were back at square one. Oh…she coughs more at night."

Joanna thought about the odor of cigarette smoke on the baby's clothing the night Max arrived at the ranch, and mentally ran through a list of possible respiratory illnesses. "Is she wheezing? Do you see any change in her color?"

Joanna heard him step away from the phone, then return.

"She's awfully pale. Wheezing? I don't know what that sounds like."

"She ought to be seen. You could take her to the E.R., or you could meet me at the clinic."

"There wasn't anything about insurance in her diaper bag. I called my provider on Wednesday, but they won't cover her without proper documentation and I sure as hell don't have any." His voice lowered in derision. "Apparently Holly didn't have time for that sort of thing on her way out of town."

If she ever met this woman, Joanna already had a few good topics of discussion. Now she had one more to top the list. "I'd better meet you at the clinic. Twenty minutes."

"Whether she has insurance coverage or not, I want her to have whatever she needs," Ben said tightly.

"Don't worry, she will." Joanna ended the connection as she pivoted and went into the cabin. Inside, a low fire crackled in the fireplace, filling the air with sweet fragrance and sending flickering light across the deep gold paneling.

The contrast with the snowy world outside the windows made her feel cozy, protected. A good book and a cup of hot chocolate in front of the fireplace would be so nice later this afternoon. "Exactly what you need, Weston," she muttered to herself as she grabbed her purse and keys. "The life of a hermit."

At her car door, she stopped in her tracks and chuckled. Talking to herself was *not* a good sign. At least only Galahad and Moose were around to hear her. She turned to check on them one last time.

Moose was hanging over the yard fence, bouncing on his hind feet in an effort to get over. Galahad—

Where was he?

Joanna tossed her keys and purse onto the front seat of the Tahoe, then spun around and ran to the fence, calling his name. The gate was still locked. She hadn't seen him even come close to the electric fence since it was turned on, and from under the wide eaves of the little barn she could see the fence charger's reassuring blinking light marking each pulse of electricity surging through the wire.

Moose whined and raced to the far side of the yard, where he barked sharply. She reached him just in time to see why.

The bottom rail of one section of fence was on the ground. With one hard blow of his front hoof, Galahad sent the middle rail to the ground as well.

"Whoa!" Joanna screamed, starting across the yard at a dead run. "No!"

Galahad didn't so much as swivel an ear in her direction. He dropped to his knees and scrambled underneath the remaining top rail. *Under* the fence?

Dislodged by his broad back, the final, top rail fell unceremoniously to the ground. Galahad disappeared over the hill and into the trees. *Again.*

With a sigh of frustration, Joanna turned toward her SUV. He'd either come home, or someone would call to let her know where he was. Right now what mattered most was a sick little girl and her worried father. Anything else would just have to wait.

JOANNA'S CABIN was two miles west of town on curvy mountain roads. Ben's ranch was nine miles south. He still beat her by five minutes, which gave him entirely too much time to worry about Max. How did other parents manage the stress?

"You used lights and sirens to get here?" she teased as she unlocked the front door and flipped on the lights.

"If I'd had 'em." He followed her into the reception area and folded down the blanket he'd tossed over Max's head when he took her out of her car seat. Max lay limply against his chest, showing no interest in her new surroundings. "Just look at her."

Joanna leaned close for a moment. Frowning, she toed off her snow boots and shucked off her jacket, leaving them in the entryway. "Bring her in."

Anxiety over Max's harsh breathing had tied his stomach in knots this morning. Joanna's frown and businesslike manner tightened them. Stamping the snow from his boots, he followed her to the first exam room and shifted the baby in his arms so he could unzip her snowsuit.

"Just let her sit on the table." Joanna helped him undress the baby down to her diaper, then picked up an ear thermometer, slid on a disposable-tip sleeve and checked her temperature. "It's 101.8°."

"So she's higher now." He hovered close, feeling helpless. "I gave her a dose of baby Tylenol drops three hours ago. Shouldn't she be better?"

"Maybe." Joanna checked the baby's ears. "Inflammation on the right side…okay on the left." She took a quick glance at her throat.

"So that means she's in a lot of pain, right?" Now guilt slid through him. "She was fussy, but she wasn't crying all night. I didn't know, or I would have brought her in sooner."

Joanna glanced up at him as she positioned her stethoscope in her ears. "Sometimes, when these infections are starting, a child might not complain much, and then again, they can change awfully fast. They might be brought in with cold symptoms, but their ears are fine. An hour or two later they've got a painful infection going."

She leaned over and listened to the baby's lungs from the back, returning several times to the left side before listening to the chest. "She's congested, but I don't detect any pneumonia. I thought I detected a faint wheeze, but only picked it up once."

"So that's good, right? Just her ears?"

"Well...she isn't very perky." Joanna put her stethoscope on the counter. "We can get her started on an antibiotic for her ears and a good pediatric antihistamine. She should begin to feel more comfortable soon."

"Is that all? How sick is she?"

"So far, nothing unusual, though that wheeze concerns me. Do you have any idea how you can track down Max's mother? I know the note said she'd be back in a few months, but I'd really like those old medical records."

"Holly told me she was from somewhere in Texas, but said she was in the process of moving at the time. I gave her my address and phone number but never heard from her. She mentioned being unlisted. I've done an Internet white pages search and haven't found a thing."

"Maybe you'll be able to find a relative who knows where she is?"

He gave a short laugh. "Not easy—with a last name like Nelson."

The optimistic light in her eyes faded. "On the upside, I hear you've been taking Max to Gina's house during the day. How's it going with Gina's baby-sitter?"

"Pretty well. Sadie's just not up to watching a baby every day, and there were no other options. Sue Ellen seems nice enough."

"I'm sure Gina wouldn't have hired her if she wasn't." Joanna helped dress the baby, then turned to write on a prescription pad. "Fill these prescriptions—follow the directions on the labels and be sure to use it all."

She handed the sheet to him. "If her breathing changes—gets more raspy, or congested sounding—I want you to call me right away. Okay?"

"Raspy?" He picked up the baby and held her at his shoulder, where she dropped her head limply against his flannel shirt. "Exactly what does that mean, compared to wheezing and just plain congested?"

Joanna smiled a little. "Why don't you bring her in tomorrow."

"Sunday?"

"No problem. I can meet you here. Or sooner, if she seems worse."

He held Max a little tighter as a wave of sudden panic swept through him. He could handle foaling a twelve-hundred-pound mare. Treat wounded cattle. Heck, in his young and stupid days, he'd even earned his pro-rodeo card and spent time on bulls who'd rather see him dead than alive.

But this tiny child was the biggest challenge he'd ever faced. She'd stolen his heart *and* his peace of mind. "But what if I can't tell? What if she gets worse but it isn't real obvious?"

"You'll hear if her breathing becomes harsher or seems tight. If she looks really pale and it sounds like she's panting, or if she just won't eat and drink. Call me if you aren't sure. I know you don't have insurance on her—"

"That doesn't matter at all. I'll do what it takes."

"I'm just warning you that if she gets worse she might need a little time in the hospital."

Ben felt the blood drain from his face. *"Hospital?"*

"Don't worry. She might snap out of it just fine." She glanced at the clock on the wall. "Use my cell-phone number if you need to call this afternoon, okay? I might be gone quite a while." She gave him a rueful grin, but when their eyes met, her grin faded into something…warmer.

The subtle change scrambled his thoughts, and he had to think for a moment before he could answer. "Galahad?"

"I'm beginning to wonder if he plots these escapes and finds it more fun to try a different method each time. First, he jumped the fence like a gazelle. The next time, I swear he picked the lock with his teeth. This time he broke two lower rails and shimmied underneath. If you see him…"

"I'll call."

She lifted a hand to brush a wisp of hair away from Max's soft cheek. "I want to apologize. I…I was awfully quick to judge you last weekend. I had no right to do that."

"If it's any consolation, you aren't the only one. I don't think there's been a hotter topic of gossip since the owner of the feed store eloped with an eighteen-year-old clerk at Elkhorn's Hardware."

"I'm sorry."

"Don't be. If nothing else, Gina tells me it's proving to be an abject lesson for the good mothers of Enchantment," he said wryly. "Everyone who thought I led a wild life before can now point out the consequences."

"Well…it's not anyone else's business."

"In a small town, it is." He gave a short laugh. "The funny thing is that I *don't* lead a wild life. I've always been careful. God knows I never wanted to be responsible for some poor kid growing up like I did, with a dad I never saw."

She eyed him thoughtfully. "Apparently Holly had your

name and number all this time—and she sure found your ranch easily enough, even in the dark. If she didn't care about child support, at least she should have told you about Max. Intentional pregnancy or not—''

''*Intentional?*'' He'd been imagining that Holly had been alone and scared, or maybe too embarrassed to come forward. He'd been feeling a pervasive sense of guilt and regret, but *this* possibility made him feel used.

If she'd been after something the one night they'd been together, it had only taken a little too much whiskey and that breast-hugging tight dress of hers for him to fall right into her seductive hands...and the thought of a woman like that raising Max made his blood chill.

''We don't know what really happened,'' Joanna continued, ''but wouldn't you think she'd be worrying, and want to make sure things were okay?''

Since Max appeared at his doorstep, he'd wondered that every hour of every day.

Ben closed his eyes briefly. ''I sure can't picture Holly as a loving mother.'' Max whimpered and stirred in his arms. ''I can't stop wondering if she'll simply never come back—or worse, if she'll show up out of the blue, try to grab Max and take off.''

''She might've discovered that solo parenthood is much harder than she thought, and just wants her freedom,'' Joanna said. ''On the other hand, she could return and fight you if you try for shared custody. You might want to consider DNA testing and also have your lawyer check into establishing your rights, if you want to be a part of Max's life.''

And that could easily cost more than he had in the bank.

Max had laid her head against his shoulder and dozed off almost immediately. Now she stirred and looked up at him, her eyes wide and trusting. Lifting a small hand to rub the stubble on his cheek, she giggled…and broke into a spasm of harsh coughing.

Money? Everything he owned was tied up in the ranch. The horses. The equipment he'd had to buy and the buildings he'd had to replace. He already supported Sadie and helped Gina's family occasionally, and now he had Dylan as well.

But even if it meant he lost everything he'd worked for, there was just no way he could let his daughter go.

GALAHAD MAY HAVE PLOTTED the perfect escape, but he hadn't counted on the devoted readership of the *Arroyo County Bulletin*.

As soon as Ben left with Max, Joanna dialed the phone number at her cabin and retrieved the messages from the answering machine.

There'd been three calls by elderly women reporting the progress of the big old gelding heading through town. A fourth from Parker Reynolds, the Birth Place administrator, who'd seen the horse trotting gaily down Copper Avenue.

The fifth call was from an irate home owner named Mrs. Purdy on the east side of town, who declared that the horse was placidly pulling laundry from her clothesline with his teeth and dropping it on the ground. She'd already called the police, she added, and there would be big trouble if Joanna didn't immediately fetch her horse.

All five callers noted that they'd seen Galahad's photograph on the front page of the newspaper last Saturday, and their messages firmly chastised Joanna for being so careless.

"Thank you, Nolan," Joanna muttered to herself an hour later as she pulled her SUV and horse trailer to a stop in front of the Purdys' upscale house.

The woman, pinch-faced and wizened as a dried apple, appeared at her front door before Joanna was halfway up her sidewalk. "He's still here. In back," she snapped. "Now that he's done with my laundry, he's chewing on the ornamental shrubbery I planted last year."

Joanna shifted the halter and lead rope to her other shoulder and pulled her checkbook from the hip pocket of her jeans. "I know I owe you for damages. I'm truly sorry."

Mrs. Purdy crossed her arms tightly across her sunken chest.

"Perhaps I can pay for you to take your laundry into town and have it done?" Joanna prompted. "And the landscaping—any idea?"

"This is *very* inconvenient. It's not just the damage he caused." The woman sniffed. "It's the time and bother."

Joanna leaned to one side, trying to peer around the house. Galahad, apparently sensing the end of his adventure, peered at her from around the far corner, his lower lip flapping and his ears at wary attention.

A pair of scarlet panties dangled from one ear.

Scarlet? Joanna darted a glance back at Mrs. Purdy in disbelief. "Maybe I'd better nab him while I can, ma'am. Then we can settle up?"

When Mrs. Purdy just scowled, Joanna hitched the halter and lead rope farther up on her shoulder and tucked it all behind her arm so Galahad couldn't see it.

She casually sauntered around the house, keeping her eyes averted as if she hadn't even noticed the presence of a horse roughly the size of a bull moose. As always, he fell for the ploy, watching her with interest and failing to sense the trap. Or perhaps he was just too eager for his reward.

"Lucky for me," she murmured as she eased the rope over his neck and slipped the halter onto his head. She draped the panties over the clothesline.

He nuzzled her jacket pockets until she produced a carrot. "I'm sure I could never catch up if you decided to take off right now."

Mrs. Purdy was still at the front of the house as Joanna led the gelding toward the street. "I'm so glad you called and left a message," Joanna called out. "Once I put up a lower strand of electric wire he should stay put, I promise."

"I certainly hope so." The older woman glanced pointedly toward a trampled planting of bougainvillea in front of the impressive house across the street. "They aren't going to be too happy, either. Mrs. Pennington ought to be getting home anytime now."

Surprised, Joanna pulled to a halt. "Pennington? Stuart and Fiona Pennington?"

"That's right. And he is going to be even more upset than her when he sees his bougainvillea."

Joanna remembered Jason Pennington's accidents and the bruises around Fiona's wrist. "He's...got quite a temper," she said carefully.

"I wouldn't know." Mrs. Purdy's eyes narrowed. "But I hear her car acomin' up the street, so you can ask her. She always pulls around behind her house."

So much for delving into the local gossip to see if her suspicions were correct. "I'll just go apologize to her. What do I owe you?"

"Nothing. Just keep that horse at home." With a sniff, the woman turned, tromped into her house and slammed the door.

As soon as Galahad was loaded in the trailer, Joanna squared her shoulders and walked up to the front door of the Penningtons' home. It was a sprawling, contemporary adobe, the leaded-glass panes in the massive front door refracting the image and light of a chandelier hanging over the entry hall on the other side. Deep, melodic chimes sounded within when she pressed the doorbell.

A safety chain jangled. Someone fumbled at the lock. The door opened a few inches and Jason stood in the door with a startled expression. "Dr. *Weston?*"

"Hi, Jason."

"You make *house* calls?"

At the expression of alarm in his eyes she smiled down at him. "Occasionally, but not this time." She took a step to one side and gestured toward the mangled bougainvillea. "I need to apologize to your mother."

"Wow," he breathed. "You did *that?*"

"Not me—my horse."

His gaze shifted briefly to the trailer and SUV parked at the curb, and a flicker of distaste crossed his face. "I 'spose it bucked you off," he said flatly.

"Nope, he escaped. And this time he caused trouble for both your family and Mrs. Purdy across the street."

Jason cocked his head and stilled. "I hear my mom coming. I think you'd better talk to her. *Before* my dad comes home." He turned and raised his voice by a few hundred decibels.

"Mo-om! You got company!" He gave Joanna the sympathetic expression of someone who'd been in trouble a number of times himself. "Good luck."

"Thanks," she retorted dryly.

He disappeared, voices raised and fell, and a moment later Fiona appeared at the edge of the door, clearly not intending to welcome Joanna inside. Frowning, she bit her lower lip as she studied the damaged flowers. "I-it's all right. I'll take care of it. I'm sure the garden center must have something similar."

She was young and elegant, in an expensively cut red maternity jacket and cream slacks, but where one might expect the casual confidence of the wealthy, there was the nervousness of a rabbit caught away from cover. She started to shut the door.

"Wait—let me pay for the replacements. I can even plant them if you'd like. I owe you that much at least."

A sleek oyster-shell-white Mercedes purred to a stop behind Joanna's trailer. The darkened windows hid the occupant, but at Fiona's indrawn breath Joanna didn't need an introduction. "Your husband?"

Fiona's gaze darted toward the street. Sure enough, a hefty man with thinning red hair stepped out of the car and scowled at Joanna's rig. After scanning the neighborhood he began marching toward the house, but his stride faltered as he approached the mangled flowers.

"Just go," Fiona whispered. "Please. It's better for you to just leave."

"I can't. What about the hoofprints in the snow?" Joanna glanced over her shoulder at him before turning to Fiona and gently taking her hand. "Come talk to me. This week."

"Fiona!" he roared. "What the hell happened here?"

"It's my fault," Joanna said mildly as she faced him. "Not intentionally, of course, but I'll certainly pay for the damages."

His pale gray eyes were the color of February sleet, and just as cold as he scrutinized Joanna. "Your horse left those footprints? Over my prize bougainvillea?"

Joanna nodded. "Afraid so."

His eyes narrowed. "I'll need my landscaper to handle it, of course. He'll need to start a search for the correct variety."

From behind her, Fiona gave a quiet sigh of exasperation.

"I figure…seventy-five to a hundred dollars, easily." He pursed his lips. "Maybe more, with the rock arrangement needing to be redone."

"Rocks?"

He gestured impatiently, but all Joanna could see were the dried plants crushed into the snow and a scattering of nondescript river rock. "I'm not sure…"

"Really, Stuart, I think I can handle this through the garden center, and we—"

"Fiona."

His wife drew in a quick breath at the low, warning tone, and disappeared silently into the house.

So I was right about him. Trying to hide her distaste, Joanna forced a conciliatory smile, not wanting to aggravate the situation for Fiona. "Do you want to let me know later on? You could drop by at the pediatric clinic in town with the receipts."

"You're the gal with the horse who was in the paper. The new doctor." His gaze sharpened, and she could see him mentally adding up what else he could try to charge her for.

"I'll only be in town for a few months." From her trailer came the loud *thumpa-thumpa-thumpa* sound of Galahad pawing. "I'd better go before my horse tears up the trailer."

"You'll be hearing from me."

Joanna returned his sharklike smile with one of her own. *And if I see any evidence that you've laid a hand on Jason, you'll very definitely be hearing from me.*

CHAPTER TEN

WITH A DAD LIKE HIS, who rarely landed at home for more than a few weeks at a time and seemed to go through girl-friends faster than a tube of toothpaste, Dylan already knew family life mostly sucked. Living at the ranch with an old lady and the noisiest kid on the planet had now confirmed his opinion.

Who in their right mind would *ever* want a baby? After almost two weeks of Max, Dylan knew it wouldn't be him.

During the day, when he was in school, Max went to some baby-sitter who watched Gina's kids. At night and on weekends, Max was at the ranch. Emptying the cupboards of pots and pans and canned goods when she was happy. Crying when she wasn't.

Actually…she was sorta cute sometimes, though he'd never admit it to anyone. She gave him these huge smiles that lit up her whole face whenever she saw him. When he picked her up, she gave him sloppy baby kisses and gig-gled, and liked to grab his nose.

But she was a lot of work, too. Someone had to watch her like a hawk or God only knew what she'd get into, because she could move like lightning toward anything she shouldn't have.

And *that* had gotten old, fast.

Now, faced with the decision to get on the school bus or follow Nate and some of the other guys downtown, the choice wasn't hard.

Dylan fell into step with Nate. "Ricardo's?"

"Nah...my uncle says one of the cops has been hanging around hoping to bust him for underage kids in the bar." Nate gave a short laugh. "I had a little trouble with Miguel once, and I ain't planning on messing with him again. We could hang out at my place, though. Ma works late Friday nights, so she won't be around."

Dylan had been there once. A rusted single-wide out at the Lazy H Trailer Park, Nate's mom tried to keep it clean and neat, but she worked long hours at a truck stop and Nate was pretty much on his own.

But even as a warning voice sounded in his head, Dylan found himself nodding in agreement. "Sure—why not?"

The two other boys, Billy and Jonah, exchanged glances, then gave Nate a hard look.

"What's up with that?" Jonah jerked his chin in Dylan's direction. "We had plans."

"Still do." Nate elbowed Dylan in the ribs. "He's cool. Right, Slick?"

Behind them, the school buses were pulling out into traffic. Dylan felt a surge of exhilaration. *Freedom.* "You bet."

The other two boys sauntered through the high-school football field, angled across Copper Avenue, then turned south on Sage with Nate and Dylan close behind them.

The sidewalks sparkled with a fresh dusting of snow, the air was sharp and damp, heavy with promise for the snowfall predicted for later tonight. At the corner of Sage and Paseo de Sierra, they passed a rental ski shop sporting brightly colored snowboards in its front windows.

A sudden yearning for his dad hit Dylan like a blow to the chest. Once, when Dad was around for a long weekend, they'd headed up to a ski resort in Vermont for a three-day weekend, and it was the best time Dylan had ever had in his life.

Just the two of them—no business meetings, no phones,

none of his dad's hot dates that left Dylan sitting home alone with the TV remote in his hand and a dark, silent condo for company. If heaven could be anything he wanted, it would be like going on another ski trip with his dad.

God knew another one of those trips wasn't likely to happen anytime soon. Philip Carson rarely had time to spare.

"Hey, do you guys ski?" He blurted it out without thinking.

The scornful expression from the other boys felt like a bucket of ice water in his face.

"Yeah, rich boy. We spend all our time up at the resorts. We just can't *wait* till Angel's Gate opens." Jonah gave an effeminate flip of his wrist. "Right, Billy?"

Both boys doubled over, laughing. Nate just looked comfortable. "That's a fancy new ski place north of town. Some of my uncles and cousins work construction up there. I got to see it once."

Still embarrassed, Dylan gave him a thumbs-up. "Cool."

A string of out-of-state, luxury cars and SUVs topped with roof ski racks purred by. At the first break in the traffic, the boys raced across the street. Two blocks farther down Sage, Jonah and Billy peeled off and disappeared into a corner grocery.

Nate kept on walking, so Dylan followed him. "Aren't they coming over?"

"Sure. After they get the stuff."

Stuff? Dylan had seen it all back home—the drug buys done in the boys' bathroom and out behind the gym at school. The casual exchanges in the parking lot of the fast-food restaurant a half block away. The parties where most everyone got high and more than a few passed out.

But he hadn't messed with that shit yet and he didn't plan to now. Seeing his only friend go to the E.R. and not come back had been one of the worst deals of his entire life.

"Hey, man—maybe I oughta get home. I forgot that I needed to—"

Nate cut a disgusted glance in his direction but kept on walking. "What, you got a problem with a little beer?"

Dylan stifled a sigh of relief. "'Course not." He fished in his hip pocket and pulled out a couple of fives. "Did you all chip in?"

A corner of Nate's mouth lifted. "Yeah. We'll put this in the kitty. Billy's girlfriend works there, so she gives us a good deal."

The other two boys, each laden with a six-pack of Bud rolled up in their jackets, arrived just minutes after Nate and Dylan reached the trailer.

Inside, with the shades drawn and lights off, Nate lit a candle on a battered coffee table and they all dropped onto the floor. Light flickered in the sparsely furnished room as they each pulled a bottle out of the pack and twisted off the cap.

The first bottles slid down in reverent silence. The second and thirds amid raucous jokes. Dylan leaned against the swaybacked sofa and grinned to himself as he tossed his empties into the trash can Nate had dragged into the middle of the room. Hanging out with the guys felt *so* good.

At the sound of approaching footsteps outside, he froze. The boys all exchanged glances.

"You said your mom was working," Jonah hissed.

Nate belched as he crawled across the room and lifted the corner of the window shade. "Holy shit." His face white, he stumbled to his feet and grabbed the trash can. "It's Miguel Eiden. That *cop*. Didn't you guys pay for this stuff?"

A sharp rap sounded at the door. The boys launched into action, tossing bottles into the trash.

Nate scanned the room frantically. At the next knock on the door he hauled the can down the narrow hallway, shoved it into his bedroom and slammed the door.

He flipped on the living-room light and squared his shoulders. "You guys are cool, right?" He narrowed his eyes at Dylan, and his voice hardened. "We just came here after school to…study."

Jonah grabbed his backpack and dumped out a handful of tattered spiral notebooks. Nausea roiling through his stomach, Dylan did the same as cold sweat chilled his skin and his throat turned dry.

After his trouble back home, this could be bad. *Really* bad, especially if the beer was stolen or this cop was hoping to nail someone.

When Nate finally ushered him in, Dylan's heart sank. Miguel Eiden was big. Muscled. From the military cut of his black hair to his dark, piercing eyes and marine-sergeant stance, he was obviously major trouble.

The cop took a deep breath—no doubt detecting the smell of beer—and scowled. "This time, I'm taking you guys in."

Nate sank awkwardly onto the couch and glanced nervously at the others.

"For what? Doing homework?" Billy scoffed. "Some crime."

"The legal drinking age is twenty-one," Miguel snapped.

Dylan closed his eyes briefly. *Good move. Make the cop angry.*

"And at a very special price, thanks to your girlfriend. Who, by the way, not only lacks a state Alcohol Server's Permit, but isn't even twenty-one herself. Your free beer is going to land all of you in a lot of trouble." Eiden's cold, assessing gaze landed on Dylan. "Who are you? I haven't seen you hanging around these guys before."

Dylan's mind raced through a dozen possibilities. None of them but the truth would work in the long run. "Dylan Carson," he mumbled, trying to look the man in the eye. "From Shadow Creek Ranch."

Now he would just have to pray Eiden didn't check his out-of-state record.

"BREAKING AND ENTERING?" Gina stared at her brother's drawn expression as she opened her front door and welcomed him inside. "Did Phil tell you about those old charges when he brought Dylan out here?"

"He mentioned some court appearances for shoplifting and vandalism, but said the charges had been dismissed." Ben followed her into her living room, his Stetson in one hand. "He blamed it all on the boy's rowdy friends. The kid has a real attitude at times, but I never guessed there was more."

"So how was Phil able to take Dylan out of state?"

"Miguel found out that the juvenile judges were lenient the first time. The second time, Dylan was on probation for eighteen months." Ben gave her a wry smile. "Guess it helps to have a dad with a reputation in the media and money for a high-powered lawyer."

"And that's an unfortunate lesson in itself." Gina motioned him toward the sofa, then sat down next to him. "What will Miguel do now?"

Ben sighed heavily. "The other boys will be going in front of the juvenile-court judge, along with the girl who gave them the beer. The owner of the store could lose his liquor license."

"And Dylan?"

"He got quite a lecture down at the police station, with a warning. If he gets in trouble again out here, he'll face the judge. The fact that he's leaving Enchantment in two months and lives out at the ranch with me has given him one more chance.''

''Does Phil know about this?''

Ben lifted a shoulder. ''I e-mailed him the minute I got Dylan back to the ranch. Haven't heard from him, but he could be far from any telephone lines, for all I know. Sad thing was, I told the boy that I was informing his father, and he just gave me this blank look and said, 'See if he even cares.'''

''That poor kid,'' Gina said. ''Dylan may come from money, but he sure hasn't had it easy.''

''Is Max sleeping?''

Gina glanced at the clock. ''Um…Sue Ellen says she fell asleep at four, so she's been down for just an hour. Want to stay for supper and just let her sleep?'' She reached over and playfully punched him in the arm. ''I've had home-made chili cooking in the Crock-Pot all day. Your favorite recipe.''

''I'd love that. But I've got to get home. Dylan is there, and Sadie has been a little under the weather.''

Regret slid through her at the weary expression in her brother's eyes. For years he'd claimed he wanted no ties, no family responsibilities, yet now he had all the burdens of family, but without the love and support of a woman.

''I just wish I could help you more,'' Gina murmured. ''If I moved, maybe I could take in Sadie…or Max…''

He dropped a kiss on her cheek. ''I've got the space. Heard anything from your husband?''

''Nope.'' She shivered. ''Thirteen days and counting. Zach made a deposit into our checking account, though, so I was able to pay the mortgage on the fifteenth.'' Tears burned beneath her eyelids.

''How are the girls doing?''

''One day they're quiet, the next they're angry and upset.

Regan thinks this is all my fault and that I drove Zach away.''

Ben swore under his breath.

"It's okay. I understand how much this hurts them. In fact…I'm beginning to think that maybe Zach was right.'' One of the tears spilled down her cheek, so she turned away. "Maybe I should give up on being a midwife until the girls are grown. Am I being selfish, wanting it now?''

Warm, large hands gripped her shoulders, and Ben drew her against his hard chest. "If it means a lot to you, then Zach and the girls need to realize that you have a right to be happy, too.''

The phone started ringing. Stepping out of his embrace, Gina reached for the receiver. Sadie's agitated voice came across the line, breathless and impatient. "Ben—is Ben there? I tried his cell phone but he didn't answer. Oh, dear…I do need to talk to him.''

Alarmed, Gina gripped the receiver tighter. "Yes—he's here. Are you okay? Is something wrong?''

"It's the baby's mother. I know I should have written something down, but the call surprised me…'' Sadie's voice broke.

Gina handed the phone to him and hovered close, watching his tense expression as he tried to calm Sadie down. "That's okay. I'm sure she'll call again. Don't worry…she's where? What happened?''

He listened for several moments, then reassured her again. "It's all right. I'm just glad to know she's okay. You did just fine, Sadie. I can check the caller ID when I get home. No, don't check it. It could be erased if the wrong button—'' Closing his eyes briefly, he handed the receiver to Gina. "She hung up.''

"What is it? What happened?''

"Holly called. We don't have a phone number, or address, and in the next five seconds probably won't have anything on the caller ID, either.''

"Was there a car accident? Is Holly injured?''

"Not a car. She apparently wasn't just out job shopping on the West Coast. She stopped in Colorado for a week of skiing with a boyfriend and broke some ribs and her ankle on the slopes.''

"Is she coming back here so we can take care of her?''

"Sadie said something about this boyfriend flying her to his place in Los Angeles, and that Holly would call us when she got there.''

"But we don't have the phone number.''

"If she called on a cell phone, the number might have been unavailable on the caller ID anyway. So even if Sadie didn't accidentally erase it, we probably don't have a name or number for the guy. Not even the resort where the accident happened.'' Ben's jaw tightened. "Sadie said Holly didn't seem very concerned about Max.''

At a sudden spasm of coughing from Allie's bedroom, where Ben had set up a crib for Max, they both stilled. The sound was different than before. Tighter.

"How was she feeling when you dropped her off this morning?'' Gina asked quietly. "Just more of the same cold symptoms as yesterday?''

"Yeah.'' Ben's forehead creased with worry. "You'd already gone to work, but Sue Ellen said it was fine to leave her. She said babies often have runny noses and cold symptoms.''

Gina nodded. Sue Ellen had raised six kids of her own, and was one of the more unflappable people Gina had ever met. Sometimes, though, she didn't take things quite seriously enough.

"How did Max sleep last night?''

Ben smiled ruefully. "Not much.''

He followed her into the darkened bedroom, and they

stood at the side of the crib listening. Even Max's breathing sounded tight, and her nostrils flared with each indrawn breath. Beneath Gina's fingertips, the child's forehead felt warm and damp. Poor little thing.

"I think she should be checked, Ben. Just to make sure."

"Of what?" His voice tinged with alarm, he stared down at the child.

There were hints of reactive airway disease, if Gina's hunch was correct, though she knew the local doctors tried to avoid that diagnosis in a child this young. To Ben she just said, "These little ones can get sick so easily. She's had coughs and sniffles since she arrived in Enchantment."

"I'll make an appointment for first thing tomorrow."

"Maybe sooner, so you can be sure." Gina glanced at her watch. "I'll call the pediatric clinic and see if the doc is still around."

Within a few minutes she'd made the call, helped Ben bundle up the baby and the diaper bag, and watched him drive away after he promised to call her later.

She leaned against the door frame for a few minutes before finally shutting the door. When she turned toward the kitchen to put supper on the table she nearly tripped over Allie who'd come up behind her.

"Whoa, sugar—I nearly stepped on you!"

Allie's eyes were dark and solemn.

"What's up? I thought you and Regan were on the swing set."

"Our uncle loves that baby," Allie murmured. "More than us."

"Oh, sweetie." Gina bent to swoop the child up in her arms but Allie stepped away, just out of reach. "Of course he still loves you. You and Regan will always be his favorite nieces."

"No." Allie's lower lip trembled. "He loves *her* best.

And now we don't got him, and we don't got a daddy either, because you were mean and made him go away."

Gina drew in a sharp breath. "Allie, I'm so sorry about your dad being gone right now. But he'll come home. I promise he will."

"You said that before." Allie's accusing voice rose with hurt and anger. "And he *didn't*."

"Allie—"

"He doesn't even love us anymore, and it's 'cause of you." She took another step, tears welling in her eyes. "I know, 'cause I *heard* you fight."

"What?" Taken aback, Gina tried to remember when Allie could have heard any of the arguments. Could she have been awake late at night? Or overheard them while playing out in the yard?

"Daddy said you want your job more than you want him, so he was going away." Allie's little shoulders were shaking now, and she swallowed hard. "I hate you, Mama. I do. And Regan does too!" Bursting into tears, Allie whirled and ran to her bedroom, slamming the door behind her.

A chasm wide as the Grand Canyon opened in Gina's heart. *What have I done?*

ON FRIDAY, Joanna was surprised to see Shanna Dodson's name on the day's schedule. She was even more surprised when Val brought her daughter in at a quarter of five, right on time.

"You said to come back in ten days," Val said from the corner of the room, her arms folded across her chest. Shanna stood next to her, a grimy thumb in her mouth and a hand twisted tightly into a fold of Val's sweatshirt. "But I'm not sure why. She looks okay to me."

Joanna gave Val a firm nod of approval. "You were absolutely right to bring her in. Can you bring her over and put her up on the table?"

Val swung the child up into her arms and plopped her on the table. When Shanna gave a startled yelp and twisted toward her with her arms raised, Val glowered at her and stepped away. "Stay there, now."

"I'll bet she'd like you to stay close. She'll feel more secure, don't you think?" Joanna waited with one hand securely resting on Shanna's leg until Val moved closer, then playfully brought out her otoscope and peered into the child's ears. "That's *much* better. Now, how are you two doing?"

Val shrugged. "Me and Shanna got kicked out of my grandma's place." Despite her insolent expression there was a hint of fear in her voice.

"Oh, no. Where are you staying now?"

"My grandma had to move to someplace smaller...so we went to a friend's house. Her mom's kinda mad about it though, 'cause it's crowded. Now..." Val sighed. "I guess we'll have to go back to my mom's."

"Sounds like it's been a hard month." Joanna gave the two-year-old a playful tap on the nose, then positioned her stethoscope and listened to Shanna's lung sounds. "Can you take a big, deep breath?" She demonstrated, and the child mimicked her, her big eyes focused on Joanna's face. "What a good girl you are! I'll bet you would like a sticker. Remember?"

Shanna's gaze cut toward the box of colorful cartoon stickers on the counter, and when Joanna lifted her down from the exam table and handed her the box, the child looked up at her in awe.

"It's okay, sweetie—find the one you like the very best, okay?" While Shanna started searching for the right one, Joanna draped the stethoscope around her neck and turned to Val. "She sounds great, and her ears are fine. Did she finish the doses of medicine?"

Val nodded.

"So…how will it go if you move back home?" Joanna chose her words carefully, not wanting to seem judgmental. "Is your mom good with Shanna?"

"Yeah…I guess."

"Do you all get along pretty well?"

"When Mom isn't on my back about something. Like she thinks I'm still twelve or something."

Shanna selected an iridescent sticker from the box and held up the box to Joanna.

"What do you say?" Val prompted.

The child frowned for a second, then she looked up at Joanna and offered her a big smile. "Thanks!"

"You're very welcome." To Val, she added, "We're starting some new parenting classes on November 9th. They're free, and we're encouraging all first-time parents to come."

Val gave her a bored glance. "I probably can't. My mom works a lot, so she can't baby-sit."

"We'll have free child care, and treats…" At Val's expression, Joanna made a snap decision. If she had to, she would foot the cost herself. "And we'll even have door prizes at each class. A gift certificate from the children's store in town, or for pizza…even one from the video store."

Val brightened. "Cool."

"The chance of winning ought to be pretty good, too. The classes won't be all that big. Can I put you down? It might be fun."

"I guess so." Val bent down to corral her daughter and put on her coat. When Joanna handed her a pink flyer with the details of the classes, she stuffed it into her purse.

"One last thing. I know I mentioned it before, but we're always here—or available through the answering service— if you have questions or worries about Shanna. And if you have financial problems or difficulty finding a place to live, we can set you up with a social worker. Okay?''

''Thanks.''

Biting her lip, Joanna watched the two of them leave. Then she lifted the tape recorder from the counter and started her dictation on the exam. One more appointment— with Max and Ben Carson, who'd just called in—and then she'd be more than ready to head for home.

''SHE WAS OKAY this morning. I swear I would have brought her in sooner if I'd known something was wrong.'' Guilt lanced through Ben as he watched Joanna examine Max.

Stripped down to her diaper, the baby seemed so tiny lying on the exam table. So utterly defenseless. What chance did she have with some incompetent rancher like him for her dad? And where the hell was her mother?

Joanna disengaged her stethoscope and draped it around her neck. ''Parenting is a complex business,'' she said as she finished the exam. When Eve appeared at the door, Joanna handed her a vial containing a swab. ''Run this over to the lab on your way home, will you? I want them to call my cell with the results.''

She gently pulled the baby's sweat pants into place once more. Max didn't fight the process as she usually did. Her glassy eyes and lethargy were frightening.

''What's wrong with her?''

''I'm not sure yet. RSV is a common childhood respiratory illness. I've done a swab for it, and we'll get those results soon.'' Joanna rested a comforting hand on the baby's cheek for a moment. ''She's had mild fever, noisy breathing and tight, dry coughing?''

Hovering over the baby, Ben nodded.

''Let's have her breathe in some medicine with a nebulizer. Maybe that will open up her airway.''

A breathing treatment? Oh, God. He scooped Max up and snuggled her against his chest, holding her tight, his thoughts racing through memories of his second cousin, Tom, and the inhaler he'd always carried. One day it hadn't done the trick, and images of that funeral had stayed with Ben for over twenty-five years. He forced the words out, dreading the answer. "Are you saying she has asthma?"

"No, but I want to follow her closely." Joanna clipped a pulse oximeter on Max's finger, waited a moment, then read the results. "She's at 94 percent right now. Not bad— she's just mildly low on oxygen."

Joanna rummaged through the cupboards and pulled out a small compressor, plus a sealed bag containing tubing and some small plastic pieces. "I'll be back in a minute." She disappeared down the hallway.

Max rested against Ben's shoulder. Her head felt heavy and hot though his flannel shirt. She stared with half-closed eyes at her surroundings, showing no interest in what she saw.

He'd had her for fourteen days now. It seemed like a lifetime. What if something happened to her? What if he missed the critical signs of something going wrong, and she paid the price? For the first time in his life, Ben was flat out terrified.

Joanna bustled in moments later with a small vial. "You're not going to pass out or anything, are you?" she said, eyeing him with concern. "You look awfully white."

"No. Of course not." He knew his voice lacked conviction.

She reached over to the hand-sanitizer dispenser on the wall and rubbed her hands vigorously with the solution. With quick, efficient motions she hooked the tubing to the machine and measured liquid into the small plastic cup at the end of the tube, then assembled the rest of the plastic apparatus. "This is a premixed bronchodilator medication.

She's too young for an inhaler and she'd probably fight a mask and just tighten down more, so I'm going to blow it by for about ten minutes or so.''

A pungent mist rose from the tip as Joanna held the T-shaped tip below Max's nose. The baby stirred in his arms, shaking her head to avoid it, but soon gave up and rested limply against his chest.

After the medicine cup had emptied, Joanna flipped off the machine. ''Not too bad, was it?''

He brushed Max's damp curls away from her forehead. ''How do you know if it worked?''

Joanna positioned her stethoscope and listened to Max's lungs. ''I'll recheck her breathing in a few minutes and again in an hour. Would you like to go into our staff lounge? There's a crib in there and the bedding is clean. Maybe you can lay her down for a while. Also,'' she added with a smile, ''there just might be some of Eve's hundred-proof coffee left. I'll bet you could use some.''

His anxiety eased at her casual manner. ''Thanks, Joanna.''

He'd settled the sleeping baby in the crib and had started his second cup of coffee, when Joanna walked in with the oximeter apparatus. Without disturbing Max, she attached the sensor to the child's finger.

''Is she better?''

Joanna nodded as she checked the screen. ''Up to 98 percent.'' She removed the sensor from Max's finger, and positioned her stethoscope and listened to her lungs again. ''Much better.''

Relief flooded through Ben. ''Now what?''

''I'd like to watch her here in the clinic for an hour or two and see how she does.''

''I really appreciate this. I'm sorry to keep you here so late.''

"It's what I do. I'm hardly ever home until eight or nine in the evening."

She looked tired, though, with dark smudges under her eyes. "Want to send out for pizza while we wait?" he asked.

"Well…"

"I haven't eaten since seven this morning, and I'm starving. My treat." Without waiting for an answer he reached for the cell phone clipped to his belt and hit the speed-dial code for Carla's Pizza.

Joanna slipped out of the room to her office, but was back in the lounge for a status check on Max before the pizza finally arrived.

The rich aroma of warm pepperoni, cheese and Italian spices filled the air as Ben opened the box and set it down on the small, round kitchenette table near the sofa. "I forgot this is Friday night," he muttered, lifting a heavily laden slice out of the box. "Carla must have been busy."

Joanna settled into a chair at the table and scooped a slice onto a paper plate, closing her eyes as she savored her first bite. "But well worth the wait. This is fantastic!"

And more than a little difficult to eat, with all the melted cheese and heavy toppings. He watched in amusement as she tried to juggle a slice with both hands. Finally, she opened a cupboard door and retrieved napkins and plastic utensils.

"It's definitely not finger food, though. The only bad thing is that now I know this pizza place exists and it's going to be hard to avoid."

From what he could see, she didn't need to worry. Though slender, she had nice—*very* nice curves in all the right places. Some women were thin as fence posts and proud of it, but while they might be beautiful, he preferred soft curves to angles.

Max stirred in the crib and whimpered.

He launched to his feet and moved across the room to massage her back until she drifted off again. "Since Max was better when you just checked, do you think she'll be all right?"

Wiping her fingers on a napkin, Joanna frowned. "The breathing treatment helped. I'm still concerned, though. She was here on—" she glanced at a calendar on the wall "—the seventeenth, and this is just the twenty-third. We'll need to monitor her carefully. If she starts into labored breathing again, you'll have to bring her in. If I'm not available, take her for an evaluation at the emergency room. Have you heard anything from her mother?"

"Nope."

"Was there anything on the caller ID?"

"Nope." He gave her a wry smile. "Sadie checked it for me, wanting to be helpful, and erased it. Though perhaps it was just one of those unavailable numbers anyway."

"So you don't have any health insurance information yet?"

"Nope."

Joanna gave him a sympathetic smile. "This has been really hard on you, hasn't it?"

Max stirred, and he lowered his voice. "The hardest thing will be seeing Holly swoop into Enchantment and take Max away. What chance does the poor kid have with a mom like Holly?"

"She seems irresponsible. But she might love Max very much. If she had surgery and has been on a lot of medication for a week or so, that could account for her lack of communication."

"I never would have dropped Max off like this," Ben said flatly. "And no *medication* would have kept me from calling."

"You're really attached to this little gal now." That familiar hint of sadness came into Joanna's eyes. "I've come to the conclusion that life is a lot easier if you just keep some distance."

"Distance. What kind of life is that?"

Joanna pushed back her chair, gathered her paper plate and napkins, and pitched them into the trash can in the opposite corner of the room. "It's a safe one, and that's what counts." She gave a little shrug as she headed out the door. "I'll be in my office if you need me. Otherwise, I'll be in to check her in about an hour."

DISTANCE. Ben had the next hour to think about it, and didn't like his conclusions.

For three years he'd done the same thing. After Rachel ran off, Ben had kept his mind on business and made sure any relationships were strictly casual. Short term. And what did that prove? What did that save?

Playing it safe no longer held much appeal.

CHAPTER ELEVEN

AT SEVEN O'CLOCK, Ben watched Joanna examine Max once again. At eight o'clock, she took one last oximetry reading and rechecked for lung sounds.

"I think you're good to go," she said. "She sounds clear. The RSV results won't be back for a few more hours, but I'd like you to bring her in tomorrow morning for a recheck anyway."

Gratitude and relief filled his chest. "Thanks. For everything." He glanced out the window. Against the darkness, the window only reflected his own image. "This got awfully late. What about your dog and that horse of yours?"

"They're fine." She used the hand sanitizer dispenser once again, then pulled the stethoscope from around her neck and laid it on the counter. "Galahad has stayed home for the past week, amazing as that sounds."

"What did you do, hog-tie him?"

"Nope—I think he just gave up." When she laughed, her serious professional persona slipped away. "And believe me—it took just two tries for me to learn that Moose can't stay in the house when I leave for the day."

"He left you presents?"

"Not exactly." Her eyes twinkled. "He ate the linings out of every pair of my shoes and figured out how to open the refrigerator. Anything he could open, he ate—including a squeeze bottle of catsup. He also had fun frolicking with my feather pillows. *That* was the first day."

Wisps of curly blond hair had escaped the loose knot at

her nape. Maybe all the stress and worry had lowered his defenses. Maybe he was just so thankful for the sense of peace at being here with an expert who could help keep Max safe from harm. Or maybe…he needed to finally feel a closer connection with a woman.

Whatever the reason, he found himself reaching out with his free hand to touch those errant curls.

She froze, but her startled gaze flew to meet his and color rose in her cheeks. Still he lingered, savoring the silky strands, reaching a little farther to her nape and snagging the pins that bound her hair, until it cascaded in shimmering waves to brush her shoulders.

"Thank you, Jo. For everything," he murmured.

"You're most welcome." She took a step back. "Look—I know it's easy to misinterpret gratitude and… um…attraction. It happens a lot, and I do understand." She turned to go. "I'd better complete Max's chart."

"Wait."

"I really don't think—"

"I just want to hear what Moose did the second day," he teased. "And find out what you did with him."

Gratitude? Yeah. But there was also something more here. What he wanted was for her to stick around. To stay and talk to him so he could hear her lilting laugh and breathe in the faint, sunny scent of her. Just having her near made him feel…whole, somehow.

A smile played at the corners of her mouth. "The second day, he unpotted every plant in the cabin and shook the dirt everywhere. He also clawed at the door trying to get out. The scene was straight out of Stephen King—like some evil force had taken over the place."

"Did you consider taking him back to the animal shelter?"

Her eyes filled with horror. "I *adopted* him. I couldn't ever do that. He's family."

"Just a tad more destructive than most." He shot her an amused smile. "And roughly the size of a rhino."

"The vet said he was acting out due to separation anxiety and would do better with sedatives. Instead, I've been closing him in a box stall when I leave. He's happy, Galahad's happy, and I've got a lot less housecleaning." She reached for the oximeter and gently clipped it over Max's forefinger again. "Can you imagine how much a Great Pyrenees *sheds?*"

He could imagine how much he'd like to spend the rest of the evening talking to her. He could imagine…curving an arm around her waist and drawing her closer.

But she'd been perfectly clear. He might be interested, but she wasn't, and he needed to keep that fact firmly in mind.

"I'LL BE BACK IN TOWN on Sunday," Zach said tersely, skipping any effort at a friendly greeting.

Standing in her kitchen, Gina gripped the phone receiver tighter at the familiar sound of his voice. Hope welled up in her throat until it was hard to speak. "The girls and I will be glad to see you again. They ask about you all the time."

"You know I've been on some long hauls." His tone grew defensive. "I called every day this past week."

Gina took a steadying breath. "I know. It's just that we look forward to having you here."

"I'm staying at my brother's house."

His words hit her like a slap across the face. Instead of trying to work things out, he was simply going to move out.

Her stunned silence lengthened, until he finally added, "It'll be better that way."

"For who? Your daughters—who'll be scared and worried about what's going on?"

"You can tell them."

Her anger rose. "Let's see…what would be the right thing to say? That you're afraid to face any serious discussion? Or that I have so little value that you don't even need to *consider* some sort of compromise?"

"Don't make me the bad guy, Gina. At least I want what's best for the family. You just want what's best for yourself."

"That's not true."

"The hell it isn't."

"We can still work this out…find a counselor, maybe. Celia Brice is really good—"

"Right." Zach gave a snort of disgust. "One of your friends down at The Birth Place? I'm sure *she'd* be impartial."

"Someone else, then."

"They couldn't tell me anything I don't already know. Until all this came up, I worked hard to support you, and you were home for the kids. Our family was just fine that way. You've changed…not me."

"And I know you don't think that's fair, but people grow. They learn new things. They can become *better*."

"So now you've become 'better' and the rest of us don't mean anything," he growled. "I'll stop over to see the girls around three o'clock on Sunday. Make sure they're home."

Long after he hung up, Gina rested her forehead against the wall by the phone as a hundred memories flooded through her thoughts. The Saturday mornings, when Zach made the girls Mickey waffles or French toast—the only two recipes he knew. The family hikes up into the mountains. Sitting together in church on Sunday mornings. Zach, his eyes filled with adoration when he watched his daughters playing in the backyard.

Sure, their marriage had had a rocky start, with the wedding planned after Gina found herself pregnant, but she'd thought they'd grow old together, holding each other's hands in some nursing home when they were ninety. She'd been sure that he loved her as much as she loved him.

Maybe she'd just been blind.

JOANNA EYED the western saddle on the hitching rail in front of her barn and shook her head. "Really, I don't want you to get hurt."

"I do this for a living," Ben retorted. "I ride horses eight hours a day, six days a week."

"What if he was sent to the sale because he was *dangerous?*"

"He doesn't look dangerous." Ben flipped a heavy Navajo blanket onto Galahad's back with one hand, then turned to pick up his saddle.

In that brief moment, Galahad bent his head around to the other side, caught the edge of the blanket with his teeth and jerked it off. He shook it vigorously, then let it drop to the snow-covered ground. Before Ben could react, the horse planted one big hoof firmly in the middle of it.

Joanna burst out laughing.

"Cute. Really cute." Ben leaned into Galahad's shoulder until he moved over and released his prize. "I wonder what else he knows."

"You think someone taught him tricks? I think he's just one really smart horse."

Ben retied the lead rope shorter so the gelding couldn't reach around, dusted the snow off the blanket and deftly saddled him. "Gotcha," he murmured, rubbing Galahad's neck. "Now we'll see what you can do."

Joanna gave the horse a dubious look. "What if he falls with you? He's supposed to be lame."

"You have to wonder why he was sent through an auction that way. Not many people would announce a lameness—especially one so mild—because it means a gelding will likely go for bottom dollar to the killers. Far as I can see, he's sound as a dollar now. No heat and swelling, no evidence of ringbone or navicular—or anything else, for that matter. Doesn't appear that he's ever been foundered. You could have him vet checked and X-rayed, though.''

''Maybe. How's Max doing? I haven't seen her since Wednesday.''

''Yesterday and today she's done well. No cough, sniffles, no harsh breathing. So far.''

''I'm glad to hear it.'' Max's RSV results had been negative, but she'd had trouble recovering from her viral upper respiratory infection. Over the past week Ben had brought her into the clinic three times—twice after business hours—and in addition to the usual payment for office visits, he'd insisted on helping Joanna with Galahad as thanks. ''You really don't have to go through with this test drive, you know.''

''Yes, I do.''

Ben led the old paint into the corral, shut the gate and checked the cinch. He gathered the reins at Galahad's withers and eased a boot into the stirrup.

Galahad bent his head around and studied Ben with mild interest, his ears pricked forward and lower lip flapping. He didn't move a muscle when Ben swung lightly up into the saddle.

''So far, so good. Maybe you can start riding this old guy and have some fun.''

She'd left work at five to meet Ben here. The whole idea had sounded like a bad one, but now…well, maybe Galahad really was going to work out as a gentle riding horse after all.

The gelding moved off into a quiet walk, his head low, then accelerated into a rough trot. Ben played with the tension on the reins, finally easing him down into a slower jog after several bone-jarring laps around the corral. "Not bad—I don't think he was ridden western much, though. He just wants to give me an extended trot. On this guy, it's like riding a jackhammer."

When Ben urged him into a lope, Joanna's breath caught in her throat. She didn't know much about horses, but this one was poetry in motion—like a rocking horse, with his neck arched and his tail raised, transformed from something ordinary into something so beautiful that she couldn't help but grin from ear to ear. *He's mine—he's really mine!*

With his black-and-white spotted coat and gangly body he was certainly no Austrian Lipizzan, but he moved with a surprising level of grace. Someone, somewhere, had trained this horse beautifully.

Without warning, Galahad exploded.

Ben apparently hadn't been expecting it any more than she had, after so many quiet trips around the corral. He nearly lost his balance on the first high, arcing leap. He caught up on the second, though, and settled in for the ride, reaching out to the side with one rein to crank Galahad's head around sharply to the left

With his free hand he whomped the gelding on the opposite side of his neck, pulling the horse into a tight turn. Galahad spun hard, dodged back to the right and blew skyward.

Joanna's heart caught in her throat as the horse reared high. *Too high.* His back hooves scrambled and slipped in the snow. He struggled to catch himself as his rangy body teetered out of control.

Horror rushed through her as Joanna watched, helpless to stop the inevitable.

Ben swore. Kicked free of the stirrups. A split second later the horse went over backward, landing against the unresisting oak fence before Ben had a chance to get away.

"Oh my God…" Joanna vaulted at the fence.

On his back, wedged against the fence, Galahad panicked, twisting and fighting to regain his balance, his eyes rimmed with white and nostrils flared.

Before Joanna could reach him, he managed to lurch to his feet and stood, spraddle-legged, his sides heaving.

He took a step toward Ben's motionless form.

"No!" Joanna raced across the corral.

But instead of pawing at the downed cowboy, the gelding lowered his head and gently nudged a boot. Took another step forward and snuffled along a leg…then Ben's jacket…then his jaw. And then he sneezed.

"Hey!" Ben coughed, winced as he levered himself up to sit with his back against a post. "What the hell…"

Joanna grabbed at the reins and pulled the horse away. After tying him to one of the posts a few yards off, she hurried to Ben's side. She dropped to her knees and leaned close to peer into his eyes. "I am so sorry. Are you okay?"

He squinted at her, and gave her a slow, lazy smile. "Real friendly, aren't you?"

His voice was a little slurred, but his pupil sizes were equal. So far. No bleeding from the ears or mouth. His color was pale. "Do you know how you ended up on the ground?"

His forehead creased.

"You fell off my horse."

His frown deepened. "Did not."

Well, *that* sounded normal. "Okay, so my horse went over backward and took you with him. Does that sound right?"

He seemed to turn that possibility over in his mind. When he didn't answer, she added briskly, "You were a good sport and gave him something soft to land on, too. Tell me what day this is."

"Uh…Thursday. October…30."

"Right. Do you know who I am?"

"The Easter Bunny." Maybe he seemed a little dazed, but he managed a brief, lopsided grin.."I think this is sorta how we met, right? Me on the ground and my horse somewhere else?"

At his lucid memory, a rush of relief turned her knees to rubber. "That first time, you told me that you went down with your horse. This time, I believe it." She gently gripped his ankles. "Let me just check you over quick. Wiggle your feet for me."

When he complied, she moved her hands up his legs, watching for any signs of tenderness. When she got to his thighs he took a sharp breath and tried to wave her away.

"Don't worry—you can just tell me if *those* parts are all right." With a smile she skipped upward, ran her hands over his narrow hips and unzipped his jacket. The firm muscle beneath her fingertips jerked when she got to his flat belly. She probed farther. "Does that hurt?"

He gasped and grabbed at her hands with one of his. "Hell, no. I'm *ticklish*. Just help me get up. Play doctor with someone else."

"No one else around here got squashed by a horse, cowboy. I can't believe you're okay."

"Sorry to be a disappointment." He gave a low laugh. "I could be better, though."

Concerned, she moved up and inspected his collarbone, shoulders and arms, but still found no pain, no guarding, no swelling or crepitation.

"Not there. Higher."

She lifted her gaze and found him watching her intently, his eyes dark and compelling.

"You could just kiss me and make me better," he murmured. "God knows you owe me after letting me get on that killer horse of yours."

"Owe you! I told you *not* to ride him."

"Yeah, but you weren't all that clear."

She laughed and started to palpate his neck. "Just be quiet and let me make sure you're okay."

"I'm fine. Believe me." With a low laugh he reached up, slid an arm around her shoulders and drew her close. Against her ear he whispered, "But the attention was sure nice."

Startled, she felt her heart flutter against her ribs. "Please…don't."

"Why not?"

He brushed a kiss across her forehead, sending currents zinging through her nerve endings. She felt the heavy muscling of her arm flex as he drew her even closer to kiss the tip of her nose.

His eyes locked on hers, and instantly it was as if she'd grabbed hold of that electric fence. A current, searing and powerful, zapped between them.

"You're…um…just confused. You—"

"That's one thing I'm not. I've been thinking about this for a good long while."

"But—"

"Ever since we met, you've been hiding behind your stethoscope and lab coat, but I figure there's one interesting woman beneath all of that."

His voice went husky and low, full of unspoken promise, and seemed to flow right through her, warming places that hadn't been warm since…when?

Her thoughts grew fuzzy when he brushed another kiss across her mouth, his lips firm and cool, tasting of snow and a hint of wintergreen.

When he pulled away, she almost felt bereft until she looked up. His heavy-lidded gaze burned into hers…and then he *really* kissed her, his arm hooked around her neck, holding her close, his other hand cupping her nape. Nothing tentative this time. Nothing gentle.

Her insides melted, pooling low in her belly, and without thought she was suddenly kissing him back, angling her mouth for deeper contact, reaching for him, trying to get closer…

It took a moment for the unexpected sensation to register. The lump beneath her fingers. Something warm and wet at the back of his head.

She withdrew her hand and pulled away from him. *Blood.* Hidden in all that thick, dark, wavy hair. "You didn't tell me about this."

"Just a bump."

"A *bump!*" Maybe that heavy-lidded gaze had been due more to dizziness than desire.

She leaned forward and peered into his eyes to check his pupil size once again. "You've got a laceration. Swelling. You could have a concussion, a hematoma, or even a skull fracture."

Was he a little less perky than he'd been a few minutes earlier? A host of other medical possibilities crowded through her thoughts.

"Can you stand? Make it over to my house?"

"'Course I can. But I'm not goin' anywhere till I get that horse unsaddled." He glowered at her. "And when I do, I'm going *home.*"

With a growl of frustration, she stood and dusted the snow off her jeans. "I'll take care of my horse. You stay there."

Joanna mentally reviewed what Ben had done to get the saddle on, and reversed the process. By the time she'd let Galahad out into the pasture, Ben was on his feet, with one arm hooked around a fence post. He didn't seem entirely steady.

"Are you feeling dizzy? Nauseous?"

"No."

"And I'm sure you'd tell me if you were." She took his arm. "Let's go, buckaroo."

"Depends on where we're going." He slanted her a woozy grin. "Will this be fun?"

"Oh, yes," she lied. "We just need to get in my car."

She hadn't been too worried at first, all things considered. He'd certainly kissed her with the focus and power of a man who was alert—and very aware of what he was doing. But with any sort of injury to the brain, the situation could worsen with time. If he had a subdural hematoma— bleeding in the brain—the increasing pressure could cause brain damage, or worse.

The fact that he allowed her to guide him into the Tahoe without an argument intensified her concern.

She made the trip to town in record time, pulled to a stop at the E.R. entrance of Arroyo County Hospital and stepped out to beckon an orderly. "We need a wheelchair, here."

"Nope, I don't," Ben growled.

She bent to peer inside the Tahoe. "Yes, you do."

Refusing assistance, he got his seat belt unbuckled after two false starts and was out of the vehicle before the orderly arrived with a wheelchair.

He did, however, seem to need a firm grip on both the door frame and Joanna's shoulder for support. "I hope that chair isn't for me, because I sure as hell don't plan to use it."

Joanna exchanged glances with the orderly, and he stepped into position to take one of Ben's arms while she took the other. Together they got Ben into the E.R., where Sandy, the triage nurse, took one look and waved them into an exam cubicle.

"Your lucky day, Ben," she said cheerfully. "We haven't had anyone come in for hours."

The orderly helped him get up on a gurney, though Ben

refused to lie down. "I'm fine. I just have a little head-ache."

"Yeah, right." Joanna shifted her attention to Sandy and gave her all the details. "I'm concerned about the hard fall he had. Who's on call?"

"Woodgrove. You're the new pediatrician, right? Dr. Weston?"

Joanna nodded. "Who's your doctor, Ben?"

Ben scowled at her. "Him."

"Woodgrove? That's handy." Joanna patted him on the leg. "He's got all your records and can do any follow-up." She turned to go.

"Hey! You're not leaving me here!"

"No…I need to move my car, and I need to make some calls so your family knows where you are."

"Don't." Ben moved to get off the gurney, but the nurse caught his arm. "You'll just worry Sadie. I'll be home soon anyway."

"What about Max?"

He gripped the edge of the gurney until his knuckles turned white. "She's with the baby-sitter at Gina's place. Six o'clock at the latest, because Gina's on call."

The clock on the wall behind him read six-fifteen.

"I'll go get her." She could see Ben's frustration mounting. "No problem, okay? She can just stay with me until you're good to go. After all, my horse put you here."

"You got bucked off a *horse?*" Sandy's voice filled with awe. "Was it, like, some wild mustang someone brought in?"

"Not exactly." Ben shot a dark glance at Joanna. "I seem to have real bad luck with horses when Joanna is around."

"Well, I'm sure you're going to be fine. I need to doc-ument your vitals, and we need to do a history and get a physical started, okay?"

Grabbing her keys from the counter, Joanna waved at them both, and headed for the door.

Maybe Ben wasn't a happy camper, but she'd had good cause to be concerned. However, even as she tried to focus on his accident and the need to pick up Max as soon as possible, her thoughts kept flitting to those moments in the corral when his kiss had stunned her.

Less than three months and she'd be in San Diego. With no regrets, no looking back…and certainly no ties.

But Lord Almighty, where had that man learned to kiss like *that?*

THREE INTERMINABLE HOURS later, Ben Carson stepped out of Joanna's Tahoe and forced a polite smile when she hopped out from behind the steering wheel and appeared at his side as he eased Max from her car seat.

"I appreciate your help," he informed her in a low tone. "But this isn't necessary."

"Yes, it is."

His frustration kicked his pounding headache up a notch. "I'm okay. It took Woodgrove hours to tell me what I already knew."

He started for the house with the sleeping child in his arms.

"Maybe the CAT scan was normal," she pointed out as she caught up and took his arm. "But you still have a concussion."

"I rodeod for a few years, Jo. This sure isn't the first time."

"All the more reason to be concerned. Someone responsible needs to just keep an eye on you overnight." She stepped ahead and opened the door for him. "Who'll watch Max? You need me."

For a woman who could kiss like no other, she could be

one persistent and irritating female. "I can handle things here."

Joanna lifted an eyebrow. "You *really* think she'll sleep all night?"

The answer to that was all too easy, and they both knew it. Max's coughing woke her up several times every night, and it took an hour or more of rocking or walking to get her back to sleep each time.

Even then, he couldn't doze off for long, with all the worry over how she was doing alone in her crib. What if he slept too soundly and failed to hear her on the baby monitor? If she was quiet for very long, he was up to check on her. If she whimpered, he was awake. How did full-time parents handle all this stress?

After three weeks of late nights, interrupted sleep and long days working with the horses, the presence of an expert to take over and the possibility of a good night's rest suddenly sounded too good to pass up.

"You're on," he said. "Thanks."

The kitchen was dark and quiet. Dylan—grounded for a week after his run-in with the law last Friday—was probably sulking in his room while serving his last day of penance. At nine-thirty, Sadie had probably already gone to bed.

Ben toed off his boots on the entry mat and moved quietly through the darkened house to the room next to his own, where he'd set up a makeshift nursery. With slow, gentle movements he eased Max onto her back in the crib and unzipped her heavy jacket.

"Need some help?" Joanna snapped on the 25-watt lamp on the dresser across the room and joined him at the side of the crib.

Max stirred as he slid off her little boots and puffy pink snowsuit. "I think I'll just leave her sweat suit on. It's almost like pajamas anyway, right?"

"Close enough." She shrugged out of her jacket and tossed it on the rocking chair before joining him at the crib. "Her diaper should be okay, too. I changed it just before we left the E.R."

He watched her lay a gentle hand against Max's forehead, and the concern and compassion he saw in her eyes touched him in some deep and inexplicable way. Strong, intelligent and level-headed, she was nothing like the flashy, superficial young things he'd flirted with over the past few years.

God knew, his fiancée's departure had left him feeling as if a herd of mustangs had trampled his heart. He hadn't ever wanted to face that pain again. Yet, an undercurrent of awareness sparking between Joanna and him seemed to intensify with every passing day, and it was getting harder to remember why caution was so important.

He'd been a little dazed in Joanna's corral—still couldn't quite recall how he and that horse had landed in a heap on the ground. He wasn't even quite sure how he'd ended up kissing her. But the moment he felt her mouth beneath his, he'd felt a dizzying rush, as if he'd plunged off a cliff. And she'd very definitely kissed him back.

Now, knowing that he shouldn't, he reached up and brushed his fingertips through her hair. Touched her chin, tipping her face toward him.

When she met his gaze, time stood still and all he could feel was the heavy beating of his heart and a surge of desire so intense, so unexpected, that he couldn't have moved away if his life depended on it.

"This isn't possible," she whispered.

"You're right." Slowly, with deliberate sensuality, he brushed his thumb across her mouth.

"I…can't be casual about these things."

But he didn't *feel* casual. Casual was kissing some sweet young thing at a dance. Casual was flirting with a gal at a horse show just because she was pretty, or fun to be with. What he felt right now was something deeper, more compelling—and it scared the hell out of him.

Her eyes were hauntingly dark, hinting at lost dreams and silent pain, and he wanted to erase all of that and make her smile. She was leaving in a couple of months, and he wanted to find some way to make her stay.

With a growl of frustration, he leaned closer. "Just this. Just once more."

Her mouth curved into a faint, seductive smile.

"And," he continued, "if it's just going to be once, it's gonna be *good*."

Her smile faltered a little, but when he took her face between his hands and lowered his mouth to hers, her eyes drifted shut. A quiver ran through her as he swept her against his chest with one arm. She opened to his kiss…responding. Inviting…

From somewhere far away, as if on a distant planet, came the sounds of approaching footsteps.

Startled, Joanna pulled away. "Sadie?"

They both turned to the door and found Dylan standing there, his eyes filled with knowing and that familiar smirk curling his lips. "Thought I better check in, *Uncle*. So there won't be any hassle about my plans."

What plans? Ben struggled for the recollection, but his brain was still drifting and his blood still ran too hot for coherent thought.

Dylan snorted and rolled his eyes. "I'm not grounded after today, and I've got plans for Halloween tomorrow. There's not gonna be any problem with that, right?"

Ben could think of a few, but none that he wanted to discuss right now. "Get on to bed. We'll discuss it tomorrow."

"Yeah." He shot an insolent look at Joanna. "I know, you're *real* busy."

He disappeared down the hall.

"Well, that was certainly awkward," she murmured. "I…um…imagine he makes dating a little difficult for you."

Mentally running through the pathetically short list of women he'd taken out since Rachel left, Ben nearly laughed aloud. He hadn't been on a date in months. "I'm trying to remember if I was like him as a teenager. I sure hope not."

She cocked her head. "I'll bet you were a sweet little boy…and grew up to be a teenager who walked a pretty narrow path."

"Right." Max stirred in her crib, and he reached inside to gently rub her back until she settled into deeper sleep. "Babies are so innocent. Makes you wonder where all the attitude and bravado comes from, doesn't it?" He turned toward Joanna. "Thanks for everything you've done for us today."

"Well, it's all my fault that you got h—"

"No. Like I told you, I ride horses for a living. If there's any fault, it's mine. Galahad seemed so placid that I got careless." He moved toward the door, beckoning her to follow. "And thanks for your good care of Max."

"That's my job," she said breezily, glancing around the room. "Is there a guest room nearby, so I can hear her if she wakes up?"

He could think of a much better answer, but instead he gestured across the hall. "That's a guest room. We keep it ready, so the linens should be all set."

"I'll listen for Max and take care of her if she wakes up, but I…um…also need to check on you now and then. Because of your concussion."

"I don't have one."

"Yes, you do. I need to make sure you can be easily

awakened, that your pupils respond equally. I won't bother
you much, really.''

That's what *she* thinks.

Going to sleep after awakening to her gentle voice and
submitting to her inspections just wasn't going to happen.
He'd be awake from one visit to the next, dwelling on other
good uses for a night alone with her.

''I'm locking my door.''

''If you do, I'll knock on it until you answer. And if the
baby wakes up because of the noise, I'll just hand her to
you, and *I'll* go to bed. Deal?''

He laughed softly. ''Not a very good one...but maybe
someday we can find a way to improve on it.''

CHAPTER TWELVE

STAYING AT SHADOW CREEK overnight had been a good idea. The right thing to do.

But heaven help her, by one o'clock in the morning Joanna wished she'd dropped Ben off at the ranch and headed back to the safety of her own cabin, with just Moose and Galahad for company.

If she'd done that, she wouldn't have spent these past two hours rocking Max, feeling the precious weight of her, breathing in her soft baby scent. What was it about this little girl that slipped through her defenses more with every passing week? Losing her heart to Max would be a mistake.

But logic didn't seem to matter. Tonight had further eroded the careful emotional walls she'd built around her heart, bringing into painful focus everything she'd yearned for since her own baby died. Joanna had rocked Max, hummed all of the age-old lullabies, stroked her downy cheeks.

And Ben…oh, my. What was it about dark, silent nights in New Mexico, where the blanket of stars overhead was impossibly bright, and the crisp scents of pine and sage-brush and freshly fallen snow filled the air? Here, she felt far more alive than she'd felt for years. As if every possibility in the world still lay before her, and anything she'd ever dreamed could come true.

Even though she already knew that dreams and wishes were a dangerous commodity, and the only sure thing in life was that you couldn't count on anything. Not on tomorrow being happy. Not on love, nor on husbands who promised forever and bailed at the first crisis.

Taking a deep breath, she settled Max into her crib, grabbed a flashlight from the bureau and went into Ben's bedroom, planning to wake him gently by lightly touching his arm to make sure he was responsive.

But when she reached his bedside, her breath caught in her throat when she found him staring at the ceiling, his hands stacked beneath his head, the white cotton sheets settled in folds at his waist.

A narrow, lean waist.

An upper body toned and hardened and still tanned from a summer of working outdoors.

He turned his head toward her, just a fraction, and murmured, "You don't need to check on me. I'm fine."

"But—"

"I mean it." His voice lowered and his eyes heated, until she was barely aware of anything beyond that voice. "Unless you want something more."

She lifted her chin. "Only to make sure you're okay."

"I won't be, with you planning to come in here every hour."

"I take it you're feeling okay? Your headache isn't worse?" She leaned closer, flicked on the flashlight and aimed it at his eyes.

"Hey!" He flinched and jerked his head away. "Put that dang thing away. Better yet, give it to me."

"Your pupils constricted equally. Your color looks good," she retorted coolly. "Tell me the name of the vice president, and I'll let you go back to sleep."

"No." His eyes turned wicked, his voice dropped to a deeper, dark whiskey range. "But I'll tell you something else."

Undoubtedly something she'd rather not hear. Not now,

not while she was alone with him in this darkened room. She started to back away but he caught her wrist gently.

"I'd like to tell you how much I appreciate what you've done for Max and me."

He tugged her closer.

"And I'd also like to tell you…" His grin was slow in coming, filled with wicked promise as his gaze swept over her. "That what you do to me just can't be legal."

Mesmerized, she felt his hard, strong hands slide up her wrists. Her forearms. An undercurrent of sexual awareness sparked to life between them, sending shivers of anticipation through her. She had no doubt about what could happen, here and now. No doubt that it would be the most incredible night she'd ever had—or ever would.

But this is what he does best, a small voice whispered in her thoughts. *He travels…he leaves a trail of women behind wherever he goes…he doesn't really care.*

She only had to remember Allen to know that her inner voice was right. Ben was a lot like Allen…wasn't he?

"You're smooth," she said lightly. "I'll bet you get what you want almost every time."

"Smooth?" His laugh was low, self-deprecating. "Hardly. I barely remember my last date."

He wouldn't need to try very hard for one. She'd seen the nurse and the X-ray technician eyeing him with blatant interest at the hospital, and Nicki still peppered her with questions about him at every turn. "Really?"

He gave her a wry smile. "Believe it or not, I'm a little more discriminating than people seem to think."

"So everyone in Arroyo County is wrong."

"Yep." His smile faded. "And usually, I don't care. Except now—when I look at you, and think about every way you appeal to me."

Just another line. But if the emotion in his eyes wasn't genuine, he was the best actor she'd ever seen.

"I'd rather just sit and talk to you over a cup of coffee than go on some hot and heavy date with anyone else."

When he pulled her down so she was sitting at the side of his bed, she raised an eyebrow. "So you just want to talk."

"I'd be happy with that. You're bright, and you're dedicated. You have a dry sense of humor. But you're also one of the prickliest women I've met. Someone, somewhere hasn't appreciated just how amazing you are. What happened?"

Nothing that he needed to know about. "Let's just say I'm probably older and wiser than most of the buckle bunnies you meet when you're out on the road with your show horses."

"I don't do one-night stands." When she cut a meaningful glance toward Max's room, he added, "Once. When I was hurting, and stupid, and too drunk to pay attention to doing the right thing. But darlin', maybe Max wasn't planned, but that little girl has captured my heart."

She tried not to flinch. A "mistake," and a beautiful little girl was born. Her own pregnancy had been wanted, and nurtured, and she'd loved her little one long before birth. Dreams upon dreams for the future—all shattered in the blink of an eye. "Some of us," she murmured slowly, "haven't been as lucky."

Ben's gaze traveled over her face, then locked on hers. She could see the realization dawning in his eyes. "What happened?" he asked softly. "Why do you look so sad?"

The deep compassion and concern in his voice wrapped around her as if he'd enveloped her in an embrace. "I lost my baby two years ago...the first of December."

"Awww, Jo."

"Some Christmas, right?" She focused on a painting of the Sangre de Cristo Mountains that hung over the bureau to the left, leashing her emotions. "Even now, 'Away in a Manger' makes me cry. And the candles…all the Christmas lights…'' She shuddered.

He levered himself up against the headboard and cupped the side of her face with one hand, his gaze still fastened on hers. ''And here I thought you just didn't like Santa Claus.''

''I don't. Not anymore. The true meaning of Christmas I just think quietly about. The rest, I ignore, because all the festivities are painful. Everyone else is so happy, and even after two years, all I can think about is how terrible it was to lose him.''

''I'm so sorry.'' He reached for her, and suddenly she found herself in his arms.

He nestled her head against his warm, hard chest, the strong bands of his arms encircling her, offering comfort and strength, until the tears she'd held back for so long started burning beneath her eyelids.

His heart pounded, steady and reassuring, beneath her face. When he gently lifted her chin, she found herself seeking, silently begging for something more, and when his warm and sensual mouth settled on hers, she felt as if she'd finally come home and found what she'd needed so long ago. Compassion. Caring. Strength.

And after all these years, she finally felt a sense of peace.

DYLAN WATCHED BEN walk into the kitchen for breakfast at eight-thirty. Eight-thirty! When did the guy ever sleep past five? Without a clock to punch at some nine-to-five job, you'd think he would slow down sometime and take a day off. But no—every morning he was up at the crack of dawn, and so damn cheerful that Dylan could barely stand it.

Dad, when he was home, usually woke up at noon.

The reason for Ben's late arrival followed a few minutes later clad in the same clothes she'd worn the day before, her hair tousled and eyes bleary. Ben didn't look so good himself—he moved like an old man, and from the careful way he held his head steady he had to have a killer head-ache...or a hangover.

Some role model. Dad had said Ben was a smart, steady, straight-arrow kind of guy. One who would be a good influence. Dylan snorted aloud at that thought. *Yeah, right.*

"Well...um...I'd better be going," the doc murmured, glancing around the room. She spied her coat slung over one of the kitchen chairs and retrieved it. "I need to check on Galahad and Moose, and listen to my messages. Now remember—call your doctor if you start showing *any* of those head-injury signs we talked about. Okay? Double vision, headache—"

Ben held up his hands in self-defense. "Believe me, we've been over this enough."

Head injury? Dylan studied him, then stifled a laugh. Naaaahhh. Just hiding a hangover. Dad had tried to do that often enough, and Dylan wasn't *that* dumb.

Joanna gave Dylan a tight, awkward nod and an over-bright smile. "Is Sadie up yet?"

"She was up early to bake her rolls, but I think she's lying down again. They're on the counter if you want one."

"Next time, maybe. Tell her I'm sorry I missed her." To no one in particular, she added, "Max is sleeping soundly. When she wakes up she'll need her diaper changed. Call me if she starts coughing again, okay?"

From the way Ben stepped closer to Joanna and brushed a hand through her hair, they had more going on than just some mutual concern over the kid. Dylan stilled, trying to hear what Ben murmured to her, but they were clear across the kitchen. Setting up some hot date, probably.

Dylan shrugged and swallowed a half can of Coke, watching Joanna out of the corner of his eye as she put on her jacket and boots. He waited until he heard her rev her

Tahoe's engine outside. "I did what you said. Followed the rules. I'm free to go with my friends tonight. Right? They're coming at six o'clock."

Ben poured himself a cup of cold coffee at the stove and stuck it in the microwave. When the timer dinged, he grabbed the cup and lowered himself slowly into a chair at the kitchen table. He seemed to think about the question far too long. "Tell me more."

"Nothin' to say, really." Deep resentment curled through Dylan's insides. Back home, he got along just fine when Dad was gone on one of his endless trips. The current housekeeper usually gave up trying to play mama after a few weeks and just let him run, as long as he turned up in his own bed by morning and didn't trash the place.

When Dad was actually home, things weren't much better—he was out late more often than not, leaving Dylan to sit home alone.

At first it had been sorta fun being around Ben—a man who actually stayed in one place—but the guy's assumption that he had some sort of control was still hard to swallow.

"No details?" Ben raised an eyebrow. "Guess you're staying home."

Anger and rebellion surged like lava through Dylan's veins. He fought to keep his voice level. Calm. "Some of the guys are getting together tonight. Just hanging out in town."

"Who?"

Dylan thought up a few good names, but Ben would probably check...and then there would be hell to pay. "Nate."

"And?"

"Billy." Dylan gave a heavy sigh. "Jonah."

"The ones who got in trouble before."

"Jonah and Billy got grounded, just like me. Jonah's mom was real mad."

"The friends you choose make a big difference in what happens, son."

I'm not your son. Dylan bit back the sharp retort just in time. "We're just gonna hang out at Jonah's. His parents and little sister will be there. How bad is that?"

Ben studied him pensively over the rim of his coffee cup, took a swallow and put the cup down.

"I'll be home by midnight. Nate has his license and he's gonna pick me up."

"You'll go straight there, and straight back?"

Dylan nodded. Anything was better than being stuck out here for another night. *Anything.* "Nate's mom is okay—she knows how to shoot pool, and she can beat the socks off most anyone who takes her on."

"Okay…" Ben hesitated. "You understand that I'm just trying to do the right thing here, don't you? Your dad wants to find you in one piece when he gets back to the States."

"Yeah."

He glanced at the clock on the wall. "I'm going out to work one of the colts. Want to come along? You can ride my gelding."

It was a generous peace offering, and Dylan knew it. Ben's old cutting horse was a blast to ride—responsive, fast on his feet, Badger could turn on a dime and spin until Dylan was almost too dizzy to stay on board, and he could lay fifteen-foot skid marks in the dirt when cued to a sliding stop. Badger was even better than Dylan's motocross bike back home.

"Yeah—sure. I just want to check my e-mail. Maybe Dad wrote."

"How long has it been now?"

Dylan's excitement faded. "Two weeks. But he's always busy. And maybe he doesn't have a phone handy."

Ben nodded in agreement. "I'm sure that's true."

At the sound of footsteps, they both turned toward the

doorway. Sadie, wearing another one of her snap-front housedresses, with her hair twisted up into some sort of ball on the top of her head, bustled in with Max in her arms. The baby's cheeks were sorta red and she was already whining. Not a good sign.

One glance and Dylan launched out of his chair. Sometimes Sadie took care of Max for part of the day on Saturdays, and if he stuck around, he'd end up helping. "I—um—need to go to the bathroom," he muttered, grabbing at the easiest excuse. "Then I need to check my e-mail and go out to the barn."

"I can make you breakfast," Sadie called after him. "Pancakes? Eggs and bacon? You need some—"

Dylan didn't stop until he got to his room and locked the door firmly behind him. Breakfast—*yuck*. At home, he grabbed a Coke and leftover pizza, or whatever he could find in the fridge. Here, Sadie tittered and worried, wringing her hands, exclaiming that he was going to "make himself sick," until he finally gave in and ate something gross just to please her. Like eggs—*eeeuwww*.

Waiting for the computer to power up he studied the calendar on the wall. Seven weeks left. Only seven! He'd be back home for Christmas for sure. Maybe Dad and he could go skiing again….

Grinning, he logged onto the Internet and found his Yahoo mailbox, then scrolled down through the new messages for any from Dad—*yes!* Leaning forward in his chair he eagerly skimmed through the message. Maybe Dad would be coming home earlier….

He blinked. His heart sank.

Sorry—I didn't expect to be over here this long—but Ted isn't coming to replace me and I have to stay through the first of the year. Maybe as late as the tenth of January. I know you're having fun at the ranch, though... I'll bet you'll hate leaving that beautiful country. Your uncle is a pretty cool guy, right?

The words on the screen blurred.

Dylan hit the power button without bothering to close out of the program, and spun his chair around to face the window and the rocky, barren hills that climbed toward the pine-covered mountains.

Oh, yeah. Staying here was just *great.* On par with that juvenile-detention hall in New York, or that crappy school he'd had to attend as a seventh-grader. And now he wouldn't even see his dad at Christmas. Anger welled up in him, hot and wild, until he felt as if his head might explode. Whirling around, he slammed a fist against the wall and felt a flash of power when the plaster and lathe gave.

Then he sank onto his bed and wondered how far he could get if he took that red Chevy pickup parked out by the barn.

FROWNING, Ben paused outside Dylan's door. He rapped lightly. "Hey, kid—are you in there?"

The boy hadn't come out to ride Badger after all. Sadie reported seeing him grab a sandwich and disappear into his room around noon, but hadn't seen him since.

Now it was nearly six o'clock, supper was on the table and those friends of his were supposedly due any minute. Ben tried the door handle. Pounded on the door. The complete silence on the other side confirmed his suspicion. *Damn.*

It had been one hell of a day—his head still pounded and his joints still ached from yesterday's fall, and with Joanna hovering close by through the night, he'd barely slept at all.

And now Dylan had gone missing.

Ben stalked down the hall to the kitchen, where Sadie was unsuccessfully trying to feed Max in her high chair.

"Is he still sleeping?" Sadie asked, looking concerned.

"I don't think he ever was. Did you see the red Chevy pickup pull out this afternoon?"

"I...don't think so..." Sadie scooped another serving of something green and waved it enticingly in front of the baby's mouth. Max's little face scrunched up and she jerked her chin away, a soggy soda cracker gripped in each chubby hand. "No, I don't remember that at all."

But Max had been fussy all day, and if Sadie had been tending her, the boy could have easily slipped away unseen. If he'd driven around the back of the house, no one else would have noticed, either. And Sadie's hearing wasn't all that good. Ben grabbed his black Stetson from the rack by the door and shrugged into his down jacket. "I'm going outside for a minute."

"But supper's ready. Aren't you hungry?"

He and Rafe had been working colts and dealing with several clients who'd come to see how their horses were progressing, so he'd missed lunch. The rich, heavy aroma of roast beef and gravy made his stomach growl. A big bowl of Sadie's fluffy mashed potatoes waited on the table as well, along with glazed baby carrots and a basket of flaky biscuits.

It took considerable willpower to open the back door. "Right now I've got to find that boy. Maybe he's out in the barns somewhere."

Ben had watched and helped Gina with her two girls from the time they were born, so little ones were less of a challenge. Teenage boys were an entirely different story. After a fifteen-minute search, Ben knew that both Dylan and the red truck were missing. *Again.*

What was it with this kid?

Back in the house, Ben ate quickly, then bundled Max

into her warm snowsuit while Sadie prepared a couple of bottles and loaded the diaper bag. Worry etched her wrinkled face. "It's my fault—I should have known Dylan wasn't in there."

Ben scooped up the baby and shouldered the diaper bag. "Not at all, Sadie. You thought he was in his room on his computer. I imagine he waited to leave until he was sure you were busy."

She wrung her hands. "He's not even old enough to be driving. What can he be thinking, going off like this?"

"Exactly. Miguel has already warned Dylan about staying out of trouble. This time, he might well arrest the boy."

Ben circled Sadie's thin shoulders and gave her a gentle hug. "It's hard on him, living way out here with his dad somewhere on the other side of the world. Try not to worry. He's in town somewhere. I should have him back here in an hour or so."

Sadie's gaze dropped to the rosy-cheeked baby in Ben's arms. "She's been cranky today. Don't you want to leave her here?"

As if on cue, Max whined and twisted in his arms, shoving at him with both hands and kicking her little feet against his bruised side. But Sadie looked tired and he knew she'd had a hard day already. "Two minutes in the warm truck and Max will be asleep," he said with a smile. "Maybe you can take a nice hot bath and turn in early."

"Well..."

"I'll ask Rafe to keep an eye on the place while I'm gone, okay?" He gave her a quick kiss on the cheek before heading through the door. "An early night will do you a world of good." Through the window set in the door he could see the distant glow of lights twinkling from Rafe's house. "Rafe and Felipe are home tonight, so you can call them if you need anything. You can also call my cell phone, okay?"

By the time he'd driven his black Ford over to Rafe's, Max was already asleep in her car seat. After briefly filling Rafe in, he drove down the long lane to the highway, while scanning the roadsides for any sign of the pickup.

Darkness had already fallen by the time he reached the highway and turned north toward Enchantment. "I sure hope you stayed on the road, kid," he muttered.

The main highways leading into town from the east twisted through the mountains, with hairpin turns providing dramatic views of rocky cliffs and deep valleys. This southern route was less dangerous, but for an inexperienced driver taking curves too fast there were still numerous places a car could slide off the road into a rugged ravine or a heavy stand of trees.

With luck, Dylan was hanging out in town. If not, Ben would need to call the Enchantment Police Department and request help. The red Chevy pickup—with its silver Shadow Creek Ranch logo emblazoned on each door— ought to be easy enough to spot, unless it was already out of the county and headed to who-knew-where.

Calling the county sheriff and the New Mexico Highway Patrol would be the next step. One Ben hoped to avoid, because it could mean a lot more trouble for an underage driver who already had a record of trouble.

Max whimpered in her sleep. The dim lights of the dashboard rendered the interior of the truck in monochrome shades of gray…but were the baby's cheeks a deeper color? Concerned, Ben reached over to rest the back of his hand against her face. She seemed warmer than she had before. A fever? Just too warm in her snowsuit?

Concerned, he turned the thermostat down to sixty-eight as he drove in to town.

Under the streetlights he could see young trick-or-treaters straggling down the sidewalk at either side of the street. Goblins, ghosts and witches, under the watchful eyes of parents, swung plastic pumpkin-shaped pails at their sides as they made their way from one house to the next. Even through the closed windows of the truck he could hear laughter and shrill cries of excitement.

Memories…he smiled to himself, remembering the years Mom had shepherded Phil, Gina and him down these same streets on Halloween. Afterward, they'd dumped their loot on the kitchen table and divvied up the treats.

Until he took off, Dad had always pounced on the miniature Snickers and Musketeers. Mom had liked the red licorice the best. They'd made a game of it. Then they'd always ended the evening with apple cider, warm, fudgy brownies and card games until midnight—even if Halloween fell on a school night.

Glancing over at the sleeping baby, Ben's heart twisted. Where would she be when she was old enough for her own family traditions? Still here—God willing. But maybe she'd be far away in some big city with her mother, where people were afraid to take their kids out at night, and the fun of Halloween was only something the kids read about in books. The thought left him feeling lonelier than he'd felt in years. What if he never got to see her excitement and her costumes?

Mindful of the trick-or-treaters roaming the streets, Ben cruised slowly down Paseo de Sierra, checking the parking lots at the Sunflower Café, the hamburger place at the edge of town and Slim Jim's, before turning up Sage. At the corner of Sage and Copper he spied a familiar, petite feminine shape bundled up in a puffy red ski jacket trailing behind two little girls.

Pulling over, he stepped out of the truck and called out to them.

"Ben!" Allie and Regan called out in unison. They rushed over and hugged him fiercely, each vying for his undivided attention.

"Hey—what are you guys this year?" Regan wore an oversize cowboy hat and jangling spurs that clanked against the ground with each step. Allie wore bright pink tights with a fluffy pink skirt that barely peeked out from under her heavy jacket. "Let me guess. Allie—you must be a fireman. Regan…" He studied her thoughtfully. "An astronaut. Right?"

Both girls giggled as he hugged them. Over their heads he smiled at Gina, but one look at her face and he didn't have to ask how things were going. "No word?" he said quietly.

Giving a meaningful glance at the two girls, she lowered her voice. "Zach called on Thursday. He told me he's coming back to town, but he's going to stay at his brother's place."

Ben looked at her in disbelief. "If and when I see that husband of yours, he's going to have a lot to answer for. What kind of jerk walks out on his wife and two of the sweetest little girls in the world?"

"You're still my big brother." Gina gave him a quick hug. "But this isn't something you can fix."

"But—"

"No. I was ready to compromise, but there isn't any room for discussion as far as Zach is concerned. He's self-centered and bullheaded. I don't think he even really loved me all these years. He probably just felt trapped."

Hearing the stress in her voice made Ben wish he could land a fist or two in his brother-in-law's face. "Some people will *never* be as lucky as him. When will he be back?"

"Just stay out of this, Ben. I mean it. I'm on the verge of finding a lawyer." She moved to the passenger side of his pickup and peered in on the sleeping baby, clearly wanting to change the subject. She forced a cheery smile. "Max is a little young for trick-or-treating, isn't she?"

"I'm out trying to find Dylan."

Gina's face fell. "Not again."

"I think he took the red Chevy."

She bit her lower lip. "I don't remember seeing it any-where…and we've covered quite a lot of ground tonight."

Regan danced impatiently, her spurs clinking on the con-crete sidewalk and the cowboy hat slipping down over her face. "Moo-om. We gotta go. It's getting late!"

"We haven't been to Sissy's house yet—or Holly's," Allie informed Ben, twisting a strawberry-blond pigtail around her finger. "And Mama promised us a burger at the Sunflower."

He grinned and touched a forefinger to the brim of his hat. "I'd better let you ladies get on your way." Shifting his attention to Gina, he continued, "Call my cell if you see the pickup anywhere, okay? And keep me posted on what's happening with you."

Ten minutes later he'd covered more ground and still hadn't had any luck, and his cell phone hadn't rung.

The dusty little theater downtown—always behind the times by at least six months and staunchly adhering to its owner's policy on strictly family fare—was showing a chil-dren's movie from last spring. The pickup wasn't parked there, but that was no surprise.

The high-school parking lot was empty.

A check of the trailer court where some of Dylan's friends lived revealed a lot of pickups, but none from Shadow Creek.

Frustrated, Ben drove to Paseo de Sierra and pulled to a stop in front of the town square. He cracked the driver's-side window while he let his truck idle.

A faint, sweet smell of burning leaves wafted inside. The littlest trick-or-treaters were off the streets now, and just the older kids remained. A gaggle of middle-school girls sauntered by wearing an assortment of grunge-rock and 1930s movie-star get-ups, their overloud laughter calling out for attention. A trio of boys across the street—none of them Dylan—whistled and called out to them.

Surely the boy hadn't left town. How far could he get on a tank of gas and a lot of anger? Unless he was in a ditch somewhere....

Awake now, Max cried out, thrashing her arms and legs, struggling to be free of the confining car seat. Her breathing sounded...harsher. Faster. Her cheeks had been pink before, but now they appeared pale under the illumination of the street lamps outside. Too pale.

How could she change so fast? The chilly night air? Another cold coming on? She'd been fussy earlier, but he'd attributed that to being tired. Now, he wasn't so sure.

He murmured comforting words to her. She settled for a moment when he gently stroked her cheek, but she broke into a spasm of coughing.

And then he heard it...a strained, high-pitched sound with every breath.

When he slid closer to unbuckle her car seat and lifted her free, he could feel her little heart racing beneath his fingers.

He nestled her limp weight at his shoulder, hoping she might feel more comfortable in a different position. Her rapid breathing remained shallow. Strained.

He hesitated for only a moment before grabbing his phone and speed-dialing for help.

CHAPTER THIRTEEN

JOANNA MET BEN at the Arroyo County Hospital E.R. fifteen minutes later, her hair windblown and her cheeks flushed. The E.R. nurse—Sandy, again—had already ushered Ben and Max into a cubicle and taken the baby's vitals.

Now, an hour after she'd arrived, Joanna walked into the cubicle with the chest X rays she'd ordered and an all-too-serious expression in her eyes.

"We've got good news," she murmured. "No pneumonia."

Sandy had brought in a wooden rocking chair so Ben could rock Max to sleep against his shoulder. Her breathing still sounded harsh and tight. "But there's something else," he said flatly. "I know she isn't *normal.*"

Joanna pulled up a chair and settled into it, resting a clipboard in her lap. "No."

"You once said you would need to follow her pretty closely." He hesitated, not wanting to hear the answer, then plowed ahead. "Do you think she's got asthma?"

"Most doctors I know hesitate to give that diagnosis at this young age. Unless it's a very definite case, they'd rather not label these kids due to insurance concerns —and many children will even grow out of the problem, as they get older."

"But she's wheezing. She's having problems."

"She's wheezing a bit, yes. She doesn't want to lie flat

because it's harder for her to breathe. When she inhales, her nostrils flare, and you can see the retractions—denting of the skin between her ribs. She makes that soft grunting sound when she exhales, because she has to work harder at it.''

"And that means…''

"We usually try to chart these acute situations as an episode of reactive airway or a viral infection with bronchospasm, unless the disease progresses.''

Disease. A cold fist settled around his heart as he considered what this all meant. He struggled to find the words to express his worst fears, but in the end he just stared at Joanna, knowing that he probably appeared just as shellshocked as he felt.

She gave him a sympathetic smile. "We need to figure out if she has certain triggers that bring this on…and we need to discuss how she can be managed when she goes home. I think we should keep her here overnight, at least. She needs to be observed, and she's also dehydrated. We need to get some fluids going.''

"An *IV?*" Ben felt himself pale as he thought about how frightened Max might be, and how much it might hurt.

"She hasn't been eating or drinking well, so she needs that. We'll also start breathing treatments every few hours, and start teaching you how to do them at home.''

The thought of hospitalization might have scared him before, but now he only felt relief. *There'll be others here to watch her…make sure she's safe.*

Joanna apparently misunderstood his expression, because she added, "I know you don't know about any insurance coverage she has…''

"Just do everything you need to do. I don't care about the cost,'' he responded. Max stirred restlessly in his arms, scooting higher until her downy head rested under his chin.

He gently rubbed her back. "What did you say about triggers?"

Joanna pulled her chair closer and tapped a patient instruction sheet on her clipboard. "Max's airways are sensitive, and may swell, tighten up, or even clog with excess mucus if she encounters certain substances. Pollens, mold, dust mites, animal dander—"

Ben groaned. "The horses?"

"Possibly, though I doubt it," Joanna admitted. "Max has been exposed to that source every day through you and your clothing, and she hasn't had these problems each day. Certain chemicals can be a problem...wood smoke...just having a cold can trigger wheezing for some people."

Smoke. "The first time she had problems, Gina's neighbors were burning leaves right next door," he said slowly. "And tonight—Max seemed to start having problems right around the time I smelled burning leaves in town."

Joanna gave a thoughtful nod. "Smoke can be a problem for a lot of people." She stood and spoke briefly into the intercom on the wall, then returned. "I've told Sandy that we're admitting your daughter. They should have a room ready in a few minutes, and once we get her settled we'll start the IV and give her a treatment. Does Sadie know you're here?"

"I called both Rafe and Sadie a few minutes ago. Rafe said he'd go up to the house and stay in the spare bedroom tonight, just in case Sadie needs something. He's calling my friend Manny to come over and help work the horses— I've got two owners coming to pick up their mares in the morning, so those horses need to be worked."

"And Gina?"

"I saw her earlier with the kids, but when I phoned her place, Nicki answered. Gina got called out to a home birth by Eagle Nest."

He debated only a moment before calling the police department and asking to talk to Miguel. If he couldn't go after Dylan then somebody else needed to before it was too late.

"YOU CALLED the *cops* on me?" Dylan gave the newspaper guy a horrified look, then shifted his attention to the window of the teen center. Outside, everything was pitch-black save for the swirling red lights of a patrol car parked at the bumper of his pickup.

"No." Nolan McKinnon slung an arm around Dylan's shoulders and peered out the window, too. "What did you do—rob a bank?"

"Hardly." Dylan stepped away from him and moved closer to the window. "I just…uh…got sorta lost."

Nolan raised a sandy eyebrow. "Lost? As in gone for hours? Days?"

"Hours. Big deal. Maybe I just parked illegally out there, or something."

He'd taken off in midmorning, hoping to make it to Albuquerque, where he planned to buy an airline ticket with the credit card his dad had left him. Some of his friends would take him in. Or even his dad's housekeeper, if he could convince her that it was okay.

Instead, he'd gotten lost on those twisty, mountainous roads outside of Enchantment and had finally found his way back long after dark by following the lights of a semi headed—he hoped—toward Enchantment.

He'd cruised the streets of town until he spied the teen center, where the lights were bright and a group of kids could be seen inside, playing Ping-Pong and pool.

He'd heard kids talk about the place and figured it was a place for losers, but the kids inside had dismissed him as if they thought *he* was one, until McKinnon had sauntered over and drawn him into a game of pool. Later, the two of them had joined a game of pickup basketball in the gym.

Dylan had found himself telling the guy about the ranch, about Ben and about his father's absence. Now he was even on a first-name basis with the guy. Go figure.

Nolan gave him a measuring look. "Does Ben know you're here?"

"Yeah, sure." At Nolan's raised eyebrow he added, "He…uh…knows I'm in town."

The guy seemed to accept what he said, but when the cop strode into the building, his expression wasn't nearly as friendly.

Dylan's heart lodged in his throat when he recognized Officer Miguel Eiden, knowing he was going to be yelled at—maybe even arrested—in front of the other kids. Kids who would blab every bit of this to everyone at school.

"Nolan." Miguel nodded toward McKinnon.

"Hey, Miguel. Busy night?"

"Fair."

Both pairs of eyes cut over to Dylan.

"I was just driving by and noticed your truck's interior lights are on," Miguel said, a corner of his mouth lifting into a semblance of a smile. "You been in here long?"

"A couple hours," Nolan interjected smoothly. "Nice kid. Ben's nephew."

Miguel nodded. "We've met. Son, let's go out and see if we can get that truck started. If we can't get it jump-started, I'll give you a ride home. Deal?"

Dylan knew he hadn't left the interior lights on and that Miguel wasn't asking, he was ordering. Relief washed through him at the man's tact. "Uh…thanks."

"Come back again, kid," Nolan called as Dylan walked out the door. "We can have a rematch."

Outside, Miguel caught Dylan by the arm and turned him around. "Not so fast, son. We both know that truck will start, but you aren't driving it home."

"I won't have any trouble. I already—"

"I know. Besides driving illegally, you've worried your

family, and half the police force is looking for you. Your uncle's been afraid that you went off the road somewhere and were injured—or worse.''

Dylan lifted his chin. ''I know how to drive.''

''Even the adults around here respect the mountains, boy. We've had twelve accidents on the roads in the last ten months. Six fatalities. Ben had good cause for worry. He also could press charges against you for taking his truck.''

''I'll…just take the truck home, and I'll promise to stay there.''

''Nope.''

Embarrassment crept up his neck, turning his skin hot. ''But—''

''I can't allow you to break the law, Dylan. Ben will need to come into town and get the truck later.'' His voice lowered to a growl. ''You understand that you'll likely have to go before a juvenile-court judge. This incident also may affect your ability to get a driver's license when you turn sixteen.''

Dylan closed his eyes.

''I'd have Ben come after you, except I know he's busy right now.'' Miguel rocked back on his heels, apparently deep in thought. ''Then again, I could haul you into jail and arrange an overnight stay…''

A cold rush of fear skidded down Dylan's spine and settled in his stomach. ''Please, no.''

''Have you given a thought to your family today? Have you even considered what they might be going through with your disappearance?'' Miguel shook his head in disgust. ''Did you know that your cousin is in the hospital?''

His *cousin?* Dylan stared blankly back at him.

''Max. She's having trouble breathing, and Ben took her to the E.R. I understand they'll be keeping her at least overnight.''

With the way she'd been dumped off at the ranch, he'd

never really thought of Max as a *relative*. When she was cranky and Sadie handed her over to him so supper could be started or a load of laundry done, he wished her weird mother would swoop by the ranch and take her away.

But Miguel was right. Like Regan and Allie, Max was his cousin. Until this fall he'd never even known he had any, and now he had *three*. Sure, they were only girls, and way younger, but since he'd never had any brothers or sisters, these three might be the closest he'd ever get to having a regular family.

Sheepish, he gave an uncomfortable hitch of his shoulder. "Is she gonna be okay?"

"I think so." Miguel glanced at his watch. "Would you like to stop at the hospital on the way home?"

Dylan nodded.

On the way back to Enchantment, he'd had a lot of time to think. Leaving had been stupid. Reckless. Ben had done nothing but try to help him out, so maybe he owed the guy more than this.

"I'VE TALKED to a local investigator," Ben murmured. "About Holly."

He'd been sitting beside Max's hospital crib all night, comforting her when she awakened and fussed, gently holding her when she struggled to avoid the mist of bronchodilator medication rising from the T-tip on the nebulizer. Now, in the dim predawn light, his lean jaw was shadowed dark with stubble and he looked exhausted.

Joanna could have gone home, leaving the treatments to the nursing staff and Ben to watch over his daughter alone, but she'd sensed his worry, his feeling of helplessness, and found she couldn't bear to go.

"I need to know where Max's mother is. In the note, she said she would return in a few months, but I just can't sit here and wonder what's going to happen," he continued.

"It's been three weeks now. And while we're here at the hospital, I want DNA testing done on Max and me. Can you arrange it?"

"I'll order the lab work this morning, if you'd like." She studied his determined expression. "I checked on this for you already…it'll cost around four hundred and seventy-five dollars to get the result back in two weeks."

"The sooner the better." He shifted in his chair and sat upright, stretching out the kinks in his arms. "What if Holly dances into town and thinks she can just grab Max and disappear?"

"Which she could well do. After not informing you about Max's birth and dropping her off like this, I'd say her track record wasn't the best."

"No kidding."

Joanna glanced at the clock on the wall. "I need to go home to feed Galahad and Moose, and take a shower. I've also got to catch up on some things at the clinic. Do you want to run out to the ranch before I leave?"

"No…Rafe and Manny have everything under control. Sadie should be okay during the day if Rafe checks on her now and then, and Dylan…" He gave Joanna a rueful grin. "I think Miguel straightened him out more in an hour than I've managed over the past couple months."

"With his aura of authority and his badge, he'd intimidate any kid into going straight. He seems like a nice guy, though."

Ben laughed. "As long as you don't need arresting."

"I'll watch my step." Joanna started for the door, but stopped and turned back. "Don't worry. Max is doing really well. The nurses will work with you this morning on the procedure for administering her treatments so you can get used to giving them. I'll be back before supper to see how she's doing. You two might even get to go home later today."

He rose to his feet and closed the distance between them in two easy strides. "Thanks, Doc."

"It's Doc, now, is it?" she teased. "Not just Jo?"

"You didn't have to stay here with me, but you did. I just want you to know how much I appreciate what you've done for us."

"No problem."

Their eyes locked, and for a moment she imagined what it would be like to put a hand behind that thick, dark hair and pull him into a kiss. Right here, with nurses moving up and down the hall beyond the open door of the room. Hardly a professional thought, she chided herself.

But Ben apparently had no such reservations. The sensual lines of his mouth lifted into a faint smile, and when he cupped the back of her head with one hand and drifted a sweet, gentle kiss across her lips, she couldn't have moved if her life depended on it.

Warmth sparked through her and she felt herself melting into him, wanting more. All thought of professionalism and distance dissolved like sugar in a cup of hot tea.

"One of these days," he whispered against her ear.

A shiver raced down her spine. He didn't have to elaborate; she knew exactly what he meant.

One of these days echoed through her thoughts as she drove out to her cabin, as she did her chores and as she took a long, cool shower before dressing and heading to the clinic.

Her new job still awaited her in California. She hadn't forgotten just how faithless men could be. But by the stars above, she wanted to experience the love of that cowboy— a man who touched her heart like no other—just once before she had to leave.

BEN HELD MAX close as he strode into the drugstore at ten minutes to five that afternoon. He glanced around, hoping there'd be few customers in the store. "Maybe I should have picked up your prescriptions before I brought you home," he whispered against the hood of her snowsuit. "The last thing you need is to catch someone's cold."

Drowsy—probably from the medications she was on—she nestled closer, her eyes drifting shut as he tipped his head back to look at her.

Other than the elderly clerk at the front register and the balding pharmacist at the rear, he saw only one other person there—or at least, the crown of a western hat moving behind the shelves of office supplies down aisle three.

The other customer rounded the far end of the aisle by the pharmacy just as Ben got there. Startled, Ben stared at his brother-in-law's stubbled face. "Haven't seen you for a while," he said shortly.

Zach met his gaze squarely. "I haven't been here. You probably know why."

Yeah—because you're treating your family like dirt. "I've heard."

"I 'spose. Your sister's side, anyway."

Max stirred impatiently in Zach's arms, and he realized he'd suddenly held her too tight. "Zach, how long have we known each other?"

"Since first grade. I think we both were sweet on Mary Beth Tucker at the time."

"You sure weren't a quitter then."

Zach gave him a brief, sardonic smile. "No…I courted that little girl all through school, and she didn't look at me twice. Least not till sixth grade—and then she gave me a black eye."

"'Cause she liked me best."

"Your *horses.* I only had a bike."

The old joke between them fell into awkward silence. They'd started out as competitors, trying to best each other at every turn throughout school. After Zach married Gina, they'd become more like brothers, even though Zach's trucking and Ben's travels on the show circuit meant they didn't see much of each other.

Zach shifted uncomfortably. "Well...guess I'd better go."

"You've got nothing else to say?" Over Zach's shoulder, Ben caught Roland, the pharmacist, watching them with undisguised interest. "Look, I need to pick up some prescriptions first—but I'd like to talk to you...maybe someplace else?"

Zach's forehead creased. "Is the baby doing okay?"

"We spent the night at the hospital—breathing troubles."

"Geez. Any word from her mom? Gina told me about the child being left on your doorstep."

Ben shook his head and glanced toward the back register, where Roland already had two bottles of liquid labeled and waiting on the counter for him. "Want a quick cup of coffee at the Sunflower?"

"My brother is..." Zach glanced at his watch. "What the hell, he can wait. I guess we'd better get this over with, right?"

Fifteen minutes later, Max was awake and securely settled into a high chair, listlessly pushing soda crackers around the tray. "Dah!" she informed Ben, offering him a piece of cracker.

He took it from her and offered it back, knowing she would want to keep her prize.

Across the dark pine table, Zach watched the exchange with a pensive expression. "It hasn't been easy," he said slowly, running a hand back through his dark hair. "After all the years Gina and I have had together..."

"So what's the deal?" Before running into Zach today he'd imagined decking his old friend for hurting Gina and the girls. Now...it was all too clear that Zach was suffering, too. "Go home. Have a good argument. Clear the air."

"She's already made her decision. She'd rather have her damn job than a good marriage. How the hell do you think that makes me feel?"

"In case you haven't noticed, a lot of wives work these days."

His jaw set, Zach stared down at the coffee in his cup. "But with me gone days at a time, what kind of family life is that for the kids? Odd hours. Baby-sitters. Who's there for them to help with homework? Bedtime? Some teenager who'd rather do her nails? An old lady who's too tired to play?"

"Kids adapt."

"That isn't how I want mine raised."

"So you're walking away from ten years of marriage—and hurting my sister—because you're too damn stubborn to compromise."

Zach swore, then flushed as he gave Max a quick glance, but she was busy mashing saltines with Ben's truck keys, apparently oblivious to his burst of temper. "You were at my house a lot when we were kids."

"Yeah? What about it?"

"My mom stayed home and my dad supported us, the way it's supposed to be."

Ben snorted. "Maybe on some 1960s sitcom."

"She kept everything running like clockwork. Supper at six sharp, laundry done. Hell, she even ironed the sheets. It was a good way to raise kids, and I want that for mine. Why should they have anything less?"

"I thought...didn't..."

Zach's expression darkened. "When Dad got laid off, Mom started working. And yeah—things sure changed. I know what it's like to come home and be there alone for three hours every day. And when Dad started drinking...I learned what it was like to keep out of the way.''

Alice, one of the waitresses who'd been at the Sunflower since time began, sauntered up to the booth with a pot of coffee in one hand and a plate of cherry pie in the other. ''You boys want something to go with that coffee? I've also got blueberry or apple...'' She leaned over and winked at Max, who stared up at Alice's bright auburn hair in fascination. ''And I have your favorite pie—French Silk. This little one would have a high time finger-painting with that, wouldn't she?''

Ben gave her a brief smile and shook his head. ''I've got to head out in just a few minutes. Thanks, though.'' After Alice disappeared back into the kitchen, he propped his elbows on the table and steepled his fingers. ''I still don't get it. You talk about this ideal family...yet think leaving Gina is going to solve anything?''

''I can support my family, dammit. I want things back like they were, when she loved me and the kids enough to stay home. Now her job is so important that we're barely even second best. Phone rings—she's out the door. No idea when she'll be back.'' Zach shoved his cup to one side, sloshing coffee over the rim, and slid out of the booth. ''I can't live like that. Not anymore.''

''I think you've got this all wrong.''

Zach reached into his back pocket for his billfold and tossed a five down on the table. ''It's over, Ben. I'm sorry. I just hope you and me can still be friends.''

Max twisted in her chair to watch him stalk toward the door, then turned back, her dark curls bouncing. ''Dah!'' she said solemnly.

''That about sums it up, kid,'' Ben said on a drawn-out sigh. ''I guess love just isn't enough in the long run.''

And maybe it wasn't worth the pain, either.

''THE TAYLOR TWINS are in room one for their six-month checkups,'' Nicki announced at the door of Joanna's office the following Friday morning. "And the Pennington boy is in room two with a sore wrist."

"Thanks, Nicki." Joanna set aside the chart on her desk and stood. "I'll be there in a second."

The girl hesitated at the door, a delighted gleam in her eye. "Have you *seen* him lately?" she whispered. "Like, has he asked you out or anything?"

Joanna didn't need to ask for clarification. "*No*. He and I are friends—no more than that."

"You two are just so *perfect* for each other." Nicki gave her a broad wink and disappeared down the hallway, her sneakers squeaking against the gleaming vinyl floor.

Apparently someone at the hospital had walked past Max's room last Sunday morning and caught that kiss, because there'd been furtive whispers behind Joanna's back whenever she stopped at the hospital to see a patient, and Nicki had been peppering her with questions all week.

The entire situation was getting old. The fact that Ben hadn't called or stopped by to see her made her embarrassment grow. She'd clearly misinterpreted his little kiss of thanks, had imagined far more than his words were meant to convey.

One of these days.

So what did that mean exactly? Obviously not what she'd thought, and she wasn't going to ask, either.

Distance could be a very good thing.

Joanna smiled at Fiona Pennington as she walked into the exam room, then shifted her attention to Jason, hoping she'd managed to mask her concern. Stuart had sent her a bill for Galahad's damage to his bougainvillea, but she hadn't seen the boy or his mother since that day. She'd been worried about how they were doing. "So what's up, big guy?"

He sat on the edge of the exam table awkwardly cradling his wrist in his other hand. "I fell."

She bent over him to exam the light bruising. "Skydiving, I bet."

"Nope. Mountain bike."

"On the street?"

"Trails. My dad and me go up into the high country sometimes."

"Enjoy that, do you?" She probed the wrist, noticing his obvious wince when she palpated the joint.

"Mostly. Unless I do something dumb."

Concerned at the undercurrent of bitterness in his voice, she searched his face. "Dumb?"

"You know, like making stupid mistakes. Crashing over tree roots, and stuff like that."

"Sounds like simple, ordinary accidents to me," she retorted. "I wouldn't call them stupid."

She gently took his other hand and held them out, parallel to each other. "You definitely have some swelling there. I'm going to send you over to the E.R. for some X rays before I decide what to do. That okay with you?"

He nodded.

"Could you go out to the waiting room for just a minute? I need to talk to your mom." At the flash of concern in his eyes, she ruffled his hair. "Not personal stuff about you."

After darting a quick, uncertain glance at his mother, he slipped off the table and headed back to the reception area. Joanna touched the intercom button on the wall and asked Nicki to keep an eye on him.

"He'll be fine for a few minutes," she said to Fiona, reaching for the door and closing it behind him. "I want to ask you a few questions."

"I can't imagine why," Fiona murmured. She eyed Joanna cautiously, then studied her nails with an air of bored sophistication. "I agree with you about the X rays. We'll run over right away and have them done."

"How are you feeling these days?"

"Feeling?" Fiona gave a brittle laugh, one hand resting protectively on her rounded belly. "Pretty good for a thirty-five-year old who's six months pregnant. But I don't think that's why you want to talk to me, is it?"

"I'm concerned." Joanna softened her voice, and hoped the woman would at least stay and listen. "About both you and your son."

"Concerned? I don't know why." Fiona reached for the strap of her purse and stood.

"I've reviewed Jason's records."

"You think I'd ever let someone hurt my son?" Fiona's voice rose, touched with hysteria.

"Not just someone," Joanna said quietly. "I've met your husband, Fiona. On the day I stopped at your house, he wasn't exactly calm when he arrived home. And I noticed just how wary you were."

"You have no idea what you're talking about."

"You had bruises on your wrist the first time we met. Jason has had a number of significant accidents. That tells me that something is going on—and that you need to find some help before your husband goes too far."

Fiona turned sharply for the door. Gasped, and took a step back. *"Stuart!"*

The door had silently opened while they spoke. Stuart's hand still gripped the knob.

"It's a damn good thing I decided to join you at this appointment, Fiona," he murmured silkily, not taking his gaze from Joanna's face. "Can you imagine—walking in to find that your lovely wife is spreading lies about our family?"

"I never—I didn't—"

He turned on her, his eyes filled with contempt. "Not now, Fiona. I know what I heard."

"I swear, Stuart. I was just explaining how Jason managed to get himself in one scrape after another. He's an active little boy, nothing more than that."

"I need to talk to the doctor. *Alone.*" When Fiona froze, he glared at her. "Now."

Her pulse pounding, Joanna eased over to the wall by the intercom, ready to call for help if he made a move toward her, but he only gave her a mocking smile.

"I don't know what you think, but I'm not a *physical* man. That's rather low class, don't you think?"

"Yes, I certainly do."

"I've never laid a hand on that boy in his life. I do, however, get a little testy when someone—*anyone*—tries to interfere with my family or tarnish my name." He gave her a thin smile. "So perhaps I can return the favor."

"I'm not sure what you mean. It's my job to look out for the welfare of my patients." Something wasn't quite right here. He'd overreacted, misinterpreting Fiona's words completely, and there was something in his eyes that spoke of far greater tension than this situation warranted. "Maybe we can set up an appointment another day, when we can discuss this calmly—"

"Or maybe I can just make myself very clear right now." He moved closer, until he was looking down at her. "My reputation means everything in the kind of business I do. I'll not have you implying anything in my son's chart or to your staff that might do me harm."

"As a mandatory reporter, I always have to ask questions if—"

"Let's put it in terms you'll understand." He spoke slowly, his eyes cold. "I know there's a very close association between Davis's pediatric clinic and The Birth Place. My wife and I have been the major contributors to

The Birth Place for the last five years because it's been her favorite project. I sit on the board there, and I know the place is in deep financial trouble.''

His condescension rankled, and Joanna had to force herself to remain calm. ''I'm not sure that could have anything to do with—''

''I refuse to allow some nosey, misguided doctor to harass me or my family.'' He lowered his voice to a harsh whisper. ''I forbid my wife and son to come here, as long as you're in town. And if you try to discuss this supposed 'abuse' issue with my wife again, or try to spread these lies to anyone else, I'll pull every penny of support we'd planned to give Lydia's little business this year.''

The venom in his voice and the odd gleam in his eyes made her take a step back.

''It will be your fault if The Birth Place folds, understand?'' He waved a hand toward the November page of the calendar on the wall. ''There are other contributors, but our donations are the highest by far. All those women will be out hunting for jobs just before Christmas, even the almighty Lydia Kane. And the moms? Hell—I guess they can just go to Arroyo or drive down to Taos to have their babies, right?'' He chuckled. ''We've had a little snow this fall, but you've seen nothing yet. Trying to make it through the mountains to reach medical help can mean risking your life, believe me.''

She stared at him in disbelief. ''This doesn't make any sense.''

''Oh, but it does.'' His eyes narrowed. ''I could just have my lawyer deal with you, but I figure a doctor has plenty of insurance to cover that sort of thing, right? But The Birth Place—now there's some damage that you couldn't easily repair.''

''You'd harm all those people—this entire community— just for some sort of revenge?''

"No. To protect what's mine. You do understand that this conversation never really happened? You have no proof."

She stared at the door long after he left, listening to him joke casually with the office staff and other patients on his way out.

She had no proof that he'd actually harmed his wife or child, either, but now she had little doubt that he was capable of it. Jason's safety had to be her first priority. And with that eerie hint of irrationality in Stuart's eyes, he might well decide to carry out his threat against her no matter what happened.

Stepping out of the exam room, she headed down to her office, locked the door behind her and picked up the phone.

CHAPTER FOURTEEN

"IT'S GOOD TO SEE you again, dear." Lydia crossed a slim leg over her opposite knee and settled into her chair, a fragrant cup of blackberry tea cradled in both hands.

Dressed in a long, off-white cotton skirt and loose overblouse cinched at the waist with a silver and turquoise belt, with that same rose pendant at her neck, she appeared as poised and dignified as ever.

"I'm glad you had a few minutes, Lydia." Joanna took a sip of her own tea, and placed the cup on the coffee table in front of her. "There are a few things I'd like to discuss."

"How are things down at your clinic?"

"Busy. Dr. Davis had better be well rested when he gets back to town."

Lydia nodded. "And your job in California...are you still planning to go back?"

"Right after Christmas. Davis offered me a permanent job here, but the San Diego position is a wonderful opportunity, careerwise. I can't let it go."

"I'd hoped that perhaps you'd come to tell me that you've changed your mind." A faint smile played across Lydia's mouth.

"Apparently you've heard about the little...incident at the hospital last Sunday," Joanna said dryly. "Believe me—there isn't anything to those rumors."

Lydia gave an almost imperceptible shrug, but amusement lit her eyes as she tactfully changed the subject. "How are the classes for new mothers coming along?"

"Our first class starts Monday, with thirteen women registered and open enrollment at the door. I'm guessing we might have three or four more drop by."

"A good start, then," Lydia said with satisfaction. "Parker and I both feel this is a positive move for the future of The Birth Place."

The administrator had spoken to Joanna several times during the planning phase, and she'd been pleased to have his full support. "We have a nice mix in the class, too. You might remember one of your clients—a teenager named Val? She's enrolled and one of your older ones, Mary Davidson, is coming as well. She already had a little girl, but says it's been six years since she had a new baby and she wants to do things right."

Lydia smiled fondly. "She's a lovely woman. She and her husband are good parents already."

"We've even got the January class half-full, thanks to the efforts of your staff and mine, plus the posters that have been sent countywide. Which means—"

Lydia's smile widened. "That Dr. Davis will have to continue what you've started. I'm thankful for that."

"There's…something else." Joanna studied the late-afternoon bars of light transecting the colorful blanket draped over the coffee table in front of her. "Regarding the financial problems you're having here."

"That's all been common knowledge these past few months." Lydia's voice turned cool, her eyes narrowed. "Kim has already done wonders with our accounts receivable and a number of other procedures in the business office."

"But there's something more to it," Joanna said. "You founded this place…you're the real leader, yet your granddaughter, Devon, replaced you on the board. Why? No one will say."

Lydia shifted in her seat and looked away. "I was never a businesswoman. I prefer working with our clients."

"I don't mean to pry, but I know someone who may hold a grudge against you—and might be angry enough to cause a lot of trouble." Joanna shook her head slowly. "I need to know if it could be true."

Lydia rose stiffly to her feet and moved to the window, where she braced both hands on the sill and rested her forehead against the glass. "Years ago, a baby born here was given up for adoption by its mother. We placed it with a wonderful father, rather than going through the usual adoption channels, and the family...chose to donate funds to our facility. The important thing is that the child has had a wonderful life." Lydia's voice grew defensive. "Just last spring, all the parties involved learned about those circumstances, but everyone is extremely happy with the outcome."

"So why would there be any repercussions now?"

"We tried to keep the adoption procedure confidential, but a few people heard rumors, and chose to see it in the worst light. Rather than risk The Birth Place's reputation, I stepped down from the board."

"But maybe that hasn't been enough...for someone." Joanna took a deep breath. "I'm afraid things might get worse for you—and that it will be my fault."

Lydia turned around, her eyes filled with apprehension. "Why?"

"I just need to know two things—what do you know about Stuart Pennington, and why would he like to see this place fail?"

THE PHONE RANG after midnight on Sunday. Gina blindly reached for the lamp on the nightstand by her bed, then fumbled for the phone. An *emergency?* Had she forgotten she was on call?

At the sound of Zach's voice she flopped back against her pillow and took a steadying breath to calm her nerves.

He'd come home for several awkward hours last Sunday, and he'd called twice since then to talk to the girls, but he'd barely spoken to her. "You scared me, calling this late. What's up? The girls were asleep hours ago, you know."

"Sorry…I'm in California. I forgot about the time difference."

She waited silently for him to continue, his distant voice an all-too sharp reminder that she was alone in their bed, his pillow scrunched up against her back because it made the bed feel less empty.

"I'll be back in town two weeks from now. The nineteenth," he added after a short pause, as if he'd had to check the date.

Gina tried to keep the anger from her voice. "Then I guess you'd better tell your brother, so he'll be ready for you."

"I'm not coming to see him."

Hope flared in her heart, then dimmed. "The girls will be thrilled."

"You and I need to talk. We can't go on this way," he added. "It's not good for any of us."

So he wants to make it final. Permanent. The death knell of their marriage reverberated through her. But she wouldn't give him the satisfaction of hearing her grovel. "Fine," she snapped.

"Gina, I'm not the bad guy, here." His voice was tired, resigned, and she could imagine him hunched over a cup of stale coffee in some shabby truck stop, his face stubbled. He hadn't had it so easy either, all these years. "All I ever wanted was to do the right thing for us. For our kids."

"We both did," she said softly. "But I guess we just got it wrong."

"Give the girls a hug for me."

There'd been no note of reconciliation in his voice, nothing that hinted at a future. Not even a goodbye. She lay under the covers staring at the ceiling long after they hung up, his pillow wrapped in her arms, and memories of the past danced through her thoughts. Then with a snort of disgust, she peeled back the covers and tossed the pillow to the far corner of the room.

Now they'd both need to face new beginnings, and she wasn't going to waste time wishing for things that could never be.

BEN LIFTED the sleeping baby from her car seat and draped a wool blanket over her. Grabbing a brown paper sack from the floor of the truck, he strode across the snow-packed earth to the corral where his old friend, Manny Cordova, waited.

Inside the corral, a magnificent white Andalusian stallion shook his long mane and nickered impatiently for the treats Manny always kept in his pockets.

"I see you didn't forget," Manny said, the wrinkles of his weathered face deepening with his broad smile. "Eighty-three good years, eh?"

"Every time I turn around you're having another birthday, it seems," Ben teased, handing him his gifts. Inside, like every year before, were a bottle of Manny's favorite Mexican-label tequila and a box of cigars.

Manny beamed as he peered inside the bag. "Thanks, amigo."

"You know, that old horse of yours still doesn't act like he's more than a three-year-old. Maybe you can get him to tell you his secret of youth."

Manny's face filled with pride as he offered the stallion a chunk of fresh carrot. "Encanto still sires the beautiful babies, still runs like the wind. He and old Guapo keep me young.''

The old dog lifted his grizzled muzzle at the mention of his name, then dropped back to sleep on the pile of hay at his owner's feet.

''Since you don't have so fine a horse,'' Manny said, ''maybe you need to find a good woman, eh?''

They'd had this same conversation countless times over the years, a distillation of their friendship going to the time when Ben, as a teenager, had worked for Manny every summer.

In his prime, Manny had been a legendary horse trainer. His patience and wisdom had meant everything to a fatherless boy who'd wanted nothing more than to become a trainer of champions. These days they were good friends who helped each other out, and dropped in on each other from time to time.

''A good woman,'' Ben repeated, as he always did. ''You find me one like your Rosa was, and I'll marry her *pronto*.''

''I heard about the woman who brought you this.'' Manny stepped closer and lifted the edge of the blanket to peer inside. ''Ah…a beautiful daughter.'' He shook his head, marveling. ''A man is lucky when he has fine sons and daughters. So—when this woman returns—you will marry her?''

Ben briefly filled in his old friend on the circumstances of Max's arrival, and his worries about her future.

''Come, old friend. We'll talk over my good coffee and keep the baby warm, eh?''

Ben had stopped by to visit during the past few months, but he hadn't been inside Manny's little house for over a year. He surveyed the changes in surprise. Manny had always kept the place clean, but he'd tended to use duct tape for home repairs and had accumulated an amazing amount of clutter in the years since his wife's death. A shabby, comfortable little place, it had been Manny's refuge during his long years of grief.

Now Ben was surprised to see new cupboard doors and new vinyl flooring in the kitchen, and fresh paint on the walls. Some of the windows had been replaced, as well. "What happened here?"

Manny gave a modest duck of his head as he measured coffee into a battered percolator on the stove. "I had that boarder here for a while last year. He didn't like to sit and stare at the mountains, so I put him to work. Maybe I lived too long as an old hermit, eh?"

Ben shifted Max to his other shoulder. By the time the coffee was done, she was bright-eyed and fully awake, trying to scramble out of his arms for a tour of the floor.

"Just hold on, amigo. I got what she needs." Manny disappeared into the spare bedroom and brought out a high chair. "For my grandsons when they visit," he said, setting it up next to the kitchen table.

From the cupboards, he withdrew a fresh packet of soda crackers. Eyeing them with interest, Max submitted to the high chair and grabbed for several at a time.

"So tell me—you say her mother is *loca* and you never saw this baby till she came to your door. You know she is yours?"

"The DNA results take two weeks, and were due Friday. When they didn't show up, the hospital called." Ben gritted his teeth in frustration. "Apparently the samples never arrived at the lab."

"It's a hard thing to wait, no?"

"We're going to the hospital for another blood draw tomorrow, so I should know by the end of November. But in my heart I have no doubt."

Manny tipped back in his chair, one leg crossed over the

other knee. "I hear there is another woman. A *doctora. Sí?*"

"For a man who doesn't get to town much, you sure seem to pick up a lot of gossip," Ben said dryly.

"And for a man who says he doesn't need a woman, you sure find them," Manny retorted, his eyes twinkling. "Tell me, is this *doctora* the one? Does she make you happy?"

Ben couldn't imagine talking about this with any other guy he knew, but Manny had been like a favorite uncle for too many years to count. "Uh…I guess so."

"*Guess* so! *¡Ay, Chihuahua!*"

Ben closed his eyes for a moment, as images of Joanna sped through his thoughts. "She's pretty. Intelligent. She's a dedicated doctor, and is wonderful with children. I enjoy just being with her, you know? But she doesn't plan to stay in New Mexico. I've…been trying to keep my distance."

Manny shook his head. "Do you feel it here?" He held a fist to his chest. "That's what matters. If you feel the love, you can figure out the rest later."

"But—"

"*No.* I nearly missed out on over fifty years with my Rosa, you know? That fiancée you had was no good. But this woman—if you love her, don't waste the chance." He chuckled. "The young ones say go for it!, and that's what you should do."

FROM ACROSS HIS DESK, Stuart gave the elderly Hispanic woman a reassuring smile. "You're best off staying with our plan, Señora Marquez. As your financial planner, I'm completely dedicated to making sure your assets are safe. I assure you, your investments are exactly where they should be."

In heavily accented English she insisted, "But

my…my…'' Her brow furrowed. "Daughter. She worries…''

"I know your daughter wants the best for you." He leaned forward on his elbows, steepling his fingertips. "It's a pretty confusing subject for most people, and you can't always believe what you read in the papers. Investing in foreign banks is a wonderful opportunity right now because we're seeing triple-digit returns. And since the money is going overseas, you don't have to worry about our government demanding high taxes on what you earn. I don't," he added in a confidential tone, "tell all my clients about these opportunities. The fewer people who know about them, the better. Right?"

Her fingers were picking at her shawl in obvious agitation, so he scrambled for reassurance with what he remembered of his high-school Spanish, and hoped like hell he got it right. ¿"Usted quiere…que su dinero sea…caja fuerte?"

Her eyes troubled, she nodded slowly. "Sí…"

He struggled for more Spanish, but gave up in frustration and extended his hands, palm up. "I just hate to see hard-working people like you have to give up so much of what they've made, you know?" He shook his head sadly. "How many years did you work at the restaurant—thirty years?"

"Sí."

"It isn't fair. Does the government need more money?" He flicked a glance at his watch, pushed away from his desk and stood. "Low-risk, high-return investments are the way to go these days, now that the interest rates on bank deposits are so low, and the accounts I've set up for you won't be taxed by the IRS."

The worry lines on her forehead deepened. She spoke only broken English and didn't understand much of this, he knew. Which made it all so much better. He gave her a confidential smile. "My own mother is doing this."

The woman's furrowed brow cleared with obvious relief. "*¿Su madre?* So my money…it is safe?"

"You can trust me to take good care of you. Very good care." He rounded his desk to shake her hand, and escorted her to the door. Outside, the cars creeping by on Paseo de Sierra left tracks in the two inches of snow that had fallen overnight. *"Buenos días, Señora Marquez."*

The phone on his desk started ringing before the door closed behind her. He smiled to himself as he strode to the desk. With Thanksgiving a week from tomorrow, things had been a little slow—many of the well-heeled locals headed for Taos or Albuquerque to shop early and beat the Christmas rush—but today he'd been comparatively busy.

Tonight, at a dinner dance out at the club, he would need to reassure Paul Thompson, his partner in the new Elk Valley Lodge project who was flying in from Colorado.

They'd bought a failing restaurant near Eagle Nest last year, and the place would soon be breaking even. Silver Butte, the small resort they'd picked up for a song two years ago, would start doing better once the nearby Angel's Gate Resort Complex was completed.

They'd done some other investing together as well. Maybe he'd had to juggle the books a little, but soon every dream of money and success he'd ever had would be realized. He'd repay all of that money, and no one would ever know

Not his oblivious little wife, whose main concerns in life were the state of her latest manicure and the clothes she bought on their trips to Dallas and Los Angeles.

Not his father-in-law, who still viewed him as an unwelcome, low-class interloper.

A cold sliver of panic slid down his spine at the thought of what could happen if anything went wrong. But of course it wouldn't.

He'd seen the flicker of disdain in Walter's eyes at their

last family gathering over Labor Day weekend, but that would change. All he needed was a little more time, and everything would fall neatly into the palm of his hand.

He let the phone ring until the answering machine picked up. And then he heard the last voice he wanted to hear.

"Hey, Stuart? This is Paul. I'm still in Colorado—I won't be able to make it to Enchantment until December first. Can we meet the next day? Say, ten o'clock Wednesday? I want to go over our books on the Elk Valley project. Oh, and Stuart? I have a few questions on the investment accounts we set up…"

Pain, sharp as a cougar's claws, caught Stuart's stomach in a viselike grip. Paul had left everything up to him until now. *Everything.* The monthly reports had been positive, and Paul had been pleased.

So why in hell did he need to nose around now—and how could he be stopped?

THE GIRLS SAW their father first. Screaming with excitement, they bounced on the sofa cushion and pressed their faces to the frosty window facing the street.

"Dad's here!" Regan shrieked as Gina came from the kitchen. "He's here, he's here!"

Both girls launched off the sofa and were waiting at the door when Zach pushed it open. He dropped to one knee and encircled them both in a bear hug, his face drawn and haggard. Over the tops of their heads, he greeted Gina with a nod.

God, she wished she could tell what he was thinking. There wasn't a flicker of remorse, or anticipation, or even anger in his dark brown eyes.

Once, those eyes had been filled with sensual promise every time he looked at her. Now, she might have been just another piece of furniture in the room.

"Long run somewhere?" she asked coolly.

Hc gave each girl a kiss on the cheek and rose slowly to his feet. "Yeah. Quite a few in a row."

Hurt welled up inside her. Six weeks. Six long, painful weeks, while she'd alternately longed for him and been angry at him. She'd known she was at fault, too. But as her guilt and uncertainty gave way to resolve, she'd told herself that it no longer mattered who was to blame.

He'd made his position perfectly clear.

"I wasn't sure you'd keep your word and show up," she said.

"Mommy, no!"

Gina looked down into Regan's terrified face and instantly regretted her words. For the girls, she would try her best to be pleasant—at least until they went to bed.

"I meant," she amended with a forced smile, "that you'd said you would stop by, but I wish I'd known what time. I could've made a special supper. I'm on call tonight, so all I made was macaroni and cheese."

"You work tonight?" His voice sounded strained. Tired.

She fought to keep hers even. "Yes, and I'm glad of it. We've had cut-backs, and I'm thankful for every hour."

"The weather…have you heard the reports? Four to six inches, starting this evening. Possibility of forty-mile-an-hour gusts."

"Then I might have some trouble getting around tonight. Are you staying here, or…?" Just saying the words twisted her heart into a painful knot. Waiting for his answer—even though she knew she shouldn't care—felt like eternity. Her sessions with Celia Brice had clarified a lot of things.

Issues of dependence.

How to deal with her anger.

How to handle the children's fears.

But while Celia had encouraged mutual sessions with Zach—if and when he returned—Gina had decided on something far less conciliatory.

Now, though, with that hurt expression in Zach's eyes, she found herself weakening, just a little.

"Girls, go wash up for supper, and wait in the kitchen. Okay? Your dad and I need to talk for a minute."

Allie grabbed Zach's hand. "You'll be here? You won't go away?" she begged, her eyes filled with tears. "I don't want you to go. Next week is Thanksgiving, and you got to be here for the turkey!"

He brushed a hand over her hair and cupped her chin. "I'll be here."

As soon as the girls disappeared down the hall, Gina folded her arms and took a deep, steadying breath. "If you have somewhere else to go, you can leave after supper. Just stay that long for your daughters."

"I don't have other plans." He glanced at the framed family photographs hanging over the sofa, then turned back to her, his expression bleak. "There's no simple 'right' or 'wrong,' here. I want to work things out. I've missed all of you."

He was a big, burly man, soft-spoken and quiet unless provoked. For him, this was a major speech, but that still didn't mean he meant it. "How can I believe you, given what you said to me before? You sure didn't seem to mind just taking off for weeks on end."

"I took runs between California and New York, Gina. I was working. And," he admitted slowly, "I was just plain mad."

"Over my job."

"Over what was happening to us *because* of your job."

"Don't you see, I deserve the chance to make something of myself. I don't want to give that up."

"I'm not asking you to give up your dreams forever…just hold off a while. I can support this family on my own—it's what I'm *supposed* to do. It's what my dad did, and his dad before him."

"It isn't just the money."

"Then think about the girls. Give them a few more years of having you at home. Would that be so hard?"

"No, but—"

"We've talked about this over and over, but nothing changes. You care more for that damn job than you do for us."

"That's not true." Frustration welled inside Gina's throat at she looked up at him.

Excited laughter filtered through the house, followed by the sound of running feet and chairs scraping against the vinyl flooring in the kitchen.

"I need to go wash up, too." He sighed heavily as he bent to grab the handle of his duffel bag. "We'll have to talk later."

"I agree but I may be gone by then. I have two moms who are due any moment, and if that storm hits and the barometer drops, they might just go into labor. Should I call Sue Ellen and tell her that you'll watch the girls?"

Zach turned and opened the front door, stepping aside so she could see the heavy white flakes drifting down in dizzying spirals. "That storm is already here, Gina. Tell Sue Ellen that she'll still need to be on call, because if you have to go out in this you sure aren't going alone."

CHAPTER FIFTEEN

JOANNA SHIVERED as she poked at the logs in her fireplace and watched a scattering of sparks fly upward. A few embers pulsed and faded. Several flames rose halfheartedly around the logs before dying.

At this rate, she'd be frozen by morning.

The electricity had gone out an hour ago, and with the falling temperature and high winds outside, she could already see her breath inside the cabin.

Frustrated, she rubbed her hands together to restore the circulation, and rummaged through the pile of split logs at the side of the hearth. None of them were bone dry—heavy snow had caught her by surprise last night, and the entire stack had gotten wet with six inches of heavy snow.

Finding one that seemed less damp than the rest, she settled it on top of the others she'd arranged on the grate, tossed some shavings into the nooks and crannies, and lit another match.

Please, she muttered as first one match and then another failed to light the fire. Dusk was fast approaching. With just a few candles for light, no electric heat and snowdrifts blocking the way to town, it was going to be a long night. Unless she left Moose out with Galahad tonight, each cozily tucked in the box stall with deep bedding, and tried to brave the drifts to reach one of the warm bed-and-breakfast establishments in town.

"*If* I could even get there," she muttered, chafing warmth into her arms.

A pair of headlights arced through the front windows, sweeping through the cabin with blinding light. Startled, she hurried through the living room and quickly pulled the curtains shut, then peered out into the gloom at one edge, her heart pounding madly.

The cell phone on the kitchen counter hadn't worked all day—maybe the cell tower in Enchantment had blown over—and the cabin phone was dead as well. If this was a burglar, she had no way to call for help. Her hands trembling, she edged toward the back door. But what chance would she have in this weather? Either way—

"Joanna! Are you in there?"

At the sound of Ben's familiar, deep voice, she exhaled deeply.

He knocked on the front door and tried the handle. Moved to one of the windows and rapped sharply. "Joanna! Are you okay?"

She reached the front windows in a split second. Pulling back the curtains, she waved to him, then went to the door and unlocked it. "You scared me," she said as he stepped inside. "I had no idea you were coming."

"I tried calling your cell phone, but the reception was too poor. The telephone lines are down a few miles down the road." He stamped heavy snow from his boots onto the entry rug. "I didn't realize you might be stranded until I called your office about some refills for Max, or I would have been here sooner. The ranch hasn't gotten this much snow yet, and our power is still on."

"How did you make it up the road?"

"I put the blade on my truck." He unzipped his bulky jacket and tossed it onto the coatrack by the door. "Whoa—you don't have any heat in here."

"The electricity is out. No heat, no lights. I've been trying to get the fireplace going but the wood is too wet. I was debating about trying to make it to town so I could stay overnight at the Morning Light.''

He studied her with an expression of concern. ''You'd never make it. I barely got up here with the Ford 350.''

He was so big, strong and inviting, with that broad chest and his heavy flannel shirt, that she wished she could bury herself against his warmth.

''Are your teeth chattering?'' He brushed his fingertips against her cheek. ''Good grief—why aren't you dressed warmer? You've shivering!''

She waved away his concern. ''I heard on my battery radio that this isn't going to stop until morning, and the snow might be interspersed with sleet. You're probably sorry you came out in all this. What are the chances that we can get out of here?''

He opened the door again. The snow was still falling in fat, fluffy flakes, and already his windshield was covered with a good two inches.

''We might be able to make it if we leave right now. I could take you to my ranch or the Morning Light, if you'd rather go there.''

She considered both options for a moment, then shook her head. The thought of spending time with Ben sent a shiver through her that had nothing to do with the cold, but she knew she couldn't go. ''If I can't get back here, Moose and Galahad will be without water. They're in the barn, and it's warm enough for them, but the water buckets will freeze.''

''You could leave the barn door open…they could manage with snow for a day…''

''But they'd go out and be cold and wet. Galahad is a California baby. His muscles quiver like a bowl of gelatine when he gets cold. You should see him.''

Ben gave an exasperated snort. ''He'll survive for one day either way, Jo.''

"A warm, comfy bed and breakfast sounds wonderful. Your ranch sounds even better. But really, I can stay here if you'll just help me start a fire in the fireplace before you go."

He glowered down at her. "The wind is picking up, Jo. You could be drifted in for days."

"Exactly my point. It's too long to leave my guys alone."

His mouth hardened into a grim line. "Did anyone ever tell you that you're a stubborn woman?"

"Me?" Joanna laughed. "Never."

"Frustrating?"

"Nope." His eyes were dark, compelling, resolute, and he smelled wonderful—of pine and leather and snow. When he moved a step closer, her stomach tightened with anticipation.

"How about…incredible?" He lifted her chin with a finger, and brushed a brief kiss across her mouth.

"No," she whispered. "But you are."

Where had that come from? She still planned to go back to California. Everything Ben cared about was here. But when Max was in the hospital, Ben had whispered, *"One of these days"* to her, and during the past three weeks those words had echoed through her thoughts, day and night.

He'd brought Max into the clinic several times since then for follow-up visits—twice because she'd started wheezing again, and he wanted to make sure he was managing her well enough with the nebulizer treatments at home. His dedication to that little girl had completely won Joanna's heart.

And he'd stopped by her cabin on occasion as well, bringing a load of split-pine logs for her fireplace one day, a load of fragrant alfalfa hay the next, and a fifty-pound bag of dog food a few days after that. Useful gifts that meant she didn't need to find time to run those errands herself.

Now, his eyes burned into hers, as if he could see straight through to her soul. "I'll get the fireplace going. And I think I'll stay here, but I'm not asking for anything…personal. Understand? If this weather gets worse, you'll need help just getting out to that barn to do your chores, and I don't want to worry about you getting lost and freezing to death up here."

"What about Max?"

"Gina and her daughters are out at the ranch tonight. The girls wanted to see their cousin. Max is in very good hands."

Joanna reached up and trailed her fingertips across the rough stubble of his cheek, then down the soft, warm flannel of his shirt to rest her hand on his hard chest. Beneath her hand she felt the beat of his heart, strong and steady. "So you'll stay and be my protector," she murmured. "What if I wanted…something more?"

Beneath her hand, the beat of his heart quickened.

"I suppose we could discuss it," he said slowly. A flicker of amusement danced in his eyes, followed by something far darker, filled with desire and promise that nearly took her breath away. "Though there would be conditions."

She stared at him in disbelief. *"Conditions?"*

"Just a few."

"As in?"

"I don't want you doing this because you feel somehow…obligated."

"I don't. What else?"

Resting his hands on her shoulders, he gave her a rueful smile. "I'm not sure I even have any protection with me. Believe it or not, I haven't had any use for it for a long time."

Well, there was the kicker, because she hadn't needed any, either. During her three years with Allen, she'd either been on the Pill or pregnant, and she hadn't been with any man since. "I'm sorry."

"Hey." He pulled her into a brief embrace that sent shivers of sensation through her. "That wasn't why I wanted to stay in the first place, remember?"

Fifteen minutes later, he had a fire blazing in the fireplace, and Joanna had gathered a tray of crackers, cheese and fresh fruit. From the depths of a high cupboard, left by some previous tenant, she even found a bottle of merlot.

"What do you think?" she asked, lifting the bottle for his inspection. "There's wine, or I could heat water in the fireplace for instant coffee or cocoa mix. There's also some cola in the refrigerator."

He gathered some pillows from the sofa and pulled a thick sheepskin from the back of a chair to arrange on the woven rug near the warmth of the fire. Golden light flickered across his dark features, emphasizing the deep creases bracketing his mouth when he smiled. "Cola's fine. I'm going outside to check the barn, and bring in more wood. Should I bring Moose in?"

"Since I'm staying here, yes. Thanks."

Ben pulled on his heavy jacket and opened the cabin door. A gust of snow-filled air swirled inside, and then he was gone.

Joanna left the food on the kitchen counter and went to the front windows to peer outside. Absolute darkness had fallen. Worry niggled through her as she watched and waited for any sign of Moose or Ben. People got lost in storms, wandering away from well-known paths only to be found frozen the next day.

When he appeared at last with an armload of split wood and Moose bouncing along beside him like a joyous polar bear, she pulled the door wide open and ushered him inside.

"I was hoping I wouldn't have to come after you," she teased, hiding her relief. "Everything okay?"

"The barn's locked tight. I broke the ice in Galahad's bucket and gave him hay and grain." He glowered at Moose, who was shaking snow everywhere. "That white dog of yours is almost invisible in the snow. I tripped over him twice."

Moose, apparently delighted at hearing his name, reared up and placed his heavy, wet paws on Joanna's shoulders. Already, he was big enough to look her straight in the eye, but fortunately, he'd finally learned to abstain from licking her face in the process. *"Kennel."*

He fixed her with a sorrowful look.

"Moose, *kennel.*"

Awkwardly, he dropped to all fours and loped across the room to his portable kennel by the front door, his massive head resting disconsolately on the frame of the open cage door and his sorrowful eyes fixed on Joanna.

"He…um…thinks he's still a lap puppy," she called out as she brought the tray of food and several cans of cola into the living room and set them down on the coffee table. "Just ignore him if he starts to whine. He's usually by my side, but I figured you'd rather not have to fight over the cheese and crackers."

"With his size, he'd probably win."

"He's less than a hundred pounds—he just looks bigger because he's so fluffy. That," she added with a laugh, "is my excuse as well. I'm just a tad fluffy."

She could feel the radiant warmth of the fire start to seep into her chilled bones. But when she glanced up and met Ben's intense expression, a different kind of heat sped through her veins.

"I'd never say you were…too fluffy. I'd say you were an incredible woman, with curves exactly where they should be." He set aside his can of cola, shoved a few pillows out of the way and moved closer, until she was nestled at his side and his arm was around her shoulders. Staring into the fire, he gave a deep sigh of contentment. "There's no other place I'd rather be."

His deep, lazy voice rumbled across her skin. The warmth and weight of his arm was at once protective and sensual, sending potent messages tripping through her.

"Maybe we can't do everything," she whispered, turning within his embrace and curving a hand at his nape. "But that doesn't mean we can't do this. Kiss me, Ben."

She pulled him down into a kiss that started soft and sweet, a searching kind of kiss that sent sensation sparking through her nerve endings.

At first he was quiet, letting her take the lead, but suddenly he was above her, kissing her back, fierce and tender and possessive, until everything around her dissolved and only Ben remained, and all she could think about was this powerful, seductive man who could fulfill her fantasies with just his kiss.

He pulled away with a low growl and looked down at her, his eyes dangerously dark and intent. "You are so beautiful," he whispered, "that you take my breath away."

The controlled tension of his muscles told her just how much he wanted her…and how much it cost him to hold back. And heaven help her, she wanted him just as much. It had been so long…so very long.

"Damn," she murmured. "I wish we had—"

A corner of his mouth tilted upward. "I checked the truck," he said. "I found a single packet." She started to speak, but he shook his head and held a fingertip to her lips. "You don't have to. It might have been easier to want something more when it wasn't possible."

One packet. One chance to finally feel whole and alive again.

But not with just anyone. Everything about this man had

touched her heart—his honor, his deep sense of responsibility, his gentleness—and something deeper, less easy to define, that made her pulse trip and her nerves tingle at his touch.

She lifted a hand to the buttons on his flannel shirt and undid one. Then another, never taking her gaze from his. "No second thoughts," she murmured. "Absolutely none."

"Aw, Jo," he breathed, closing his eyes at her touch. "I want to make this good for you. I don't want you to ever forget."

In a tumble of buttons and zippers and laughter they managed to undress each other, until at last they stood before the golden light of the fire with the dark velvet night surrounding them. Only the crackle of the fire and the rush of wind-driven snow against the rooftop broke the silence.

He looked down at her with such intensity, such need, such tenderness, that any remnant of hesitation faded.

I love you, Ben. The thought came out of nowhere, catching her unaware.

And then she stepped into his arms.

If she'd had a choice, they might have been snowbound for a week. But up here in the mountains, road crews were well prepared for two feet of snow, and the road leading up to Joanna's drive was open by noon the next day. Even with that quick attention, there'd been enough time to find out things about Ben that she hadn't expected.

Once, she'd thought him just another footloose, uneducated cowboy, but he'd surprised her at every turn. Who would have guessed that he'd have such a keen intellect, or be so competitive at chess? After the start of their first match on Sunday night—when she'd patiently explained the rules and coached his first moves—she'd looked up to see laughter in his eyes, and a smile playing at the corners of his sensual mouth. Then he'd beaten her two out of three times.

She'd discovered that one night with him just wasn't enough.

The following week passed in a blur of heavy scheduling at the clinic, and evenings spent with Ben on moonlight rides up into the mountains, dinners at the Silver Eagle, dancing at the Legion…but the best evenings were spent in the warm, flickering light of her fireplace with mugs of hot chocolate and Moose curled up at their feet.

Now, at noon on Thanksgiving Day, Joanna arrived at Shadow Creek with a sense of anticipation.

"I'm so glad you could join us, dear," Sadie exclaimed, reaching out to envelop Joanna in a hug. "You're always welcome here."

Joanna stepped into the kitchen and took a deep breath. "There's nothing like the aroma of roast turkey and gravy. This all smells so wonderful!"

"Nearly ready, too. We'll be eating in a few minutes."

"I'm just sorry I couldn't get here sooner to help. I needed to attend an emergency C-section at noon."

"We had lots of help," Sadie called briskly over her shoulder as she headed to the stove. "Thanks to Dylan and Gina."

At the kitchen counter, Dylan stood mashing a big pot of potatoes. "I never knew this was so much work," he grumbled. "Three of us all day! At home, my dad and I just go *out*."

His expression didn't match his words, Joanna noted with surprise. The surly jut of his chin was gone, and he'd lost most of that rebellious tone in his voice.

Sadie gave Joanna a satisfied look. "He's finally starting to come around," she said in a low voice. "I think it was Max who did it—that little girl sure did take a shine to him. He's been helping Ben with one of the colts, too, and

Ben says he's got real talent. Hearing lots of praise can do a lot for a young fella's outlook.''

Gina popped in the doorway, with Max on her hip, her face flushed. ''Hi, Joanna. My girls and I just played a game of Twister. I need to help Sadie with the gravy—could you take Max for a bit? She's been crawling all over the place, and now the girls are out playing Old Maid with Ben and their dad.''

Joanna held out her arms for the squirming baby. ''How's it going with Zach?'' she asked in a low voice.

Gina glanced over her shoulder toward the door to the living room, then moved to the stove and began whisking the drippings and flour with a vengeance. ''Fair. He's had a few shorter runs, but mostly he's at our place. And he did go out with me on a maternity call one night—when he was worried about the weather.''

''That's promising, isn't it?''

''I guess. But you know what? I was on the verge of quitting my job just to make peace with him, and then I decided that it just wasn't fair.''

''So…''

''I told him that the arguing and tension is hard on the girls, and that I've spent way too much time feeling guilty, and worrying, and trying to make amends.''

''You gave him an ultimatum?''

''Yes, I guess I did.'' Gina smiled sadly. ''I told him that I wanted to settle this before December, so we wouldn't be arguing clear through Christmas.''

Sadie bustled past carrying the golden-brown turkey on a platter, its mouthwatering aroma in her wake.

''Whoa!'' Gina took the heavy load out of Sadie's arms. ''I'll take this. It's a twenty-five-pounder,'' she explained to Joanna as she carried it into the dining room. ''Sadie wanted to make sure we had some leftovers this year.''

Ten minutes later, the dining-room table was laden with a bountiful Thanksgiving feast, and everyone had arrived.

Gina and her little girls, and Zach—who sat across from them with a pensive expression in his eyes. Rafe and his father, Felipe, who bantered with Sadie and brought a blush to her wrinkled cheeks. Dylan, whose usual cocky attitude had indeed faded into something more subdued. Was he just tired, or could he be missing his father on this traditional family holiday?

Ben sat at the head of the table, flanked by Sadie and Joanna, and everyone joined hands as they recited a simple table prayer.

As Ben carved the turkey, Sadie helped fill the serving platter. Joanna watched and felt suddenly melancholy as the heaping bowls of mashed potatoes, sweet potatoes, salads and green-bean casserole were passed, followed by fluffy homemade rolls, relishes and even more side dishes.

Ben's warm hand clasped hers beneath the table. "I'm glad you joined us after all," he said, the laugh lines at the corners of his eyes deepening. "We were going to send a posse after you if you'd decided not to come."

Just his touch, or the sound of his deep voice had the power to heat her blood and spur visions of their time together this past week. Sensual, seductive, powerful—he was also the most tender man she'd ever met, and each memory of him would stay with her for a lifetime. But she shouldn't have come here for Thanksgiving dinner.

Conversation ebbed and flowed between these people who had known each other for a lifetime, and would know each other until the day they died. Joanna caught Dylan's eye and wondered if he felt the same way. These hours were pleasure, but they were also just temporary. A brief glimpse of a Norman Rockwell sort of family life that she'd probably never have.

She smiled across the table at Dylan and he smiled tentatively in return, and she could only wonder what his holidays were like with just his father for company.

A lot like mine, probably. Nice restaurants…good service…and an empty house when you go home. No leftovers, either, to extend the pleasurable holiday spirit another few days.

As wonderful as these months had been, she had that same solitude to look forward to when she moved back to California.

A life that would seem far lonelier when she left Ben Carson behind.

CHAPTER SIXTEEN

"SO, HOW ARE YOU feeling today?" Gina said to the woman seated in the chair across from her. Mary Davidson, due in January, was one of her favorite patients, and had enjoyed a relatively easy pregnancy thus far. "Any concerns you'd like to discuss?"

"Just that yesterday's turkey dinner made me feel as if I ought to deliver early!"

The pager at her hip buzzed. Lifting it, she felt a flicker of surprise as she read the number. *Home?* The girls and Max were there with Sue Ellen, but none of them were to call unless there was a problem. If Max was getting sick again...

"Excuse me, Mary. I need to make a quick call. I'll be back in a minute."

"Don't worry about it." Mary nodded toward the little girl and picked up a children's book from the end table by her chair. "I'll just read Sammy a few stories."

Gina hurried across the hall and slipped into the midwives' office, shutting the door behind her. Zach, to her surprise, picked up on the second ring. "I thought you were going on a run to Denver today."

Silence stretched between them, uneasy and laden with too many things that they hadn't dared say to one another since their last argument before Thanksgiving. Like tightrope walkers, they eased through the days, afraid to take a misstep.

"I can't," he said finally. "I started, but I had to come back."

"Why?"

"I need to talk to you."

"I'm working, Zach. I've got clients booked until noon."

"Can you come home for lunch?"

Sue Ellen would be there. And though she was a dependable baby-sitter, she would also be listening. "Can you come here? We could talk in my car. Or we could drive over to the Sunflower."

"I'll be there at noon."

Throughout the morning, Zach's words pounded like a drumbeat in her head. *I need to talk to you. I need to talk to you.*

By the time she stepped out of the door at noon, her stomach was in knots and she had a headache two aspirin hadn't cured. For all her firm convictions, there was a lot of emotion tied up here. The love that she'd felt for Zach for years. The children they shared. None of this was going to be easy.

He was waiting for her, leaning against the door of his silver Dodge pickup, his arms folded and his handsome face a pale mask that probably mirrored her own.

Inside the truck, he offered her a takeout bag from the Sunshine. "Veggie burger and milk, is that okay?"

Nodding, she accepted the bag but held it in both hands, unable to think about eating. "What's this about?"

"Us."

Gina took a steadying breath and wished she could slow her pounding heart. "And?"

He set his unopened burger on the seat of the truck and draped a wrist over the steering wheel, his gaze fastened on something outside. "I haven't been happy."

"Well, I haven't been happy, either. It isn't right for you to think that only your opinion counts and that I don't have equal rights in this relationship."

"I know."

She silently steeled herself for the inevitable. She'd gained strength over the past months, and no matter what he said, she could handle this and move on.

Reaching over to take her hand, he gave a rueful shake of his head. "Male pride runs pretty deep, I guess. I wanted to be the provider. To have you home with the kids. I didn't want things to change." He turned her hand over and traced the lines on her palm. "When I went out on that call with you during the snowstorm I saw what you do, how much you help these people. How much," he added in a lower tone, "you love what you do."

She silently watched him struggle for words as his emotions played across his face.

"I-it scared me, Gina. That this all mattered so much. What was left for me and the kids?"

"I never stopped loving you all. I never stopped doing everything I could for you."

"I know." He lifted her hand to his mouth and kissed her fingertips. "I just had some growing up to do, I guess. I couldn't leave town today without telling you that. I want us to stay together, Gina. I promise things will be better."

The sleepless nights and endless days she'd endured melted away as she looked into his eyes and saw that he'd suffered just as much as she had, and that he meant what he said.

"To new beginnings," she whispered, moving over to capture his mouth with a kiss.

He eased from behind the steering wheel. His arms were trembling when he wrapped them around her. "New beginnings."

And then he kissed her until she melted beneath his touch.

DURING THE DAY, when he was saddling, working and cooling out one horse after another, Ben thought of Joanna. At night, he tried to be with her whenever he could. He delighted in her intelligence, her radiant smile. She was everything he could ever want.

And she was slipping away.

He sensed it in the way she moved, in the brief hesitation when he left her at night. It was there, in the shadows in her eyes, and in the way she held him after they'd made love.

And he didn't know what to do about it. When he talked about the future, she changed the subject. When he tried to get her to talk about her feelings, she turned away. Frustrated, edgy, he'd hung around the ranch tonight later than usual, working a couple of three-year-old colts up in the snow-covered foothills and then riding out to check cattle when he knew Rafe had done it earlier.

It was after dark—he'd just unsaddled his old gelding—when the cell phone at his hip rang. *Another customer,* he muttered to himself. The last thing he wanted to do was talk business. Most of his customers liked to settle into interminable conversations about their horses, about the market, about who was leading in the standings on the show circuit. Usually he could handle it. Today—

Just the same, he grabbed the phone and read the caller ID. *Arroyo County Hospital.*

He hit the answer button on the fourth ring.

"Hey, Ben." Dr. Woodgrove's voice boomed through the receiver. "I've got some news for you—don't know if it's what you want to hear or not."

Max. "The DNA results?"

"That's right. I made a note to myself to call the lab today, since they screwed up last time. You'll be getting the report in a day or so."

His heart stilled. "And?"

"Positive." Woodgrove hesitated. "The child is yours."

He'd hoped. He'd figured she had to be. But until now, doubt had curled through him at odd moments, gripping his insides as he imagined what it would be like to see Holly take Max away and never return. With a shout of joy, he hurled the phone in the air and caught it on its way down. "You're sure? Absolutely sure?"

"This is what you *want?*"

At the hint of disbelief in Woodgrove's voice, Ben laughed aloud. "This is the best news I've had. Ever."

After ending the connection, Ben jogged to the house.

Sadie was asleep in front of the television. Gina had taken Max into town to buy her some clothes. Dylan, he remembered belatedly, had stayed after school for pizza and a game at the teen center. Ben's footsteps on the tile floors echoed through the emptiness of the rambling adobe.

Frustrated, he grabbed the keys for the truck and took off. By the time he hit the highway he'd started singing along with the radio and tapping out the beat with his thumbs on the steering wheel. Joanna would share his joy, he knew.

Of all people, she would know just how much this meant.

SHE DIDN'T ANSWER the door.

He let himself in, calling her name, and made a quick search of the place before going outside to stand on the porch. Moonlight changed the snowy meadow into a sea of sparkling white sequins, and threw dark, jagged shadows from the base of the pine trees at its perimeter. Overhead, stars blanketed the heavens.

From some distant peak came the lonesome call of a wolf howling at the moon. A host of juvenile voices joined in, and then another pack answered with yips and howls of its own. Joanna's SUV waited in its usual parking spot near the cabin.

Turning his collar up against the icy breeze coming over the mountains, he headed for the barn, though no footstep marked the path. *She hasn't come this way recently,* he realized with growing concern. *Where the hell can she be?*

Inside the barn, he flipped on the single light that hung in the center of the small building between the two box stalls and the open area used for hay.

Galahad nickered softly and moved to the front of his stall to hang his head over the half door, blinking at the unexpected light.

If not for that massive white dog of hers, he wouldn't have seen Joanna sitting in the shadows, up on the hay bales, with Moose curled at her side.

"Joanna?"

The dog raised its head and looked down at him but didn't stir.

"Joanna." He scaled the six-bale height to where she'd curled up in the shelter of higher bales, her feet tucked beneath her. "Honey—are you okay?"

Her eyes fluttered open, though he couldn't read her expression in the shadows. "What are you doing here?"

"Trying to find you." He gave her an affectionate nudge with his shoulder. "Decided you'd sleep out here tonight?"

"No…"

Something wasn't right. "Let's go up to the cabin and make some coffee."

Uncurling from her nest in the hay, she moved as if she'd sat there far too long. He took her arm when they stepped outside, where his own tracks were already obliterated by the blowing snow. Moose, apparently sensing something was wrong, followed with his head and tail low.

"You didn't call, so I didn't think you were coming," she said as they trudged through the drifts. After another few steps, she pulled to a halt and stared up at him, her eyes empty and her voice devoid of emotion. "It's okay—you don't need to when you're busy."

With sudden clarity, he recalled another conversation they'd had. "This was the night," he said softly. "The night your son was born."

"Yes."

"Oh, honey. I'm so sorry." He reached for her, wanting to provide comfort, but she pulled away, her spine stiff and erect.

"It's all right. I'm fine."

He hooked his arm in hers and started again toward the cabin. "And that's why you were sitting out in a dark barn at night? Because you're *fine?*"

She didn't answer until they reached the cabin door. "I went out to do chores, and just sat there watching Galahad eat. No big deal."

He reached around her and opened the door. "Let's go in and have a cup of coffee."

"No—"

He cradled her face in both hands. "Please."

After a long hesitation, she shrugged and waved him inside. This time, the cabin was snug and warm, but he went to the fireplace and started a fire all the same. By the time he had it going, she'd come from the kitchen with two steaming mugs of coffee.

"You didn't tell me your news," she said as she handed him one and sank into the soft leather sofa with her own cup cradled in both hands.

He'd come to her intending to share his joy. Now, bringing good news about his daughter while Joanna was mourning the anniversary of her son's death seemed cruel.

"Nothing, really," he hedged, easing down onto the sofa next to her and beckoning her into his arms.

"The DNA test results were due today." Her mouth

curved into a smile that didn't reach her eyes. "I'll bet they were positive."

He nodded, his joy tempered by her obvious pain. "Life is strange, isn't it? And so unfair. I've just gained a daughter, but your son was taken away."

"I'll never understand," she whispered.

They watched the fire burn down to embers. When the last ember died, Ben shifted his weight, expecting to see that Joanna had fallen asleep.

Instead, she met his gaze with a steady one of her own. "Please, stay with me," she whispered. "I'd...rather not be alone."

And then she led him to her bedroom and shut the door.

STUART RUBBED the back of his neck as he shuffled through the papers on his desk, then flipped on his computer to check the stock market. While waiting for it to boot up, he surveyed his office with a deep sense of satisfaction.

He'd done pretty damn well on his own. There were people who thought he'd married into money and had had an easy ride, but everything he had, he'd earned himself. Fiona's father had never parted with a single dime to help. Mahogany furniture. Lush, pearl-gray carpet. Original native art on the walls. A pretty, young secretary—who was home with the flu today—at the front desk. Every trapping of success.

The bastard hadn't even used Stuart as his financial planner, which would have been a visible show of support and might have brought in a number of the old man's rich friends.

If that had happened, maybe Stuart wouldn't have had to finance this place on credit. Obvious success, after all, was a reassuring thing to potential clients. Who would trust an adviser who drove a battered car and worked out of some hole-in-the-wall?

Today his crisply pressed shirt was already plastered to the cold sweat on his back despite the raw winter wind outside and the sixty-five-degree setting on the thermostat.

During Paul's last visit to Enchantment, Stuart had managed to avoid him on the pretext of going out of town for a business seminar in Tucson, but the man's phone calls were becoming increasingly insistent and finally Paul had announced that he would be flying in on the morning of the nineteenth. He'd said, in no uncertain terms, that he intended to stop at Stuart's office for a serious discussion regarding their investments. *Just another week to go.*

Stuart glanced up at the clock for the fourth time in five minutes, then shoved away from his desk and strode to the front door to peer outside. Anxiety gnawed at his gut as he contemplated just how far he was from making those investments pay off.

But if everything went to hell, he did have that nice little nest egg in an offshore account, courtesy of Paul's lack of attention to details early on....

And then he saw Fiona walk past.

She was due the middle of January and already had the awkward walk and heavily rounded belly. He hadn't wanted another kid, but she'd pleaded...and one day, she just *happened* to turn up pregnant, claiming that her birth control pills must have "failed." He was still angry at her deception.

Another woman crossed the street and stopped Fiona just beyond the edge of the building. Curious, Stuart scraped at the frost on the window for a better view.

It was that damn doctor...and she seemed to have a hell of a lot to say, because the two of them stood talking for three minutes. Four. *Five.*

With every minute, Stuart's blood pressure rose and his anger grew. He'd seen the censure in that woman's eyes.

He'd *heard* the doc discuss "abuse" with Fiona, and urge her to get help. *Help,* for God's sake!

Even now, fury licked through his veins at such preposterous accusations. And fear lingered there, too, because if Fiona's father got wind of such lies…

It was time, he realized, for Fiona to remember who was boss. Maybe Stuart couldn't get his own hands on her money—her father had auditors check every penny annually—but he could sure control the way she used it.

He smiled to himself as he opened the front door of his office and called Fiona's name.

Startled, she whipped her head around to stare at him, then she turned to the doc and apparently said hasty goodbyes.

He should have done this before, really. It was so perfect. Fiona would receive proper warning, that nosey doctor would bear the blame, and Lydia Kane would face financial hardship, all with a few strokes of Stuart's pen.

LYDIA'S FACE WAS A GRIM, pale mask as she spoke quietly to Parker Reynolds and Kim Sherman outside Kim's office on Friday morning.

Waiting for her next patient to corral her toddler, Gina stood near the receptionist's desk and watched the three from the corner of her eye. Their voices were low, strained.

By the time mother and child made it up to the receptionist's desk, Parker had gone into his office, but Gina still caught the words *funding, this morning,* and *Pennington* as she led her patient to an exam room.

Funding concerns sounded bad. Really bad, for The Birth Place staff and patients. Gina was still at thirty-six hours a week, but she and Zach were together now and they could survive if her hours were cut. Some of the other employees would be in serious trouble, though.

In the exam room, the patient shooed her two-year-old

into the corner where an overflowing basket of toys would offer some distraction as they talked.

Gina consulted the folder in her hands. "Twenty-eight weeks along, already. How are you feeling?"

"Better. I didn't know morning sickness could last so long, but I think it's almost over now." The woman gave her son a quick glance, then lowered her voice. "Tell me something—I've been so worried."

Frowning, Gina glanced at the last progress notes in the chart, wondering if she'd missed something important. "It looks like you've had a very healthy pregnancy so far. What's the problem?"

"I keep hearing about troubles here—this place will still be open when I deliver, won't it?" She bit her lip. "I just don't know what I'd do, otherwise—my car isn't the best, and I know all of you. It would be hard going someplace else."

Gina gave her arm a reassuring pat. "Of course we'll be here. The Birth Place will be in operation when your grandchildren need it. Whatever you've heard is just gossip and nothing more."

But long after the woman left, Gina stared after her and wondered if the rumors were true.

CHAPTER SEVENTEEN

HE'D KNOWN THIS DAY might arrive. He'd prepared for it, deciding on what he'd say and how he would say it. But when a gray Focus rental tooled up the lane and parked at the tips of his boots, Ben's throat turned dry and he could only stare as a leggy brunette climbed out, fluffed her heavy mass of hair and gave him an uncertain smile.

"Hi, Ben." Her voice was softer, more breathy than he remembered, though maybe she was still recovering from those broken ribs. "It's…um…been a long time."

She wore dangly silver and turquoise earrings with a matching silver squash-blossom necklace, and one hell of a lot of makeup. Her coral-tipped nails were way too long for handling a baby. Fancy overlay western boots, skintight jeans and body-hugging denim jacket completed the picture of a city girl who'd decided to play dress-up for a trip out West.

"Holly." He tried to remember being with this woman. Tried to remember what she'd been like, but could only recall vague images…and absolutely no emotional attachment at all.

He bent to peer into her car, expecting to find her new boyfriend, but saw only fast-food wrappers on the front seat and two pieces of luggage in the rear.

Favoring her left ankle, she moved forward with a tentative smile and offered her hand. "It's good to see you again."

He forced his mouth into a pleasant smile. "You, too. We haven't spoken since…"

"That sale in Houston." A faint blush crept up her cheeks.

"It's been a long time."

"Why didn't you tell me about Max?"

Her eyes filled with confusion. "Who?"

"The baby." He reined in his impatience. "We've been calling her Max."

"I couldn't." She studied the tips of her turquoise boots. "Lost your number."

She was a terrible liar. From the sulky defiance in her voice, he could well imagine her deciding she wanted a baby, and finding an expedient way to achieve her goal. "I wish I'd known, Holly."

"I…um…finally did come across your number. I thought about calling." Her chin lifted. "But by then it just seemed sort of, you know, late to be announcing something like that."

"I would have helped you out. I could have been a part of Max's life from the start."

Her chin lifted a notch higher. "I didn't need any money, or anything." She met his eyes for a split second, then gave the barns and house a speculative glance. "Really nice place you have here."

"You'll stay with us, won't you? We have a guest room, and it's quite a drive back to Enchantment."

"You said 'we.'" She looked at him uncertainly. "Are you *married?*"

"No. But my aunt and a nephew live here, plus a hired hand."

"Guess a baby would be a big surprise if you were married, right?" She chuckled. "Though I suppose she was anyway."

Holly was probably in her late twenties, but she didn't

seem to have a clue regarding the enormity of what she'e done—keeping the baby a secret, then dropping her of with total strangers.

"Before we go in...I need to ask what your plans are.'

"I can stay overnight. After that I'm heading back to th airport in Albuquerque, I guess," she said breezily as sh retrieved the luggage from her car and handed him th larger piece. "Thanks for the hospitality."

Panic rippled through him at the thought of how easil she could disappear. The investigator he'd hired hadn' even come close to finding her. "What are your plans be yond that?"

"I hope you're not going to get all huffy about watchin; my kid for a while. I've had her all the rest of the time.'

She hasn't even asked about where the baby is—or hov she's been during the past few months. The thought sen warnings flashing through his thoughts. Would she mak sure Max had loving baby-sitters? Would she care enoug to monitor Max's health?

"It was great having the baby here," he said firmly "Are you settled somewhere in California now? Do yo have a job?" At her frown, he added, "I'd like to keep i touch."

"I've been laid up with these ribs and my ankle. Whe I get back I'll start hunting, I guess. My boyfriend say he's got some connections."

"What about Max? It sounds as though—" he hesitatec searching for the right words "—you enjoy a pretty excit ing life. Does she tie you down?"

"She's my daughter. That's why I'm here."

Not exactly the declaration of motherly love he'd hope for, but it wasn't a hint that Holly would easily give he up, either.

At the house, Ben ushered her inside and made intro ductions. Sadie paled and reached out to steady herself wit a hand on the edge of the sink. Dylan's eyes grew round and his cheeks reddened as he gave her a head-to-toe glance. He stammered out a feeble "Hi."

Joanna stared for a split second, then flushed. "It's so nice to meet you, Holly. I was just leaving, but I hope we'll have a chance to visit sometime. I…just need to say goodbye, and then I'll be going."

She disappeared toward Max's room and returned a few minutes later, her face tense and eyes suspiciously bright. With a quick wave, she fled out the door.

"Well," Holly said brightly into the stunned silence of the kitchen. "Nice to meet you all. Where's the kid?"

JOANNA MOVED through the next few days like a robot, devoting every available moment to her work at the clinic and her classes at The Birth Place.

The classes were going well, thank goodness. Val Dodsen had been to every one of them, and had shown real interest in learning to care for her daughter. Now she brought Shanna into the supervised playroom, during class time, clean and well dressed, and was showing much more open affection toward the little girl…in no small part due to the effective parenting modeling of the woman who was there to provide the child care.

Still, despite the long hours and hard work, Joanna's thoughts often strayed to Ben. *If he wants to talk to me, he'll call.* But now it was already Friday afternoon, and he hadn't. And why would he? He'd had an affair with Holly and she'd borne his child. And she was hot, hot, hot, if Dylan's response was any clue.

Joanna swiveled her office chair to stare out at the snowy bluffs behind the clinic and felt her eyes burn. Had Holly decided to take Max? The poor thing wouldn't understand, first temporarily losing her mother, and then being taken away from people she'd come to know over the past few months. What kind of stress was that to inflict on such a sweet little girl?

Maybe Holly has already left with the baby.

The thought filled Joanna's chest with a heavy, aching sense of loss.

Or maybe Ben and Holly are trying to build their old relationship into something much more, for Max's sake. With Ben's sense of honor and responsibility, it was certainly a strong possibility.

The thought blindsided her. Left her feeling impossibly empty. For weeks she'd tried to avoid becoming attached to Max and Ben. But of course that hadn't worked. Not with Max's beautiful dark curls and trusting hazel eyes…and despite her firm intentions, Joanna's feelings for Ben had grown far beyond those of simple friendship.

In the dark of night, when she was alone with her thoughts, she'd imagined staying here for a lifetime. Growing old in his arms, in this small town, where people knew each other. Watched out for each other.

Where she and Ben, God willing, might even be lucky enough to adopt brothers and sisters for Max, rather than risk the kind of tragedy she'd faced when Hunter had died.

At a knock on the door, she swiveled back and found Ben standing in the doorway, one shoulder leaning against the frame and his Stetson in one hand at his side.

"Where's Max?" Joanna asked. Afraid of the answer, she heard her own heart beating. Felt time slow until each tick of the second hand on the wall clock barely moved.

He walked in and settled in a chair facing her desk, crossing one boot over the opposite knee. He looked as if he hadn't slept in days.

Because he'd been with Holly?

"Holly is out shopping. Gina's baby-sitter has Max."

"The *baby-sitter?*"

"Yeah. Holly is some mom, huh?" He gave a disgusted

snort. "I had horses to work every day this week—three are going to a sale next weekend, and an owner is coming to pick up the fourth tomorrow. When I can't watch Max, Holly has her with the sitter."

Hope flared in Joanna's heart. "And the future?"

"Holly changed her airline tickets to next Tuesday. She wants to get back to her boyfriend in time for Christmas. And," he added heavily, "she says she's planning to take Max."

The hope faded to ashes. "You've told her about the DNA?"

"She pointed out that in a court of law, biological fathers lose all the time. Especially if they're single. More so if there's been no contact since birth, and the mother has had custodial care."

Joanna leaned forward, crossing her arms on her desk. "But you can fight that. Anyone around here would testify to what a great father you've been."

"Yeah. I can, and I will. Max deserves better than a mother like Holly. But my lawyer says these things can take a year or more, and even if I win, the decision can be contested."

"A long, hard battle."

He sighed, and rose to his feet. "I just thought you'd want to know why I haven't called…it's all just been so…"

"I know." So unfair. So utterly unfair. He'd been wonderful with Max, caring and loving, and he deserved more than this. "Wait," she called out as he walked out the door.

Her mind raced through a dozen possibilities. Past the fact that he didn't love her, that she had a golden career waiting in California, that maybe her own feelings were simply…infatuation.

He turned in the doorway and looked back at her, his eyes bleak.

"I know this sounds crazy. But maybe it would help— and God knows, Max belongs with you. We could tip the legal tables in your favor."

"I'm not going to attack Holly's character in court, if that's what you mean."

"Nope." Joanna stood and crossed the room, then gave him what she hoped was a jaunty smile. "Ben Carson, how would you like a wife?"

"PERFECT, isn't it?" Stepping up to the guardrail edging the parking area of the scenic overlook, Stuart gestured across the deep ravine at his feet.

The view was a breathtaking kaleidoscope of rocky buttes, jagged spires, towering cliffs, snow-frosted pines. Several miles away, on the opposite side of the ravine, the Sangre de Cristo Mountains towered above the pine log buildings comprising Silver Butte Resort. The roofs gleamed in the last rays of Saturday's sunshine slipping behind the hills to the west.

"When Angel's Gate opens, we should attract a lot of overflow skiers," he continued, trying to curb the desperation in his voice. "We can undercut their rates and hit the ski magazines with an advertising blitz. A flashy Web site ought to help, too. I know we'll make a killing on this deal."

"I still need to sell out, Stuart." Paul tossed his car keys on the front seat of his Lexus and joined Stuart at the wall. "You've got the money to do it—I've studied those reports of yours, and we've done well in the market. You could own it all, do what you want. What do you say?" He waved a hand toward his car. "I brought my documents along so we can get started."

Still fit, tanned and mentally sharp at the age of seventy, the retired dentist had had money to burn and a penchant for buying investment properties in the mountains when he'd first approached Stuart five years ago. Now, he had a wife battling cancer and a son battling an addiction to methamphetamines.

His worries over medical bills and treatment centers for the two of them couldn't have come at a worse time.

"I think you're jumping the gun a little here, Paul. Another year and Silver Butte will be worth three times what it is right now." Nausea coiled through Stuart's stomach. "And the Elk Valley Lodge project—"

A stiff breeze ruffled his white hair as Paul held out both hands, palm up. An embarrassed smile creased his windreddened cheeks. "I know we had plans. Lots of plans. I figured you and I would end up being one of the strongest resort corporations this side of the Mississippi."

"We can still do that. Just give me another month, Paul. *Please.* I'll be gone next week because of Christmas, but after that I can put together some more figures."

"Thanks for the tour today, but my mind is set." The amiable light in the older man's eyes hardened. "I need audits done on our projects, and real-estate evaluations done on the properties. If you want to buy me out, I'll be happy to get our lawyers together and make a deal."

If not for you, I wouldn't have ever gotten in so deep. I wouldn't have taken the chances I did. The future opened before Stuart—a chasm of debt, of potential legal problems. Once Paul delved too deeply into their jointly held assets and investments, there would be hell to pay.

Stuart had only planned to borrow some of it, for a while, but he knew what Paul would say. What the lawyers would say.

Fraud was such an ugly word.

"Of course. I understand completely," Stuart murmured.

He'd chosen this scenic view of Silver Butte with care. Crooked Peak Road was plowed infrequently over the winter. It led up into the most remote area of the mountains and ended at a small parking area used only by summer backpackers. Those wanting lodging or winter sports took a different route, the one leading past Silver Butte and on to the Angel's Gate construction site.

He'd chosen the site just in case—and it was perfect.

Doubling over, he wrapped his arms around his middle and moaned. And hoped like hell he remembered the right symptoms.

"What is it? Your heart?" Paul moved closer and reached for Stuart's arm, his voice filled with concern. "Do you carry anything?"

Stuart staggered backward a step. Then another. "N-nitroglycerin. M-my back pocket."

It was all so easy.

One moment, he faced the loss of his home. His future. Complete humiliation. The next, a troublesome old man was hurtling over the edge of the ravine and Stuart suddenly had a far brighter future.

It took only a few minutes to don a pair of gloves. and search the Lexus. He removed Paul's briefcase and other potentially incriminating items, then shifted the car into gear and sent it over the edge. The car bounced end over end against rugged boulders on the way down and disappeared into a heavy stand of pines far, far below.

A passing hiker—or an investigator—might easily assume that the old man had driven it over the edge and had been ejected from the car on its way down.

Perfect.

There might be inquiries, of course. Enough people knew about their association that Stuart would surely be questioned regarding Paul's visit to Enchantment. And later, there would be the legal complications of dealing with the partnership.

But anyone could see that an old man facing his wife's cancer and his son's addiction might contemplate suicide, and this would buy Stuart the time he needed. Satisfied, he scanned the area for any evidence, then he backed his own car out of the lot and started down the highway to Enchantment.

It took a full ten minutes before the enormity of what he'd done hit him. Anxiety clawed at his stomach as he floored the accelerator and darted a nervous glance at the rearview mirror. People knew that he and Paul were partners. There'd be questions if Paul's body was ever found.

But Fiona was going to give Stuart any alibi he needed—she wouldn't dare do otherwise. He just had to hope like hell that no one had seen him on this road.

"GALAHAD AND MOOSE are *where?*" Joanna dropped her face into one hand as she wrote down the address and directions. "They haven't gone missing in ages. Why now? I have a date in an hour!"

The deputy on the line snorted. "Some Saturday night, eh? Maybe your *date* would like to play cowboy and help you round them up? These people were plain scared of that ole horse of yours. One of these times, somebody is gonna get hurt and sue."

Within fifteen minutes of ending the phone call, she'd changed from a silk dress and a strand of pearls into jeans and a sweater, hitched up the trailer—something she could now manage in five minutes—and skirted the north edge of town. The road narrowed, curved up two hairpin curves, then straightened across an open meadow.

Dusk was fading to darkness, without even a glimmer of moonlight slipping through the heavily overcast sky. *More snow,* she sighed. More and more and more…

Suddenly from an unseen curve just ahead, wildly swinging headlights blazed into view. The car fishtailed and skidded sideways toward her—a flash of silver—a vague glimpse of a man's pasty face. Shock and terror slammed through her as she clutched her steering wheel and waited for the impact. But somehow the vehicle's tires gained enough purchase for it to sway back into its own lane.

It disappeared around the next curve, leaving her alone on the road once again.

She feathered her own brakes and pulled to a halt at the side of the road. Her heart still in her throat, she rested her forehead on the steering wheel, waiting for her pulse to slow and her stomach to finally settle into place. *So close.* A drunk, maybe? The guy was definitely out of control.

A half mile up the road she found Pinion Lane and turned in at the first house, where a police cruiser was still in the yard. As soon as she pulled to a stop in the driveway, Miguel Eiden stepped out of the house with a middle-aged man and two young boys close on his heels.

"Your horse and dog are tied to some trees in the yard," Eiden said. "They've given these people quite a scare."

"We looked out the window," the tallest boy exclaimed. "It was like, way cool! We saw this white thing floating in the air, taller than any human, and it had these glowing, shiny eyes…like *aliens* looking in our windows!"

"'Bout scared my wife to death," the home owner growled. "She went to see what the boys were up to, and that scream of hers nearly took off the roof."

"It was your horse," Eiden said curtly. "He was peering through their windows. They saw his white blaze floating about six feet from the ground. Fred ran to get his shotgun, and you're just lucky he didn't blow Galahad's head off."

"*And* his eyes were really shiny! He—"

"He was watching TV!" The younger boy's voice rose with amazement. "He was watching right through the window!"

"And he was standing," the man snapped, "on my wife's roses. They're all covered up for winter, so I sure don't know what kind of damage there'll be."

Another car pulled in to the driveway and parked next to Joanna's truck. "Hey, we meet again, Doc," the driver called out as he climbed from his vehicle. He shouldered a camera case and strode through the snow to stand at Joanna's side.

"It's been a slow news day, so I've come to check out the aliens." He grinned at her. "The last photo got picked up on the AP wire. This ought to be guaranteed. If you and that horse keep this up, you'll put Enchantment on the map."

CHAPTER EIGHTEEN

WHEN JOANNA CALLED to cancel their dinner plans, Ben's first thought was that she'd had serious second thoughts about her unexpected proposal the night before. When he found out she was on the way home with that crazy horse and dog of hers after yet another one of their adventures, he'd laughed aloud…with unexpected relief.

Not that he was even considering her offer.

Now, because she'd been delayed, they'd skipped the candlelit supper at the Silver Eagle, and were sitting in a secluded booth at the Sunflower, listening to old-time country rock on the jukebox and eating burgers with fries. And Ben was finding that Joanna didn't easily give up on her ideas.

"It makes sense," she said flatly, looking him straight in the eye.

"No, it doesn't. Marriage is supposed to be till-death-do-us-part, not a *convenience*."

"If both of us understand the situation, what does it matter? We can stay married until you've had Max for a year. That way you could easily show a judge that you're able to provide a loving, stable home."

"Stable. As in…temporary as hell?"

"A year," she retorted, "is longer than some real marriages last. But this would be better for Max because we wouldn't have all the bickering that goes on in a failing marriage."

"It's still a lie. What if you find someone else you really

care for?'' He'd started the question, half teasing, but the thought fell like an anvil to the pit of his stomach. If some other guy even tried to lay a hand on her—

''I won't find someone else,'' she said firmly, dismissing the idea with a casual flip of her hand. ''I'm not looking. But if you do, we could dissolve our bargain. In the meantime, we could stay at your place or mine, to make sure it all seemed real. Dr. Davis has called a couple times, wanting me to stay on after he comes back to town, so I'd still have a job.''

Ben enjoyed being with her. He enjoyed her company, her conversation, her dedication to her patients. There was a whole hell of a lot more that he enjoyed, too, and he could imagine what it would be like to have her in his life permanently. A temporary arrangement could lead to a lifetime....

But if she could so casually dismiss what they had— what he'd *thought* they had between them, he'd probably been traveling down the road to major disappointment. Alone.

''I appreciate your offer, Joanna.''

''Then it's a go?''

''It's a let's-think-about-it.'' Softening the sharp edge in his voice with a belated smile, he glanced at his watch, then reached for the wallet in his hip pocket and tossed two tens on the table. ''Almost midnight. They close in a few minutes.''

''Sooo…are you coming over?''

It's what he would have done any other time, and the lure was almost irresistible. But spending more time with her right now—especially if he stayed the night—would only make it harder to make the right decision. ''Better not. Rafe is away, so I've got to do all the morning chores myself before church. I'll be up before five.''

Joanna gave him a level look as she shrugged into her heavy down jacket. "That's fine."

But it didn't seem so fine to him as he walked her out to her SUV and watched her drive away. What was better? A relationship—a *marriage*—doomed from the start? Or no relationship at all?

Maybe twelve months with Joanna would be worth the inevitable pain of seeing her leave.

"So WHAT DO YOU THINK?" Ben stepped back and studied the Christmas tree. "Did we cut the right one?"

With a Mannheim Steamroller Christmas CD playing softly in the background, they'd started decorating after Sunday dinner, and now had just finished stringing lights. This year, for the first time since Allie was a toddler, they'd once again placed only the unbreakables on the lower branches.

"It's beautiful," Sadie breathed, nodding her approval. "Best one ever, I'd say."

Dylan gave a nonchalant shrug. "Not bad. We only covered the north pasture. If we'd gone higher..."

For all his efforts at feigning boredom, the boy had been like an exuberant ten-year-old out there—loping his horse from one pine to the next, studying each from every angle. He'd wanted to cut the tree himself, and he dragged it home behind his own horse.

"If we'd gone higher we'd still be out there looking—in the dark." Ben laughed. "What do you say, little one?"

Max stood a couple feet away, gripping the edge of the coffee table in front of the sofa. She grinned up at him. *"Dadadadada."*

Everyone burst into laughter except Holly, who was curled up on the sofa doing her nails.

"Sounds like a thumbs-up to me." Dylan bent to ruffle the baby's soft, dark curls. "Look—she's letting go!"

Her knees wobbling, Max lifted first one hand, then the other from the end of the coffee table. Her eyes widened as she started to sway.

"Come on, baby!" Dylan said, dropping to one knee. "You can do it!"

Holly set aside her bottle of nail polish and leaned forward. "Here, sweetie. Come here."

Max swung her gaze from Holly, to Ben, to Dylan, to Sadie, her eyes rounded, as all of them leaned forward and beckoned to her with outstretched arms and murmurs of encouragement.

"Dadadadada!" She took one step away from the table. Teetered. Then another step, her knees lifting high and stance wide.

"She's walking!" Sadie straightened and clasped her hands in front of her. "In time for her first birthday, too."

The baby chortled, clearly proud of herself as she managed another step. The momentum seemed to get the better of her. One…two more steps, and she fell into Ben's waiting arms. "Da!"

"Guess we know who she likes best," Dylan said, grinning broadly.

"I think I was just en route to the tree." Ben lifted her up to the tree so she could bat at the shiny ornaments. "What do you think, sweetie? Pretty lights?"

Holly settled back on the couch and inspected her nails for any damage. A delicate frown marred her forehead. "She's just going to break them, if you aren't careful," she said without looking up.

"Let's see if you'll walk to Mama now." Ben crossed the room to within a few feet of Holly and carefully set Max on her feet, holding her lightly as she took two steps and collapsed against the sofa.

"Good baby," Holly said. "But I can't pick you up, or you'll have polish all over your clothes."

Sadie cleared her throat. "Well. I'll bring some cocoa out for all of you, and then I'd better start supper. Dylan, would you set the table?"

Holly waited until they left the room. "It's been nice being here this past week. I'll be a little sorry when I get on my plane tomorrow."

Ben had considered a dozen ways to discuss the future. He'd tried starting the conversation at least that many times, wanting to establish his plans to at least share custody with Max. Each time, Holly had skated away from the issue, feigning exhaustion, announcing that she had plans to run into town for shopping, or suddenly offering to help Sadie in the kitchen.

He couldn't imagine a future with Holly in the romantic sense, but losing Max…

"Quit pacing!" Holly snapped her fingers at him—one of her less endearing habits. "This isn't easy for me, you know. Maybe you should just sit down."

He took a chair across from her. "I want you to know—"

"No." She waved away his words with a slash of one hand in the air. "I want *you* to know something. And if I don't get this out right now, I might not be able to."

There were tears sparkling in her eyes, but she didn't seem to notice. "I'm listening," Ben said.

"I…haven't been that great of a mother."

"I'm sure you—"

"*Please.* Let me be honest, here." She tentatively touched one polished fingernail, and held them all out for inspection before folding her hands in her lap. "I wasn't ever planning to tell you about Max. I wanted a baby, and I wanted her for myself. No strings. No complications. I…um…told you I was on birth control when we…um…"

Ben winced. He'd been so drunk that night that he didn't remember much of anything, but given the state of the world these days, he should have been alert enough to use protection no matter what Holly said.

She gave a short laugh. ''I discovered this whole parenting deal is a hell of a lot more responsibility than I figured.''

''I would have paid child support from the very first, Holly. And now, I—''

''Just let me say what I need to say, okay? When I dropped her off, I wasn't coming back. But after I got hurt, I had a lot of time to think. What if you were a real jerk? What if you just gave her away, or something?'' She picked at a piece of lint on her emerald green sweater, not meeting his eyes. ''So as soon as I could, I bought a plane ticket, just to make sure she was okay.''

For all her flashy clothes, overdone makeup, and irresponsibility, he could see true sadness in her eyes now. He wanted to curve an arm around her shoulders. Provide comfort. But that would only complicate things more.

''A-and when I got here, and saw your nice place and pretty girlfriend, I suddenly felt so...so...*jealous.* I was going to take Max with me out of spite.'' Holly's lower lip trembled. ''But you *love* her. You really do—and she already loves you. She'd be better off here, wouldn't she? She was sick a lot, but I never knew just how sick this...this...asthmatic stuff could make her. Your girlfriend is a doctor, so Max should be safer here. Hey—maybe you two will even get married someday. That would be way cool for Max.''

Marriage.

Joanna's generous proposal had seemed so empty, given the circumstances. Especially since the entire conversation made him realize how much he cared for her. What could be better than waking up with Joanna every morning, and going to sleep with her every night? And what could be worse than doing so while knowing that she really didn't love him, and never would?

For Max's sake, he would have done almost anything. But now...

"What do you think?" Holly urged. "I mean, if you don't want the baby..."

"Yes—of course I do."

"I..." Holly swallowed hard. "My boyfriend and I are skiers. We've talked about backpacking through Europe next summer, and maybe checking out some jobs on cruise ships. If you want Max, I think she'd be a lot better off here with you. Permanently."

"You're giving me *custody?*" The shimmer of tears in her eyes told him she wasn't as blasé as she wanted to appear. His next words lodged in his throat. "You understand that...we could work out child support, so you wouldn't have to give her up?"

"I've got until my plane leaves tomorrow afternoon. Call your lawyer and see if we can meet, okay? At least we can get this ball rolling." Her voice broke. "It's the right thing to do. I thought about using an adoption agency, but you're her real dad, and I know you love her. And maybe...someday I can come back to see her?"

"Absolutely." He stepped forward and gave Holly a quick hug, then stepped back with his hands cupping her shoulders. "Max will be loved here, Holly. I swear—she'll have the best childhood I can afford."

"ARE YOU BUSY? There was no one up front...I hope it's okay that I came in."

Joanna looked up from the chart on her desk to see Fiona hovering tentatively in the doorway. "Please, come in."

Well into her eighth month now, her leather coat no longer buttoned in front. But she didn't have the rosy, contented glow of impending motherhood. In fact, her white-knuckled grip on the shoulder strap of her purse and the grim line of her mouth were anything but relaxed.

Joanna gestured toward the chairs that faced her desk. "Since Christmas is only three days away, we didn't schedule the last hour of appointments today. I figured Eve and Nicki would have shopping to do in town before the stores close."

"I can just stay for a minute. I told Stuart that I needed to drop off some insurance forms today—he's waiting out in the car."

Fiona shut the door behind her, then eased her bulk carefully into a chair. "I've been such a fool. Such a complete and utter fool. You tried to warn me, but I just ignored you." She dabbed furiously at her eyes with a crumpled tissue.

Joanna picked up a box of tissues from the credenza behind her desk and handed them to Fiona, then settled back in her own chair. "What's wrong?"

"Everything!" Fiona blew her nose loudly. "I've been so angry. So *furious* since the day Stuart withdrew our financial backing from The Birth Place. I couldn't believe he did that!"

"It's unfortunate," Joanna said slowly. Gina had told Joanna about the financial woes of The Birth Place. "But I suppose he has the right to choose the recipient of his company's money."

"But it isn't his money. Not really." Fiona reached for another tissue. "He manages my trust fund. I've always wanted our support to go toward The Birth Place…and he liked being known around town as a big donor, I suppose."

"I'm not quite clear on what happened."

"Through the trust, we've given large donations every year. But *Stuart*…" Her voice filled with loathing. "It's always control with him. Me… Jason…his business…anything for power. *Anything*. He told my father all sorts of lies, then diverted that money elsewhere. Do you know how much this will hurt The Birth Place?''

Joanna knew well. There were a number of corporate and private donors who helped keep The Birth Place afloat, but the Penningtons had been the biggest donors of all. Staff hours had been drastically cut during the past week, and gossip about possible closure had been circulating through town.

''You can't explain this to your father?''

''My father thinks I'm ignorant when it comes to business,'' she said bitterly. ''And both he and Stuart have had some run-ins with Lydia in the past. Dad was more than happy to renege on his promise to me about supporting her facility.''

''Maybe if you talked to Stuart?''

''W-when I confronted him last night, he *slapped* me. Never, in all our years, has he ever laid a hand on Jason or me.''

Right. Joanna thought about the various injuries documented in Jason's medical chart.

Fiona lifted her chin, her expression grim. ''I know what you're thinking, but it's true. Stuart has always ignored Jason. Belittled him, saying he's a real pansy. When I'm not there to intercede, he'll drive the boy to do things he shouldn't—the more advanced hills at the ski resort, riding a new show horse with a little too much fire. When I complain, Stuart tells the entire family that I've overprotected Jason and made him into a clumsy mama's boy. They all believe Stuart is doing the right thing.''

''So every injury has somehow been *your* fault.''

Laying a protective hand on her belly, Fiona's eyes filled with deep sadness. ''I'm not putting up with this anymore. For Jason's sake, and for the sake of this little brother.''

''You're leaving?''

''No.'' She opened her purse and pulled out a bulky

envelope. "I've been going through some of Stuart's records…and I found a recording on our answering machine."

"This is about The Birth Place?"

"Much worse. I think maybe I've known for some time and just couldn't admit it to myself."

"Known?"

From the front of the clinic, a door opened. "Fiona! What the hell is taking you so long?"

She drew in a sharp breath. "I've got to leave."

Heavy footsteps started down the hallway. "Fiona?"

"Please." She dropped her voice to a whisper as she awkwardly rose to her feet and shoved the envelope at Joanna. "I want this to go the police department—you can just shove it through their mail slot in the front door. They won't know who it's from."

"Shouldn't you go and talk to them?"

"No. Stuart works downtown, and he also watches me like a hawk. If he sees me go there…" She shuddered. "I don't know who else I can trust. I need your help."

She hurried to the door, where she pasted a bright smile on her face before going out to calmly greet her husband in the hallway. Seconds later, Joanna heard the two of them leave by the front entrance.

I hope you know what you're doing, she thought grimly as she hid Fiona's envelope in a bottom file drawer and locked it. Some men were full of bluster and ego, but Stuart Pennington was a man who definitely sent an uneasy chill down Joanna's back.

On her way home, she would drop off the envelope for Fiona, and pray that everything turned out all right.

BEN PACED THE LENGTH of Joanna's rustic living room, then stood at the expanse of glass facing the mountains and shoved his hands in the pockets of his leather jacket.

He'd thought long and hard about her offer of a marriage

to help him pursue at least partial custody of Max. What had that cost her? She'd spoken before about her marriage. The husband who'd failed her when she'd needed him most. The crushing grief following the loss of her baby, and how she never wanted to face that risk again. She'd said she never planned to remarry.

Her surprising offer had made him realize something that he'd refused to see until now.

When had he fallen in love with her? That first day, when she'd insisted on helping him off the mountain to her car? The late nights when she'd tended to Max with such loving care? Or maybe it was just her laughter, her smile. Her sharp mind and dedication. He wanted to be with her today, tomorrow and all the tomorrows after that.

And her selfless offer had given him hope.

Surely she wouldn't have offered if she didn't have *some* feelings for him. Would she? Tonight, he was going to discuss this with her over a good steak dinner at the Silver Eagle. She was supposed to leave town right after the holidays, but he was going to ask her to stay.

Joanna's cell phone started ringing on the kitchen table.

"Hey—would you get that for me?" she called out from her bedroom. "Just take a message."

He caught it on the third ring.

"*Ben?*" Gina faltered, then laughed. "For a minute I thought I'd dialed the wrong number."

"I just stopped by to pick up Joanna. What's up?"

"Harry, our local FedEx guy, is here at The Birth Place looking for Jo. The pediatric clinic was closed, and he knows the two places are affiliated, so he stopped here. He has an overnight package she's supposed to sign for. Will you two still be there in fifteen minutes or so if I give him directions?"

"No problem."

"I got a glimpse of the return address…it's from that

fancy clinic in California.'' She paused. ''You know about that, right?''

''She mentioned a job, yes. I'll tell her you called—''

''Wait! Don't hang up. I'm trying to *tell* you something here.''

''Her mail isn't my business.''

Gina gave a long-suffering sigh. ''Look, I know you really care for her. I can *see* it, and I just don't want you to get hurt, okay?''

Uneasy now, he glanced toward Joanna's closed bedroom door. ''Thanks, sis. I'm fine.''

''Well, she may not have told you, but she has an incredible opportunity waiting for her in San Diego—something she dreamed of when she first started med school.''

''I know.''

''Dang it, not just a *job*. I heard her tell Lydia that it's a position at one of the most prestigious pediatric clinics in the country, with field research she'll be doing through the university. They're expecting her the first week of January.''

Ben closed his eyes briefly. *She offered to marry me, to help me keep Max. She was willing to sacrifice her future.*

Ben stared at the phone long after the call ended.

Sure, he wanted her. Hell, he *loved* her. He could imagine their lives together at the ranch, with Max growing up into a beautiful young woman and maybe some brothers and sisters along the way.

He'd come here tonight wanting her to agree to a *real* marriage, not some sham. But now…what was best for *her?* A small, isolated town and a guy who trained horses and sweated for every dime? Or the chance to make a name for herself in a field that she loved?

Joanna walked out into the living room moments later. ''Are we all set?''

She wore a simple, silky black dress that fitted snugly,

showing her perfect figure. A diamond choker sparkled at her neck, picking up the brilliance of a set of matching earrings. A diamond bracelet twinkled on one wrist. Her pale blond hair was caught up in some sort of loose bun on her head, with several curly tendrils that dangled provocatively.

"You look...fantastic," he growled.

"So do you." She drew closer, and rested a hand on his lapel, tipping her face up for a kiss.

He brushed her lips softly once, twice, then settled in for a deeper exploration of her mouth. Desire flared in an instant when he drew her closer and discovered the back of the dress was bare clear to her waist.

"If you wanted to go anywhere tonight," he whispered against her ear, "a different dress might have been a good idea."

Laughing, she pulled away. "Not so fast, cowboy. I'm looking forward to staring into those brown eyes of yours over a good rib eye steak. We can talk about this marriage of ours afterward. So many decisions, so little time. The courthouse? The church? Do we want any bridesmaids?"

Her words jerked him back to reality in an instant. His heart began to shatter before he said the first word.

"About that marriage," he said. "It isn't necessary."

Her laughter died on her lips. She stared up at him with wide eyes. "What?"

"I know it's not something either of us wants. I've never wanted any commitment, and you've said the same. Hey, short-term relationships are what I do best."

"But Max—"

"Holly's given me custody of Max. She left this afternoon without her, and everything but the legal paperwork is settled. Apparently, dropping her here permanently was her original plan." Ben managed a broad grin. "So you don't need to sacrifice yourself to another marriage, and I can still play the field.''

"I see.'' Her hands were trembling, but she lifted her chin a notch. "You got everything you wanted, then. I'm happy for you.''

"Thanks. You were a real trouper to offer to help me, Jo. Thanks.''

She seemed to sway on her high heels for just a moment. Then she squared her shoulders and gave him a forced smile. "No problem. We're just friends, after all.''

CHAPTER NINETEEN

"WHAT'S WRONG with you?" Dylan asked, studying Ben across the breakfast table. "Don't you feel good, or something?"

"I'm fine." Moving like an old man, Ben picked up his plate and silverware, and headed for the sink. "I'd better get outside, I guess. I've got eleven colts to work today."

"You don't sound fine." Frowning, Sadie bustled over to him and took his plate. "Do you have a fever? Chills? I hear there's flu going around these days."

He gave her a weary smile. "I just didn't sleep well, that's all." He lifted his gaze to meet Dylan's. "Since you're off on Christmas break this week, would you like to help me? I'll pay you six bucks an hour. You've turned into a darn good rider—you could work some of the older colts."

Dylan couldn't stop that sappy grin that probably made him look like some little kid on Christmas morning. Ben had let him ride one of the Shadow Creek colts whenever he wanted to, but never anything belonging to a customer. "Cool! But you don't have to pay me."

"If you do a man's job, you deserve a man's pay. Just come out when you get done in here."

Sadie waited until Ben pulled on the boots and coat he'd left by the back door and went outside, then she moved over to Dylan and gave him a quick hug. "I've never seen him let anyone but Rafe or Manny work his young stock.

He's real particular about his trainin' horses. You must be doing a great job."

Dylan ducked his head. "Only because he's been working me just about as hard as those horses."

And surprisingly, he'd come to love it. Feeling like a part of this ranch—feeling needed—had made him feel good inside. He'd even quit counting the hours and days until Dad got back, and instead imagined what it would be like to stay here. The crowds and noise of the city couldn't compete with looking at the Sangre de Cristo Mountains every day. What he'd thought cool before—hanging out with the guys, acting tough—now seemed dumb and childish.

A distant, impatient cry came from the other part of the house. "Max is awake," Sadie murmured as she scurried out of the kitchen. "I'll bet she's hungry."

Dylan cleared the table and piled his dishes by the sink, then strode across the kitchen and tugged on his boots. Outside, a car door slammed, and Blue started barking. Another thing Dylan would miss. Blue followed him everywhere around the ranch, even when he went riding up in the hills....

The back door burst open. Dylan stared in shock at the man standing just a few feet away. *"Dad?"*

Phil tossed his stocking cap onto the kitchen counter and set aside a duffel bag, then moved forward and enveloped Dylan in a bear hug. "Thought I'd surprise you," he said when he released Dylan and stepped back. "I didn't think I'd make it for Christmas—but here I am!"

Seeing his dad again filled Dylan with joy. "This is so cool! Wait till you see the horses—and Max—and everyone else!"

Phil held out his hand and gripped Dylan's. "Ben was telling me what a great kid you are, son. He says you're turning into quite a horseman, too. Sounds like you and I have a lot of catching up to do!''

Suddenly the joy left him. His stomach felt as if it was tying itself in knots. "Are...we leaving now?"

Phil tipped back his head and laughed. "I get the feeling that you like being here, and I'm glad to hear it. No, we aren't leaving just yet. I have two weeks of vacation, and then I have to go overseas again. So you have a choice— but we can talk about that later. I flew the red-eye from New York and then had to drive up from Albuquerque. I think I need something to eat and a good quiet place to catch a little sleep."

"Choice?" Dylan persisted, suddenly wary. "Like what?"

Phil toed off his boots and hoisted the duffel bag to his shoulder. "I'll be gone a few more months and then plan to stay home for good, so you and I can get settled some-place more permanent. In the meantime, do you want to go back to our place out East? I've still got that same house-keeper—she can keep an eye on you."

"Or?"

Phil shrugged, but here was a distinct twinkle in his eye. "Or you can stay here. Ben says it's fine with him, but I don't know...I remember some of your e-mails when you first arrived. Something about this place being 'godfor-saken' and this being 'at the ends of the earth'?"

Dylan grinned at him. "I think those were just typos."

Abandoning any effort at playing it cool, he moved for-ward and gave his dad another hug. Who would have thought? He'd been happy here, for sure. He was thrilled to be staying longer. But having Dad arrive the day before Christmas Eve had to be the best present in the world.

IN HER DREAMS, Joanna heard *pounding. Pounding. Pound-ing.*

Hammers thundering inside her skull. She eased herself

to the edge of the bed and sat there, her stomach churning and her head aching.

If she'd been drinking last night, she might have thought she had the mother of all hangovers. Since she never drank and instead had lain awake most of the night counting the rustic pine boards on her bedroom ceiling, this had to be the result of exhaustion…plus her usual bout of mid-December depression, with a good dose of embarrassment and heartache thrown in.

Exactly how pathetic had she appeared, throwing herself at Arroyo County's most eligible bachelor? Had he seen the emotion in her eyes when he'd come to pick her up last night?

She'd offered to marry him to give him a better chance at shared custody of his daughter. She'd started out with that altruistic motive, anyway, but the more she'd thought about it, the more the prospect of marrying Ben had filled her with heady anticipation. She'd even dared dream that in time, they might become a real married couple—in love, and into the marriage for the long haul.

Instead, he'd greeted her with outright relief that the charade could be abandoned, and he could go back to playing the field. It had taken every last ounce of her strength to straighten her spine, gather the remnants of her pride and go out with him for one of the most interminable evenings of her life.

Another wave of nausea hit her midsection as she remembered the effort it had taken to chat nonchalantly about nothing, as the rib eye on her plate turned cold.

The pounding began again. Awake now, she finally realized that someone was at the front door. Someone extremely insistent. Moose lumbered to his feet from his place by her bed and whined, his ears lifted and head turned toward the door.

"Some watchdog you are," she muttered, jerking her nightgown over her head and pulling on a sweat suit. "Come on—at least you can *appear* ferocious."

At the front door she peered through the security peephole, then flung the door open in surprise. "Officer Eiden?"

"Yes, ma'am." He took his western hat off in that charming display of manners that was so ingrained in most of the men she'd met here.

"Is something wrong?" She looked past him to the two people standing next to his patrol car. They seemed to be scanning her pasture. One of them gestured toward the corral and then both of them started crunching through the snow in that direction. "Who are these people?"

Eiden pivoted toward the corral and shaded his eyes. When the taller person raised a hand in a thumbs-up signal, he turned to face Joanna with an impassive expression. "These people flew into Albuquerque last night after receiving a lead on their stolen property."

She stared at him in disbelief. "*What* stolen property?"

"I'm sorry, Doc, but I've got to take you into town for questioning."

"This isn't funny."

"No, it isn't. Especially not out here. You might want to confine your dog and find your purse, because I have a feeling these people are going to press charges unless you have some fairly compelling proof."

"*Proof?*"

"They've just positively ID'd their horse, ma'am. That gelding is a champion Olympic event horse that was stolen from their training stable in October. He's worth well into six figures, and the Faradays, his owners, are not happy about his disappearance."

STUART DREW FARTHER into the underbrush and ducked low when Eiden stepped out of his patrol car. What the hell was going on here? Had Joanna called the cops?

His stomach twisted into knots and cold sweat trickled down his back.

He was sure Joanna had seen him driving home down Crooked Peak Road Saturday night. Not that it should have mattered. There would have been others up and down that road over the past month, and by the time Paul was found—probably not until the snow melted and hikers started using the more isolated trails—the exact day of his death would be impossible to figure.

But now…his hands turned cold and sweaty inside his leather gloves. A shudder swept down his spine. This morning, after Fiona left to volunteer at the elementary school, he'd opened the locked file cabinets in his office at home, intending to shred all the papers that held the truth of his dealings with Paul.

Once they were shredded, no one here would find any motive to link him to Paul's death. And after a little trip to Paul's house in Colorado Springs this week, there wouldn't be anything there, either. No statements that didn't quite match the originals, or any evidence of their more recent communications.

But those sensitive files in Stuart's own cabinet were missing. *Missing.* He'd felt honest-to-God chest pain—a crushing, searing pain—when he'd stared in horror at the place he'd always hidden them.

Frantic, he'd pawed through the contents of every drawer. Spun around to check the piles of business papers on his desk. Searched his bookshelves. He'd raced to his office in town and conducted the same wild search.

And he hadn't stopped shaking since.

With a top-notch security system in place at both his home and office, no one could have breached his defenses to steal those files…except maybe Fiona. She'd been asking too many questions lately. Pointed questions, and he'd seen her watching him with narrowed eyes whenever he disappeared into his office and shut the door.

It hadn't taken more than a minute's thought to remember her meeting with the doc about insurance papers yesterday…and how edgy she'd been when he'd interrupted their discussion. Had Fiona given the files to Joanna for safekeeping?

Maybe Fiona thought she could use them as a threat during a bid for a divorce. Or use them to wield power over Stuart in the years to come. His mind had raced with the possibilities.

The one he couldn't ignore was that those documents could lead an investigator right to Stuart's door if Paul's body was ever found.

Now watching Joanna's cabin from his hiding place, he swore under his breath. The conversation between the deputy and Joanna abruptly ended. She disappeared into the house, and came out a few minutes later with a small purse. After enclosing her big white mutt in the horse barn, she climbed into the patrol car. The other couple got in their blue sedan and followed as Eiden drove away.

Oh, God. Had Joanna called Eiden to tell him everything? But if so, why didn't she have any files in her hand?

Stuart stared at the empty lane leading down through the hills toward Enchantment. After fifteen minutes, he tentatively stepped out into the open meadow, circled behind the cabin and tried all the windows. *Locked, dammit.*

He found a decorative collection of rocks by the foundation—probably for some sort of flower bed in the summer—and lifted one high. He pitched it at a window. Glass shattered across the hardwood floor inside like a scattering of diamonds.

Icy tentacles of fear had slid through him when he first saw Eiden pull up at the cabin. Now that fear dissolved as his rage grew.

If the files were here, he would find them. If not—he would visit the pediatric clinic after hours and search there. His entire future—his freedom—depended on destroying that information before it fell into the wrong hands.

And nothing—*nobody*—was going to stand in his way.

TWO HOURS LATER, the Faradays pulled up to a stop in front of the pediatric clinic. Mrs. Faraday turned in her seat and offered her hand to Joanna. "I'm sorry for all the ruckus we caused today, dear. You just can't imagine how worried we've been about Pilot."

"I understand." Joanna accepted the handshake and gathered her purse and coat. "He's quite a character. I'm going to miss him. Not," she added dryly, "the times I've had to chase after him, maybe, but he is awfully cute."

"I'm sure he was just trying to get back to his stable-mate, Whiskers. That goat sleeps in his stall, and even travels with him on the show circuit."

Mr. Faraday glanced at Joanna using the rearview mirror. "Our investigator is already tracking down Pilot's seller, using the name on your sales receipt. I'm pretty sure he was working for a stable manager we fired not long before. We threatened her with legal action over some financial matters, and she probably figured taking the horse to a sale a hundred miles from home would be a safe way to take revenge."

Mrs. Faraday's expression turned grim. "Selling Pilot as a lame gelding meant only one thing—she wanted to make sure he wouldn't sell as a riding horse, so he'd go to a kill buyer. We're so thankful that you've given him such loving care."

"Just one question—a local rancher tried riding him once, and—"

"A man, right?" Mrs. Faraday laughed affectionately.

"Pilot is a sweetheart, but he has rather firm ideas about who can ride him."

"We figure he was abused by an earlier male owner," her husband added. "You sure you don't want a ride home to pick up your car? It's no trouble."

"Thanks, but I have clinic hours right now, so I'd better get in there." Joanna stepped out of the car and bent to peer in at them. "My secretary said she would give me a lift home after work. You'll be taking Galahad—I mean, Pilot—tomorrow?"

"Early morning." Mrs. Faraday withdrew an envelope from the glove compartment. "I hope this will cover what you spent on him?"

Joanna hesitated.

"You must, dear. You gave him wonderful care and a safe home, and we can't even begin to tell you what that means to us."

Joanna reluctantly accepted the check as she got out of the car. It could be the start of a college fund for Max, maybe. A parting gift. *I should be relieved. Everything is falling into place.*

Any relationship she'd had with Ben was over. Now she wouldn't need to worry about Galahad escaping into suburbia when she moved to California. All good things, right?

Yeah, right.

Instead of relief, she felt only an aching, hollow sensation in her chest as she trudged up the steps of the clinic. For all the problems he'd caused, she loved that old horse and would miss seeing him hang his head over the fence to beg for treats.

And that sense of loss didn't even *begin* to cover the depth of what she felt about Ben.

ALL DAY JOANNA SMILED. Cooed at babies. Bantered with teens. Reassured the parents, provided careful, accurate medical advice. But all day, her thoughts kept straying to Shadow Creek Ranch, to Ben and Max and all that would never be.

"Hey," Nicki said as the last patient of the day left. "Busy day, huh?" She frowned when Joanna only gave her a curt nod. "Things aren't going so good?"

"Fine. Really fine."

"What about Ben? He used to call at least once a day."

"He must be busy," Joanna said vaguely, waving her last patient chart of the day. "I need to review this. I'll be in my office."

Nicki glanced at the darkness outside, and then at the clock on the wall. "It's already five-thirty, and the drugstore closes at six. Would you like a ride home now, or should I run my errand and come back afterward? Either's fine."

Galahad wouldn't be leaving until morning. Everything would still be the same out at her cabin, but the thought of going out there alone intensified her sense of loss. There would be no phone calls from the ranch. No casual visits from Ben that extended into late-night conversation in front of the fire...and more. "Later would be better—if you don't mind."

"I could even go finish the last of my Christmas shopping and, come back at, say, seven?" Nicki's mouth curved into a conspiratorial smile. "And if you want to talk about anything, I could help. With Ben, I mean."

The last thing Joanna wanted was more romantic advice from a nineteen-year-old with stars in her eyes and a head full of notions about the glories of mad, passionate love.

Love hurt. It disappointed. It failed. And no earnest advice was going to change the fact that in two weeks Joanna would be on her way to California, alone.

She gave the girl a gentle smile. "Thanks, Nicki. I know

you hoped Ben and I would ride off into the sunset together. But I do need to leave in a couple weeks and he needs to stay here.''

''If you never had any hope of working things out between you, why have you been so down lately? You don't eat, you don't even look like you feel good. People can make changes, you know,'' she added doggedly, clearly unwilling to give up.

Joanna shooed her toward the door. ''Come back at seven. Don't worry if you get busy and need more time— I've got lots to do here.''

Heaving a dramatic sigh, Nicki pulled her car keys from a jacket pocket and headed for the front door, muttering under her breath.

When the front door opened and shut, Joanna heaved her own sigh of relief as she switched on the computer on her desk and opened the patient file in front of her.

Silence. Blessed silence—except for a cold breeze whispering through the pines, and the soft brush of branches against the building.

Something scraped against her window.

The fine hairs prickled at the back of her neck. Her heart thudding against her ribs, she stilled.

Listened intently.

Slowly swiveled her chair.

Mirrored against the night, she saw only her own reflection in the windowpane.

Only a branch, she chided herself. Still, she reached up and jerked the cord of the miniblinds, sending them cascading over the window, and quickly close the vanes.

There it was *again.* Just the wind—or something more?

Her foolish imagination, surely, but on unsteady legs she rose and quickly checked the lock on the back door of the clinic, pivoted and headed for the reception area.

The blinds were down on the multiple windows on three

sides of the waiting room, but all were at an angle so that anyone could peer inside. Until tonight she hadn't given it a second thought. Now…an eerie sense of foreboding chilled her blood as she reached the front door.

Too much caffeine, Weston…and a little too much Stephen King last night. She reached forward to close the dead bolt.

The door swung open, knocking her hand away, and crashed against the wall. A scream died in her throat.

Fiona stood there—wild-eyed, disheveled, her hair tangled and a pocket partially ripped from her coat. "Oh, God," she said frantically. "Hurry!"

She whirled around and slammed the door shut, ramming the dead bolt home. Her face was a pale mask of fear. "The blinds—shut the blinds!"

"*Stuart?* Is he following you?"

"I—I don't know."

"What happened?"

"I—I just got home an hour ago…I helped at the school, then took Jason to an overnight with his grandparents. I—I wanted to finish wrapping Christmas gifts t-tonight." She swallowed hard. "My house—oh…" She was crying now, her tears flowing as they both rushed from window to window, closing the blinds. "While I was gone today, Stuart must have discovered those files were missing. He tore the place apart trying to find them. Are they still here?"

"I dropped them in the mail slot at the police department, just as you asked…around eight o'clock last night." Joanna gently grabbed her shoulders. "Just calm down…the doors are locked. Have you called 911?"

Fiona didn't seem to hear her. "Everything was trashed. His office. Our bedroom. I was standing there in shock when he came up from the basement. I've never seen him so angry—I think he would have killed me if I hadn't gotten away!" She took a shuddering breath. "He took my car keys from the kitchen table, so I just ran. I—I did try calling 911 on my cell phone…but I was running, and I tripped, and I lost it in the dark…and I—I knew I had to come here. It was the closest place I could think of.''

STUART STARED in frustration at the wreckage of his house. His life.

He'd gone through Joanna's cabin and hadn't found his files. He'd searched his own house and hadn't found them here, either. The combination of guilt and panic on Fiona's face tonight had told him all he needed to know. The bitch had betrayed him.

Closing his eyes, he imagined the horror of being sent to prison. Anyone who studied those documents would likely find enough proof of fraud to send him away for a good ten years. If Paul's body was found, it could be for life.

And he sure as hell wasn't going to let that happen.

The pediatric clinic would be closed by now. He could drive there in five minutes, slip in, find what he was after, then be home in a half hour, easily. Where else would Fiona try to stash something? Not at her father's place—Richard lived over an hour away, and she wouldn't have had time to get there and back.

She certainly wouldn't dare give the files to any of their mutual friends, who would surely mention her actions to Stuart.

Stuart tossed Fiona's car keys in the air, caught them and smiled to himself. He'd get his business files back, and he would deal with his wife later. She wouldn't have gone far. And when he was through with her, she'd never try ruining his life again.

THE LIGHTS were still on at the clinic when he arrived, but there were no cars in the parking lot. Stuart studied the building for a few moments, watching for any shadows of movement behind the closed blinds, then he drove to the end of the block and walked back.

At the front entrance he tried the handle, found it locked, and gave a light knock. Waited. Then knocked louder.

When no one answered, he circled around and tried the back door. Then he tried each window, standing on tiptoes to peer through every narrow space in the blinds that he could find. Through one of the side windows he thought he saw something move inside a room. *Damn.*

If the doc was in there, he'd have to wait and wait…

Searching wildly through the darkness around his feet, he found a small flower planter under a mound of snow, pried it away from the ground, and dragged it to the window. He stood on it to look inside the room again.

It wasn't just the doc in there. Fiona was there, too, gesturing wildly.

He didn't have to hear the words to know that his darling wife was trying to seal his fate. Cursing violently, he stepped off the planter and rushed to the front door once again. He had to stop her before it was too late.

SOMEONE JIGGLED *the front-door handle.*

"Hey, Fiona—I know you're in there. I'm sorry about our little fight back at home. Can we talk?"

Her eyes filled with terror, Fiona swung her head wildly toward the door. "I went through backyards and down an alley. I thought I'd lost him!"

"Fiona—don't be so silly. I'm sorry. I know you've been a little irrational, with being pregnant and all." Stuart's voice took on an eerie, singsong note. "Does Joanna know about your hallucinations? We just need to talk…and maybe get you some of those pills that calm you down."

"That's not true!" Fiona cried against her fist. "He's *lying.*"

"Stay put. We'll be okay," Joanna whispered, struggling to keep her own voice calm. "The dead bolts will hold—and I'm calling the police right now."

Fists battered against the door. A heavy blow—probably from a boot—sent a shower of plaster particles from the ceiling.

She hurried to the receptionist's desk and dialed 911 before lifting the receiver to her ear.

Nothing. The line was dead.

Another hard kick landed against the door. The wood shuddered, and a framed La Leche League poster hanging next to the entryway crashed to the floor.

"Come with me," she said firmly. "My cell phone is down in my office. We can lock that door and shove a desk in front of it. We'll be fine until help arrives."

Joanna took Fiona's arm and helped her waddle down the hall. Halfway there, Fiona groaned and leaned against the wall, her face sheened with perspiration as she panted through a sudden contraction. "I must have—" she took a shaky breath "—moved things along a little."

Joanna quickly retrieved a small plastic box from an exam room and returned to her side. "We'll call the hospital, too, okay?"

They'd just made it into her private office when they heard the sound of shattering glass and a heavy thud.

"He's coming through a front window," Fiona cried. "Oh, God—he'll be in here any second."

Joanna slammed the door shut. Locked it, and eyed the oak, four-drawer file cabinet just to the right. "I'll tip this over to block the door—you get the cell phone in my purse and call for help."

Fiona stood frozen in the center of the room.

"Now, Fiona. *Now.*"

Tears filled Fiona's eyes. "I n-never should have taken

those files. He'd hidden them so well, I figured he wouldn't notice until the police had time to do something…''

"Make that call!" Joanna swept the books from the top of the file cabinet and pushed at the top corner. It didn't budge. She took a deep breath and rocked the cabinet until it crashed lengthwise in front of the door.

Over by the desk Fiona cowered over Joanna's purse, the cell phone held limply in her hand.

"Did you call?" Joanna mouthed.

Fiona's head jerked. She punched in the numbers with shaking fingers.

"I think Fiona gave you something of mine," Stuart cajoled from the other side of the door. "Just business papers…*confidential* papers. I only want them back. I don't want to hurt anyone."

His voice was higher now, and sent icy fingers of fear down Joanna's spine. If he got through the door…

She spun around. Dragged a heavy oak end table across the room and jammed it against the cabinet in front of the door. From behind the desk, Fiona gave her a wobbly smile and a thumbs-up. "The police are on their way—ten minutes, tops."

"Ten *minutes?*"

The hallway was oddly quiet. Too quiet. Joanna eyed the door uneasily. If Stuart chose to set the place alight, they'd have to go out the window, and with a pregnant woman who was possibly in early labor…

The window.

Horror leaped up Joanna's throat as she flew across the room. The bookcase? Fastened to the wall. The desk?

An explosion of glass from the window showered into the room. A concrete block thudded heavily onto the floor at her feet.

And in a split second, a pair of meaty, freckled hands reached inside, fumbling for the window latch.

Fiona screamed. Backed against the opposite wall.

Joanna grabbed the plastic box she'd tossed on the desk. She closed her eyes briefly, praying for strength as she withdrew a scalpel and ripped off the protective sheathing.

"You make one more move, Stuart, and you'll be sorry," she said with deadly calm.

He continued to fumble wildly for the latch. His fingers landed on it. Twisted it open. "You can't do a damn thing. But when I get in there—"

"Maybe I need to be more clear." She bit her lip. Shuddered. "I've got a weapon here. You try to come through that window and I'll slit your throat."

He gave a harsh laugh as he shoved the broken sash upward. "You wouldn't—"

Everything in her opposed violence. The oath she'd once taken to do no harm had become her personal mantra over the years. But she had no doubt what Stuart would do if he got into her office.

His forearms appeared on the windowsill. He leaned forward and his head appeared. She grabbed his lanky, thinning hair with one hand and twisted hard. With the other, she rested the scalpel tip at a point just below his ear.

He yelped as she twisted harder.

"You'd better not lose your balance," she whispered. "Because any move you make will bury this scalpel in your carotid, is that clear enough? I really don't want you in here."

He started to twist away, but Joanna pressed the scalpel closer until it drew a drop of blood. He instantly stilled. "Personally, I wouldn't mind seeing you die," she said gently. "I'm sure a court would consider this self-defense. Breaking and entering. Intent to cause personal injury. Spousal abuse. There must be more…and I'll bet it's all in those files you want, but they aren't here."

Distant sirens wailed.

Twigs snapped as footsteps came around the side of the building and came to a halt outside the window. "What have we here?"

In the darkness, she couldn't see his face. The voice she recognized in an instant. *Ben.*

Stuart squirmed against her tight hold on his hair and the threat of the scalpel. "She's crazy," he hissed. "I came here, trying to help—"

"Let him go," Ben ordered.

"No—he tried to break in. He—"

"I know. Let him go."

Reluctantly, she complied.

Stuart suddenly flew backward and disappeared. The *thwack* of a fist hitting flesh sounded just once. After a moment, Ben appeared at the window.

"Stuart isn't going anywhere," he announced with satisfaction. "Are you okay?"

The sirens grew louder. Swirling crimson lights flashed through the tree branches. The sound abruptly died as two patrol cars slammed to a halt in front of the clinic. Three officers circled the building, their flashlights sweeping in arcs through the underbrush.

Within a half hour, Stuart was on his way to the police station, and one of the officers was helping Fiona into his cruiser.

"I'll come to the hospital in a few minutes," Joanna reassured her, patting her hand. "If this is a false alarm I'll stay with you tonight at your place, okay?"

Fiona raised her tear-streaked face and gave Joanna a tremulous smile. "It's all just…just…"

"I know, I know. Everything will be all right. I promise."

Joanna stamped her feet in the snow, trying to warm them as she watched the last cruiser pull away. Now, only she and Ben were left behind. With a little luck, he would go now, too, and this uncomfortable moment would end.

"Thanks," she murmured. "Though I'm still not sure why you happened to stop here. I thought we'd settled everything already."

Something flickered in the depths of his eyes. His expression cooled. "I was in town, and Nicki stopped me—she said you wanted to see me."

So that was why Nicki had been so willing to take her time before coming back to the clinic. She'd hoped to set up a meeting. "I think she still harbors this foolish belief that you and I are...could be..."

"Foolish," he echoed. "When you proposed to me, you thought it was foolish?"

"I mean, you're not interested in commitment. I've got a job back home." At his bemused expression, she added, "You said so yourself." Joanna stared at Ben, memorizing his dark, rugged face and laconic smile. Wishing that she had an album of photographs to take with her so she would remember exactly how he looked at this moment.

Tomorrow she would spend Christmas Eve at the ranch as planned, because the alternative of staying alone in her cabin was just too depressing to consider. After that, she'd leave for California and never see him again.

And then she'd have one more sad Christmas memory to add to the rest.

CHAPTER TWENTY

AFTER CHURCH SERVICES on Christmas Eve, the family gathered at the ranch for their traditional supper of ham and Swedish meatballs, followed by Sadie's rice pudding and Scandinavian cookies.

When the dishes were done, everyone filtered into the living room where the Christmas-tree lights twinkled and a warm fire blazed in the fireplace. The sweet scents of cinnamon and burning pine logs filled the air.

Max immediately wiggled out of Ben's arms and toddled over to the tree, where she squatted in front of a large package and poked at its iridescent bow.

"Who's first?" Gina said from her place on the sofa, nestled within Zach's embrace. "Regan?"

"No—me!" Allie dropped the gift package she'd been inspecting and hurried over to the scarred upright piano tucked away in a corner of the room.

Chewing her lower lip, she carefully two-fingered her way through an accurate—if a little choppy—rendition of "Away in a Manger." When she climbed off the piano bench, she curtsied, her proud smile revealing two missing teeth.

"Wonderful job, honey," Zach said amidst the family's applause. "Just perfect."

She beamed at him as she scrambled up into his lap and tucked her head beneath his chin. "I learnt it just for you, Daddy. 'Cause you came back."

Regan plinked out a more practiced version of "Jingle

Bells,'' followed by a halting attempt at ''Joy to the World.'' Bowing to the applause, she grinned. ''Mom says we can get lessons now. That's one of my 'grateful' things this year. But the best is that Daddy is here.''

From his place next to his dad, by the hearth, Dylan gave Ben a curious look.

''We always talk about what we're grateful for during the past year,'' Sadie explained, reaching over to pat his shoulder from her rocker. ''Before we open presents.''

A shadow passed across Dylan's face. ''I know I was sort of a jerk at first,'' he said slowly. ''But I guess I'm grateful to be here. You guys are cool.'' His voice hitched a little, and he looked down at his hands. ''I never had holidays like this. It's always just been Dad and me.''

Joanna felt a lump build in her throat that only grew larger when she saw Gina and Zach exchange glances over Regan's head. The love in their eyes was visible, even from across the room. ''We're thankful for each other,'' Zach said simply. ''Nothing is more important than that.''

''True,'' Gina agreed, ''though I did hear some pretty good news today. Lydia called everyone into her office this morning. She said that our staff hours at The Birth Place will soon be back to normal.''

''Hey, that's great!'' Ben rose and lifted Max away from the tree and set her on his shoulders. ''What happened?''

''Fiona Pennington was at The Birth Place today—she's been having false labor. She told Lydia and Parker that her family's support of The Birth Place will resume.''

''That's wonderful,'' Joanna said.

''There's more.'' Gina grinned broadly. ''Kim has finished renegotiating some of our health-care provider contracts, which will help us a lot. And the board is considering a special fund-raising event.''

Amidst the family's cheers, Sadie smiled softly. ''I'm just grateful to be here with all of you.'' She gave Joanna a slow wink. "And to have such wonderful news at the end of this year. I hope."

Ben cleared his throat. "I've been so blessed this year—with all of you. With the ranch business going well. The chance to meet Dylan." He swung Max down into his arms and kissed her cheek. "And with a new daughter."

He handed Max to Gina, then reached out for Joanna's hand and pulled her over to his side. "I was going to wait until later…but maybe this is the right time after all. Someone proposed to me not too long ago, and I really blew the chance."

The warmth of his large, strong hand sent shivers of sensation through her. Startled, she looked up into his eyes.

"Maybe I spoke too soon. Maybe—" he reached up and brushed gentle fingers through her hair "—I should have listened to my heart instead of my head."

"But—"

"And maybe that's been our problem all along."

He feathered a gentle kiss against her forehead that sent shivers coursing through her, and then he deepened the kiss until she melted against his hard-muscled chest and lost herself in the sensations that spun through her.

"I know you have a wonderful job opportunity waiting in California," he continued when he ended the kiss. "But there's a need for good doctors here, too."

Feeling a little dizzy, she just stared up at him.

"I…realize this is sort of sudden, but sometimes life can speed by so fast that you've just got to move or it might be too late."

Joanna's knees started to quiver. "Too late?"

"I know you haven't wanted to settle down. I know how losing your baby hurt you, and how much Allen hurt you after that. Personally, I think he's the greatest fool on God's green earth."

She felt a smile tremble at the corners of her mouth. "That's one thing he'd never believe."

"Which proves my point." He released her and withdrew a small box from his pocket. "Joanna, you can open this later, if you want to. Whatever your answer, I'll still believe you're the most wonderful woman I've ever met, and you will always own my heart."

With shaky fingers she accepted the box. Closed her eyes. "I don't know what to say."

"Then don't," he said gently. "Just think about it."

She took a steadying breath and slowly opened the box to find a gold ring inside. An old-fashioned gold ring with an emerald-cut solitaire diamond surrounded by a circlet of small rubies.

She'd once thought her heart shattered beyond fixing, but now those pieces fell into place and expanded to fill her chest with a deep, forever kind of joy. "I-it's beautiful."

"It was my grandmother's," he said. "Years ago, she left it to me with a note saying she wanted me to find the kind of happiness she shared with my grandfather."

Amid the whoops and hollers from everyone in the room, he took Joanna's hand and kissed it, then searched her face. "I believe I have."

BY MIDNIGHT, the gifts had been opened, the wrappings collected. Gina and Zach had taken their girls home, and Sadie and Max were asleep. Dylan and his father were talking out in the kitchen.

Joanna curled up closer to Ben as she stared at the dying embers of the fire. "It's been quite a day, hasn't it?"

"It has."

His voice rumbled beneath her cheek, and she could feel the steady beat of his heart. He'd spoken of how blessed he felt, and she knew exactly what he meant. She'd come here intending to stay awhile, then move on to her new life, to a job that mattered. But what mattered most of all was being here, with him and Max.

Only now she had to tell him something that he might not like at all.

"I talked to Miguel today," he said against the top of her head. "It...wasn't something I wanted to discuss in front of the others on Christmas Eve, but I thought you should know."

"About Stuart being charged?"

"Over more than we thought. Someone was out trail riding yesterday and found a rental car down in a ravine."

"Was the driver okay?"

"No. The investigator was waiting on autopsy results, wondering if the guy had died of a heart attack and gone off the road. After someone at the police station started checking those files of Stuart's, they discovered the man had been his silent partner in some business deals. Deals that are definitely shady."

"To Stuart's benefit?"

"Exactly."

Joanna shuddered, remembering Stuart's rage the night he'd tried to break into the clinic.

She levered herself up and turned in Ben's arms. "You probably saved my life, you know. And Fiona's, too."

He chuckled. "I think you had things under pretty good control. Stuart seemed worried about that skimpy hair on his head and the well-being of his carotid." He frowned a little, studying her. "What is it? Something else?"

"It's been a hard week," she murmured, trying to ignore the pulse hammering at her wrists. "An emotional week. I've been feeling tired. I figured it was a result of everything that has happened."

His eyes filled with worry. "Are you okay? Do you need to be seen by someone?"

She managed a small smile. "Not yet. I...stopped in at

the clinic this morning to see a patient with possible strep throat. When I got there, I found a package Gina left for me on my desk. She'd left a little note saying she has a sixth sense about these things, and that she'd bet me a dinner at the Silver Eagle that I'd have something to tell her.''

"Are you talking about a Christmas present?''

"Not exactly. And I guess I owe her that dinner, because she guessed right. I hadn't been keeping track of dates, really, because there hadn't been any point for so long…''

Realization dawned in Ben's eyes.

Remembering Allen's horror at hearing she was pregnant a few years ago, she held her breath. When Ben didn't say anything, she stumbled on, her words coming faster and faster. "I don't know how it happened. We were extremely careful from the very first. There hasn't been anyone else. I didn't intend for this to happen. And I didn't know about it last night, when you…um…proposed.''

"You don't want this baby,'' he said flatly, pulling away.

"Of *course*. But do you?'' Her voice sounded tense to her own ears, and she could no longer meet his eyes. *Please say you do. Please. Please.* "All I can think is that on our first time, the old condom you found in the truck failed. And now—''

He relaxed, and smiled down at her with such love in his eyes that she almost had to turn away. "What if this baby has the same heart abnormalities Hunter had? What if we go that far, only to lose him?''

"Or her.'' He reached for her and pulled her back into his arms. "Aw, Jo. I know you made it clear from the start that you were afraid of taking this risk again. But just for the record, I'm not sorry at all. There are tests, right? Ultrasound or something that can tell us if things are okay?''

She nodded, a small ember of hope flickering to life inside her chest.

"There's a good chance everything will be fine. And if it isn't—we can deal with it. *Together*. I love you, Jo—whether we have a dozen babies or just have Max, I'll love you until the day I die."

A rush of relief and love flooded through her. "And I'll love you even more," she whispered, as that ember burned brighter, warming her heart and filling her with a joyous sense of peace.

Please turn the page for an excerpt from
C.J. Carmichael's

LEAVING ENCHANTMENT

the fourth title in Harlequin Superromance's
THE BIRTH PLACE *series.*

Watch for it next month.

CHAPTER ONE

HOME LATE FROM THE OFFICE, Nolan McKinnon, editor and owner of the *Arroyo County Bulletin,* was just about to dig into his second slice of pizza, when a police call came over the scanner sitting next to his toaster. Nolan recognized the voice of his good friend, Miguel Eiden.

"10–45 on Switchback Road. Get an ambulance and backup. Now."

Geez. It wasn't even ten o'clock. Wasn't it too early for a traffic accident on a Saturday night? Nolan grabbed a notepad and pencil and waited for the details.

"10–45, Miguel," said the dispatcher. "How bad is it?"

"It's a mess. Single-vehicle accident about ten miles past Manny Cordova's place. Looks like the driver lost control and ran into a rock wall going full speed or more."

Nolan's full-time reporter, Cooper Lorenzo, had been on call last weekend. Which meant this "mess," as Miguel had put it, was all his. Sighing, Nolan closed the cardboard box over the still-hot pizza and went for his camera.

Generally he loved everything about owning and managing the local newspaper. But late-night calls, especially for stories such as this—accidents, home fires and the like—were never fun. Still, people expected newspapers to cover these personal tragedies.

Fortunately they didn't occur often in a town of only five thousand people.

A minute later, sitting high in the seven-year-old Explorer he'd just bought from an old friend of his father's,

Nolan zipped out of his neighborhood, bypassing the commercial heart of Enchantment. Sometime between now and when he'd picked up his pizza, it had begun to snow. The white flakes battered his windshield as he left town limits. Switchback Road cut into the sparsely populated Sangre de Cristo Mountains that bordered the northwest side of Enchantment. The narrow, twisting route was picturesque during daylight hours, but it had a checkered history. Every year the townspeople could count on at least one bad accident, most caused by excessive speed.

As a teenager, Nolan had done his share of wild driving. But shortly after he'd begun work full-time at the *Bulletin,* he'd reformed. God but he'd seen some grisly sights in the past ten years, and he really didn't want to experience another. He thought of his pizza cooling on the kitchen counter, and the game on TV that was only half over.

Shit. What a life.

Nolan took a sharp corner slowly, his tires jostling on the poorly maintained pavement underneath the layer of fresh snow. Ahead he spotted the flashing lights of emergency vehicles in the dark.

The left side of the road was cordoned off. Without the luxury of wide, paved shoulders, police had done their best to leave a narrow corridor open. Two officers stood at either end of the wreck, directing the sporadic traffic.

Nolan pulled over to the far left, just as an ambulance took off from the scene, sirens blaring.

Once the coast was clear, Nolan inched forward again, parking behind one of several police cars. He had a view of the accident now. The vehicle—some kind of SUV— had driven off the road and crashed into the rocky outcrop.

He'd have to get a photo.

About to uncap his Nikon, Nolan froze. He could see the

rear license plate of the mangled vehicle. The numbers taunted him. He'd seen that particular pattern before.

And then it hit him.

This was his sister's car.

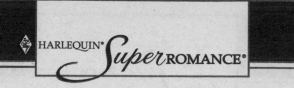

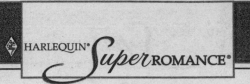

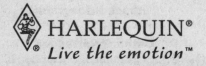

The Rancher's Bride
by Barbara McMahon
(Superromance #1179)

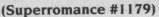

On sale January 2004

Brianna Dawson needs to change her life. And for a Madison Avenue ad exec, life doesn't get more different than a cattle ranch in Wyoming. Which is why she gets in her car and drives for a week to accept the proposal of a cowboy she met once a long time ago. What Brianna doesn't know is that the marriage of convenience comes with a serious stipulation—a child by the end of the year.

Getting Married Again
by Melinda Curtis
(Superromance #1187)

On sale February 2004

To Lexie, Jackson's first priority has always been his job. Eight months ago, she surprised him with a divorce—and a final invitation into her bed. Now Jackson has returned from a foreign assignment fighting fires in Russia and Lexie's got a bigger surprise for him—she's pregnant. Will he be here for her this time, just when she needs him the most?

Available wherever Harlequin books are sold.

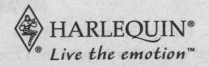

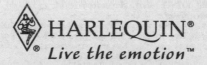

COMING NEXT MONTH

#1170 LEAVING ENCHANTMENT • C.J. Carmichael
The Birth Place
Nolan McKinnon is shocked when he's named his niece's guardian. He knows nothing about taking care of a little girl—especially an orphan—but he still would've bet he knew more than Kim Sherman. Kim's a newcomer to Enchantment—one who seems determined not to get involved with anyone. But Nolan can't refuse help, even if it comes from a woman with secrets in her past....

#1171 FOR THE CHILDREN • Tara Taylor Quinn
Twins
Valerie Simms is a juvenile court judge who spends her days helping troubled kids—including her own fatherless twin boys. Through her sons she meets Kirk Chandler, a man who's given up a successful corporate career and dedicated himself to helping the children in his Phoenix community. Valerie and Kirk not only share a commitment to protecting children, they share a deep attraction—and a personal connection that shocks them both.

#1172 MAN IN A MILLION • Muriel Jensen
Men of Maple Hill
Paris O'Hara is determined to avoid the efforts of the town's matchmakers. She's got more important things to worry about—like who her father really is. But paramedic Randy Sandford is determined to show her that the past is not nearly as important as the future.

#1173 THE ROAD TO ECHO POINT • Carrie Weaver
Vi Davis has places to go, people to meet and things to do—and the most important thing of all is getting a promotion. So she's not pleased when a little accident forces her to take time out of her schedule to care for an elderly stranger. She never would have guessed that staying with Daisy Smith and meeting her gorgeous son, Ian, is *exactly* the thing to do.

A great new story from a brand-new author!

#1174 A WOMAN LIKE ANNIE • Inglath Cooper
Hometown U.S.A.
Mayor Annie McCabe cherishes Macon's Point, the town that's become home to her and her son, and she's ready to fight to save it. And that means convincing Jack Corbin to keep Corbin Manufacturing, the town's main employer, in business. Will she be able to make Jack see the true value of his hometown...and its mayor?

#1175 THE FULL STORY • Dawn Stewardson
Risk Control International
Keep Your Client Alive is the mandate of Risk Control International. And RCI operative Dan O'Neill takes his job very seriously. Unfortunately, keeping his foolhardy client safe is a real challenge. And the last thing Dan needs is the distraction of a very attractive—and very nosy—reporter named Micky Westover.